Stages

Also by Lamar K. Neal

Novels:

A Misc. Eden

Poetry Collections:

Charm Bracelet

We All Need Therapy

[Pale]

The Ghost Charades

Acknowledgments

I dedicate this book to everyone who has inspired me:

My Mom, Ashley, Dizzle, Patty, Autry,
Regina, Zoe, Big Zay, Danielle, Dan, David
Andrew, AC, Jonna, Matthew Elisha Williams,
Neto

Lanie Mores, Ron Artis Jr, Melody Mann,
Terran Brice, Anthony Custode Jr

JPEGMAFIA, Kanye West, Michael Jackson, Big K.R.I.T
Scarface. Poets of the Fall.

Stages

Lamar K. Neal

Chapter 1
Hendrix

Him dying felt real this time.

When my dad finally caught his breath, after coughing incessantly, he forced me into a deep embrace.

"Goodbye, son," he said.

"I'm going to class, dad," I said, "not war."

"Every day is war. A war with ourselves. A war for equality. A war with those grades." In a swift motion, he snapped a picture of me. The flash forced my eyes closed.

"Come on, dad. A heads up would've been nice."

"It's the first day of the semester. You know the routine."

My vision returned with white spots floating about. "See you after class."

"I'll be right here- unless the Lord has other plans." He glanced at the driveway, which, for now, only had his car. "Or your sisters."

"Maybe I shouldn't leave. What if, you know, it happens?

"You know what I hate most about 'what if's?' We get so caught up on what might happen or what could happen, we end up missing out on what's happening. Go. Live today for today, not what could be. And I don't want to hear no lip."

I dropped into the driver's seat of my White Honda Accord. "Love you, dad."

"Oh, by the way, I found a place." He pulled a folded brochure from his back pocket, handed it to me, and waited with a grin for me to read through it all. "It has palm trees."

I glanced at the palm tree towering over our house. It made sense. And it was probably the responsible thing to do at that stage in his life, rather than putting up a façade that life was good.

"I should," I said, starting my car, "uh…Get going."

"I'll be right here when you come back, Hendrix." He winked. "Right here."

. . .

With my world falling apart, school was the last place I wanted to be.

I stepped into the classroom and froze. As I looked across the room, I connected eyes with the few people who'd already claimed their seats for the rest of the quarter.

The concrete floors and walls, browned and covered in streaks, the stuffy air of a collective breath and must from the lack of windows, and the fuse boxes beeping and hissing, made up the so-called classroom. I would spend every Tuesday and Thursday for the next ten weeks in a glorified dungeon.

Without hesitation, I slid into the desk closest to the door.

Continuously waving my hands didn't stop the half dozen flies from trying to land on me or flying crookedly near my face- of all the places in the room.

Whenever someone walked into the classroom, we awkwardly connected eyes before they found a seat. I knew most of them, not by name but from their faces. We took multiple classes together over the last two years, and I was sure they would be in my other courses that quarter. After the fifth person, I looked now and then, having spent most of my time admiring the room. As more people arrived and noticed friends they had met in previous quarters, the noise grew out of control. The room had terrible acoustics, and everything echoed: the rustling of bags and backpacks, the sound of zippers, and individuals as they conversed and laughed.

The class was supposed to start at 6 pm, and it was now 6:05 pm, and the instructor hadn't arrived yet. Students flooded into class, sighing in relief as they noticed the instructor was just as late. I knew one of them, once again, by face, but not name. Her curly brown hair almost looked black with light brown tips and pulled back into a ponytail, bushed at the top of her head. A year ago, we had taken a class together; the name sat on the tip of my tongue. My mind fluttered through those mostly chilly days. Her scarves would flail behind her as she rushed from class as soon as it ended. It was just as rare to see her without a scarf as it was seeing her with the same one twice. A chuckle came over me as I imagined a drawer so stuffed with scarves it barely opened or closed.

She didn't wear a scarf today. That's because it was about 80 degrees outside, 95 in the classroom. Her light pink blouse, hanging off her shoulder, showed off her entire tattoo sleeve. Colorful vines, leaves, sprouting flowers, and other unrecognizable images made her left arm a canvas from shoulder to wrist. She had another tattoo on her thigh, though undistinguishable through the small rip in her jeans.

She listened to music through AirPods. We connected eyes for a brief moment, and she greeted me with a closed-mouth smile before scrunching her face in disgust at a fly closing in.

She claimed the only seat still available: behind me.

At 6:15 pm, the instructor, a short woman with gray hair, wearing an unbuttoned oversized flannel that had paint on the sleeves and a white shirt underneath, walked in. Her unbuttoned cuffs hung over her hands. The only thing she had with her was two water bottles.

Like most first days of class, the instructor read over the syllabus and let us go well before the scheduled dismissal. Before we could leave, she asked us to place a piece of paper with our names, ID numbers, the Class section number, and the date on the desk in front of the class. Everyone got up and flocked around the desk, reaching over one another to turn in the assignment before cluttering at the door.

I waited in my seat for the stampede to clear out. After, I turned in my paper, taking notice of the woman wearing a scarf making her way to the desk. We connected eyes, and she flashed the same closed-mouth smile. I smiled back with teeth. As I dusted the dirt from the floor off my backpack, I heard the woman say, "Jimmy, right?"

I turned around, swinging my backpack over my shoulders. "Close."

"Johnny?"

"Hendrix."

"The best guitarist to ever live. I was just listening to 'Machine Gun' on my way to class."

"I swear my dad played that and 'Burning of the Midnight Lamp' every day."

"Sounds like you have a Father of the Year candidate on your hands."

"I doubt you'll ever meet him, but on the off chance you do, let's keep the compliment between us. His head is big enough."

"Your secret is safe with me."

"I'm not saying my father isn't great because he's the best, but how do you know my father isn't terrible, which he isn't for the record."

"Easy. Your dad has great taste in music."

"Okay? And that means what exactly?"

"Great music taste means everything. You can tell a lot about someone by the music they listen to."

"Is that right?"

"Well, yeah-at least it does for me. I like to think of music as a reflection of who we are."

"You're passionate about your music. I can't imagine how you grilled your husband on the first date."

She gave me a weird look, one of confusion and surprise. "Who says I'm married?"

"Your ring finger."

She held back a secret in a chuckle. "He survived."

"Hopefully, you didn't do my boy too bad."

"Don't feel sorry for him. The man has questionable taste." She must've spotted my confusion. "My home is solid, though."

"You love to see it. So, what does your musical taste say about you?"

"I don't know. You tell me. I like Erykah Badu, Janelle Monae, The Temptations, Smokey Robinson, Miles Davis, and of course, Jimi Hendrix."

"It could mean anything to anybody."

"I didn't ask anybody. I asked you."

"I'll get back to you on that."

She must have seen me racking my brain for her name because she said, "Victoria." As soon as she said it, I remembered. She and I were in a group for whatever class we took together last year.

"I haven't seen you around the Behavior Science building lately-not that I'm some kind of creep or something. It's just, you know, college tends to treat us like livestock. Social science majors over here, math majors over there, science majors' get back in the lab.' You kinda get used to seeing the same faces around."

"The duties of a mother never end. I thought it was time for me to go to school; my son thought otherwise."

"Good to know he changed his mind. Hopefully, he doesn't again."

She checked her phone. "Speaking of kids, I should go. Mommy duties never end" She zoned off just long enough for me to wonder if everything was okay at home. "What I would do for a weeklong vacation to Cinque Terre. Or anywhere international with palm trees."

A weight, probably that of a palm tree itself, collapsed onto me. "If I see another palm tree in my life, it would be too soon."

"Whatever you do, don't look down."

I looked down and noticed the two palm trees--one on each side--printed on my button-up. "They're everywhere."

She sucked in a smile. "It was nice officially meeting you, Hendrix."

"Same"

She pulled out her phone, putting it to her ear. From the size and glistening of her wedding ring, her husband had money. It looked uncomfortably expensive. At first, I thought she was talking to her husband because she kept saying, "baby," but her tone became increasingly motherly each time she said it. She went from nurturing to assertive back to nurturing, and it reminded me of my mom.

I hated thinking about my mom.

Outside the class, I fumbled with my headphones, trying to untangle the wires. Before class, I had wrapped the cables around my phone, and now, I cussed at myself, insisting I wouldn't do it again like I do whenever they get tangled. When I untangled them, I scrolled through my music. There were so many different musicians to describe me by my taste. Was I open-minded and diverse? I fell deeper and deeper into endless possibilities, and I asked myself questions like: would someone know I was open-minded if they looked through my phone, was I even open-minded, what else could someone say about me from my taste in music.

Whatever, I thought.

...

The street that led into the school curved into a horseshoe. Individuals hopped in and out of cars like clockwork. The individuals waiting for their rides either stood on the curb or sat on stone benches.

Victoria sat by herself on one of the benches, listening to music as she looked around for the right car to appear through all the rest that bottled necked at the pick-up area. In waves, students flooded to and from school, and new cars pulled to the curb. None came for her.

I went to my car, which took me way too long to find, and checked the traffic on my phone. To no surprise, it was at a standstill. It was always a mess at that time. For the next twenty minutes, I sat in my car listening to one of my favorite podcasts until I had to pee. On my way to the nearest restroom- inside the Bookstore- and back, Victoria still waited.

I thought about offering her a ride, and just as quickly, I talked myself out of asking. Don't come off as a serial killer, I told myself.

So, there I was, standing less than fifty feet behind her, in the middle of the school's lawn, staring. One minute I convinced myself to ask if she needed a ride, and the next, I convinced myself it wouldn't be a good idea. I already knew her response: *Oh, no, thank you. My ride is just running a little late. Thanks though.*

I started my long walk through the parking lot. I could have easily cut through the lawn. Instead, I decided to walk to the pick-up area, where Victoria and the other individuals waited. When I walked past Victoria, I stopped, took a deep breath, and turned around.

"Hey," I said, "are you still waiting on your ride?"

"My mother-in-law is running a little late. She didn't expect me to be out of class so early, so here I am waiting."

"Rookie mistake. It's the first day of class."

"I know. I have to get back into the swing of things. What about you?"

"What about me?"

"Why are you still hanging around? I swore I saw you leave right after class. Well, after you went to war with your headphones." She laughed.

"Every day is a war. A war with health. A war with family. A war with my headphones. I beat em' though"

"You really should invest in a pair of wireless headphones. I'm not saying they would make your life easier. Well, actually, yeah, I am. You were having that same problem last time I saw you."

"I really need to find out the name of that class. It's starting to bug me."

"Is it that important?"

"My curiosity gets the best of me sometimes, so now it kinda is."

"I think it was Deviant Behavior, but I'm not one hundred percent sure."

"It could have been." My head lowered a bit. I snapped, looking up. "It was. It was Deviant Behavior. I remember we had to say one deviant act we did, and I think you mentioned how you got pregnant at 17."

"Whoa. Now, I'm one hundred percent sure. I don't make it a habit of shouting that I was a teen mom from the rooftops. So, what was your deviant act?"

"I can't remember."

"You don't remember yours, but you can remember mine?"

"I guess so."

"Either you do your fair share of deviant acts, or you're noisy. Or both. I guess you have to tell me something you did, Mr. Hendrix."

"I don't have to do anything, Mrs. Victoria."

"You're right. I just thought it would make for great conversation."

"And here I was thinking we were already having a great conversation."

"It's good, not great. Great conversation is the slow burn of solving the mystery that is the human mind."

I took a deep breath. "Fine." I sat beside her. The stone dug into my bone, and I put my hands on the bench and adjusted myself. "Alright, so my dad used to be what you would call a man of order and routine. My sisters and I called him OCD on a good day and crazy on the bad. Everything had to make sense. He was one of those people. Our entire day was planned out, from when we woke up to when we went to bed. And let me tell you, we woke up early and went to bed just as early. As kids, we may have whined and begged about not wanting to do our chores or having to go to bed so early, but when you're a teenager, you don't just whine and beg. You make a stand. There was this time I'll never forget because I just got my license."

"The ultimate symbol of freedom and adulthood for a teenager."

"Unless you lived in my house. So this one time, my dad grounded me for not doing my chores. It was my way of fighting the power. He didn't care about the needs of a teenager, so I was going to make him."

"Public Enemy would be proud."

"So I'm grounded, right? The same weekend Joseph Powell was throwing a party. Now, one thing about Joseph Powell was he threw the best parties. Well, so I heard. I never got the chance to experience one myself, being a kid with a curfew."

"So, Joseph Powell threw a party."

"I snuck out. Since I didn't have a car, I took my dad's. Everything was going according to plan, up until I got outside."

"This sounds like it's gonna be good."

"I live a house down from this blind corner in the neighborhood that inspiring NASCAR drivers would hit like they're in a Fast and Furious movie. It was like clockwork. They whip around the corner, scare a few kids playing in the street, and annoy parents in the process. Nobody ever got hurt, so it was what it was until it wasn't. There I was, car in neutral, backing it from the driveway, mere seconds away from a social awakening, when some dick in a mustang hit the corner so fast that I couldn't even see my life flash before my eyes. I just heard the metal shrieking of the damned. The HOA installed speed humps a week later. Tragedy will always be the great equalizer for a lack of common sense."

"That sounds like that could have ended badly."

I stared at a parked mustang. "If God decided that was my time, I would've thanked at the pearly gates."

"You must've been terrified."

"It all kinda happened in slow motion, to be honest. When I saw the car hit, I didn't remember getting out of dodge."

"How did your dad react?"

"Just know I spent that entire summer working at a local grocery store to pay off the damages. That's the G-rated version."

She laughed. "Of all the possibilities, that's what did you in? It was the easiest part. You were in the clear, but some guy, who was doing everything but looking, ran into the car." She laughed harder. "It's pretty funny."

"No, it's not."

When she stopped laughing, we continued discussing random topics, never staying on one subject for too long. At first, she asked when I was going to graduate. I told her after the current quarter, and she congratulated me. Then we discussed our majors. We both majored in Sociology, and neither of us had a plan after graduation. I barely knew why I chose the major. For the entire conversation, my heart raced.

As if she knew I needed to hear it, she assured me that life had a plan for us. She had no idea what that plan was, but she was confident there was one.

"That's the beauty of life," she said. "It's all a mystery, an intricate puzzle you have to put together."

I couldn't stop thinking about what she said, how she said it, and the look on her face; she was so optimistic. It all eased me. My heart stopped racing. At that moment, I knew everything would work out.

Neither of us spoke. Victoria pulled out her phone and called a woman. I heard the woman's voice but didn't listen to what she said. Victoria wasn't upset or irritated when the call ended, and if she was, she hid it well.

"Ride still running late?" I asked.

"She's shopping, and when she shops, she takes her time. My mother-in-law doesn't miss her deals."

"Not to be weird, but I can give you a ride if you need one. I'm not doing anything but killing time until traffic dies down."

"I appreciate the offer, but I don't mind waiting. It's a nice reprieve from the mundane."

After a summer of listening to my dad cough and groan day in and day out, I forgot how peaceful life could be--when we let it. "It really is."

"How much longer are you going to wait?"

"Until seven. Normally, the freeway isn't so bad around then."

"So, twenty or so minutes. Good, we have some time." She turned her body to me. "Let me see your phone."

"Why?"

"Relax, I'm not going to scroll through your pictures. I just want to see what you listen to."

"I don't think I want to. I'm not a fan of being judged because of my musical tastes."

"I'm not going to judge you. And even in the small chance that I do, we don't know each other; who cares if I feel a certain way about what you like?"

"Be gentle." I handed her my phone.

She scrolled through it with little to no expression, which made me nervous. A smile occasionally broke the look on her face. When she finished, she handed back my phone. "So," I said, putting my phone back into my pocket.

"So."

"Thoughts? Opinions"

"I thought you weren't in the mood for me to judge you."

"Come on. I'm ready for my execution."

"Good thing for you, I'm a pacifist."

"I'm counting my blessings as we speak."

She stood and looked down at me. "You don't have a lot of Erykah Badu, Janelle Monae, or Miles Davis, but you listen to a lot of Outkast. And I know a lot of Outkast."

"What can I say? Other than greatest hip-hop group of all time."

"Alright. 3 Stacks or Daddy Fat Sax?"

I turned my nose up in disgust. "Come on, now. Are you really asking me to pick between two of the greatest rappers to pick up a mic? Both."

"Okay. Someone who gives Andre and Big Boi their flowers. You love to see it."

"So, what does my music taste say about me?"

Walking to a white Nissan Altima that pulled to the curb, she turned around to say, "You're pretty Southernplayalistic, Hendrix," before stepping into the car.

The street light, hooked above, lit the car enough to see inside. An older woman drove. Two boys sat in the backseat, screaming, "Mommy," loud enough that it sounded like they stood next to me. They had the biggest smiles on their faces.

Watching Victoria tickle the two boys, I zoned out to thoughts and images of my mother. My phone vibrating brought me back to reality.

My sister. She didn't want anything.

I let the voicemail answer, and as soon as my phone stopped ringing, she called again. I didn't answer. I went to send a text message, but before I could, she sent her own: Hendrix, where are you??!!! Just got home!!! It's dad. Call me right now!

My heart stopped, and my throat tightened. It felt like I swallowed needles every time I breathed. My legs kept shaking, and the cold, deep shiver took over my entire body. I trembled too much to see straight, let alone call back.

Hendrix, it was only a matter of time, I said to myself.

I took deep breaths, holding them in for a few seconds before exhaling. My throat loosened, and it no longer felt like I was swallowing needles. Just as I built up the strength to call my sister back, my dad called. I answered immediately.

"Dad," I said, breathing heavily.

"Calm down, son," he said and laughed. "I'm okay. I'm okay. Just breathe. You're supposed to bury me, not the other way around."

"Dad, you can't scare me like that. I thought-I thought-"

"I thought you knew Eve's natural inclination is to panic. I tell you, those drama classes were a bad idea."

"So, you're alright?"

"I'm alright, son."

"You tend to underreact."

"Aren't you supposed to be the cool one? Vanessa has already cursed me out; she did enough for both of you, so cut me some slack. Can you do that, dad?"

"She's already on the warpath, huh?"

"You know your sister. She could make Ares run with his dick tucked between his legs."

An entire weight lifted from my shoulders. I sighed. "Well, I'm glad you're okay."

Vanessa screamed at the top of her lungs in the background while Eve cried. She called dad selfish. I couldn't catch everything else because her voice went in and out from dad laughing under his breath, and eventually, she heard him because she called him out for it. She called him selfish a few more times and immature. A door slammed, followed by silence—no screaming or crying.

I assumed my dad sat in his happy place: out on the porch. Whenever he was stressed, upset, or sad, he smoked out there for hours. He would never admit something was wrong, but he only smoked when something troubled him. I heard the spark wheel roll, his inhaling, and when he exhaled, he sighed. It always sounded like he was letting go of all his stress the first time he pushed smoke through his lips. I listened to him smoking with a sharp pain in my chest and a tightness in my throat.

"Dad," I said.

"Hmm?"

I didn't say anything; I couldn't.

"Hello?" He asked.   "I'm still here."

"Forgot what you were going to say already?"

"I guess so. Hey, I'm about to head back. See you when I get home."

"See you soon."

"I'm glad you're okay, dad. We have a few more memories to make."

"Why do you think I haven't keeled over yet?"

I ended the call. On the car ride home, I listened to "Machine Gun" and "Burning of the Midnight Lamp" on repeat, thinking back to a time when it all made sense.

Victoria

Something about Hendrix felt off.

As my Mother-in-law drove away, Hendrix stared, like a lost puppy, into the car. As we drove away, I watched him in the side mirror and kept looking until he was another figure lost by distance.

My mother-in-law cleared her throat and elbowed my side.

"So who was that?" she whispered.

"A friend from class."

"Just a friend, huh? Are there any types of benefits in this friendship?"

I stammered. "Okay, that's a wildly inappropriate assumption." I leaned in closer. "Do you think I'm cheating on Hershey? Does he think I'm cheating on him? I don't have friends with benefits. Did he tell you I have a friend with benefits?"

"What's a friend with benefits, mommy?" Martin asked.

I turned around to look at them. Martin wiggled his loose front tooth.

"Honey," I said. "Stop playing with your tooth."

"Fine."

"Thank you. Now, a friend with benefits is just someone." I stopped and thought about Martin going to school and sharing the lie I was about to tell. All the other little kids would go around the playground, referring to one another as *friends with benefits*. Then, I wiggled his toes. "How about we make a deal? When you are ten, I will tell you what it means."

"Okay, but only if you promise to stop playing with your tooth."

"Always."

"Friend with benefits," Daniel said and giggled. He stressed every syllable, and it would have been adorable if he wasn't screaming it at the top of his lungs.

"Hey, hey, hey," I said to Daniel, "stop all that screaming."

Hendrix

Traffic was pretty light, so I got home in about thirty minutes. Eve and Vanessa's cars were in the driveway, forcing me to park on the street. Dad sat in his wicker chair on the porch. A cloud of smoke masked his face.

He waved.

I didn't wave back. I finished listening to "Burning of the Midnight Lamp" before I got out and walked to the porch. I watched the smoke rise above him as it thinned out and disappeared.

"Someone looks troubled," my dad said. He sounded winded. "Sit down with your old man and tell him what's wrong."

You're smoking, I thought. That's what's wrong.

But I couldn't tell him that, not then at least. I was upset when I saw him smoking after receiving the news, but I didn't say anything out of the fear of sounding like Vanessa. The more he had smoked, the more upset I got, and eventually, I became numb to it all. I was more upset at myself. I knew I should have said something, but like now, I didn't say anything.

If I did say something, it wouldn't have mattered. Life and age set him in his ways. Surprisingly, he would never argue. He would listen to all your points and reply with, "okay" or worse: tell a joke. He wasn't always like that. A few months ago, he was more vocal. There were times when he looked for a chance to argue. When he had learned how to work the internet, he became a troll, picking fights in the comment section of news articles about gun violence and ended each post with, "Owner of a dozen guns and still haven't shot up a pre-teen." At home, he used to walk around with a gun holstered to his belt. Ask him why, he would reply, "because it is my God-given right!"

I sat in an iron chair beside him. The cushion had seen better days that it did nothing to protect me from the iron pressing against the bone. I leaned forward, putting my arms across my legs.

"Sounds like all is well in the Harper residence," I said.

"Now you jinxed it."

"Vanessa and Eve...this quiet? Jesus is King."

"Ain't he good? The legend goes, if you listen hard enough, you can hear both of them mumbling under their breath."

We stopped talking to listen. The silence further exaggerated my dad's wheezing and heavy breathing. After about a minute, we heard Vanessa talking under her breath, complaining about being the only responsible person in the family. We laughed.

"I wouldn't trade that girl for the world," he said. "She has a passion in her."

He fell into a coughing spell. Dry and hoarse coughs. As he coughed, leaned forward with an arm covering his mouth, I noticed how much weight he had lost. He was never a thin guy, but now it looked like he was being sucked dry or collapsing from the inside.

And yet he's smoking, I thought. Then again, you're letting him.

Vanessa was still yelling-- this time about me. Like everyone except herself, I fancied being irresponsible because I didn't answer Eve's call. She and Eve changed the subject to dad. They mentioned how terrible he sounded.

He did.

"I'll be back," I said.

My dad wasn't coughing anymore. Now, he inhaled and exhaled in bliss.

"Duty calls," he said, shooing me towards the door. "Your turn to feel the wrath."

Pictures of my sisters and I hung in the entryway. The majority of Vanessa and Eve's pictures captured their lives up until high school graduation. Meanwhile, Dad and I had photos from as late as last year. I stared at this picture of Eve and me going down a slide- we were probably four years old.

Eve and Vanessa came from the kitchen and stopped halfway down the hall, glaring at me. Vanessa was tall and skinny with dreads, and her cheeks were darker than the rest of her face. Eve was the lightest in the family, so Vanessa and I used to tell her she was adopted-she would cry every time. She had long eyelashes and short hair. Her hair used to be down to her back, but she cut it off after seeing Samira Wiley from Orange is the New Black.

"Eve called you five times, Hendrix," Vanessa said.

"I was in class-"

"I'm not trying to hear anything from you except 'I'm sorry,' because not only did you show me that you are irresponsible, you showed that you could care less about your sick father. So unless you are apologizing, I suggest you save all of the excuses, Hendrix, because I don't want to hear them."

"Hey to you too, Vanessa." I waved. "I'm doing well."

She stared.

"What?"

She shook her head and stormed into the kitchen.

"Hi, Hendrix," Eve said and then hugged me.

"It's nice to see one of my sisters still has love for me."

"We shared a womb for nine months. It'll take more than a few missed calls to break our bond."

"Come on, Eve. We all know you're adopted. You never wondered why you're a shade darker than milk?"

She slapped me on the arm. "Shut up."

"You know I'm playing."

"I know. I know. I'm not saying you aren't funny; it's just time for a new joke." She went to walk away.

"Hey, sorry I didn't get back to you. I was going to call you back, but then dad called. He said he was fine, so I didn't think there was anything wrong."

"You never think anything is wrong," Vanessa yelled, walking from the kitchen as she dried her hands with a towel. "That's your problem. You never think anything is serious! Our dad is dying, Hendrix-of cancer! When your sister calls and texts you, telling you that something is wrong with our father, you don't get to decide if nothing's wrong!"

"He called me and told me he was fine." Her nostrils flared, her teeth ground together as she breathed heavily. She stammered. "I don't give a damn what he said! Dad is the same man who told me he was fine, and I get here to see he looks like life ran him over twice. He is not fine! He looks like he's dying."

Well, if you came around to see your father more often, you would have known. You went off to live your life and forgot that life was more than work and friends. I wanted to say those words so badly. They were on the tip of my tongue; I just chose not to say anything.

I didn't care that she left, but dad did. He would call her every other day, and she could care less. I thought back to the day we received the news. He called Vanessa as we left the hospital. She answered, only to hurry him off the phone, even when he told her it was important. Either she didn't care or already hung up at that point because dad took the phone from his ear.

"Can you stop yelling, Vanessa?" Eve asked. "He gets it."

"Does he?" Vanessa asked. "Last time I checked, this is the same person who took an entire month to let us know that dad was dying!" She looked at me. "Did you know dad is talking about stopping chemo?"

I sighed and nodded. "Yeah, but-"

"Of course you know. Dad decides to kill himself, and it's one big secret. I don't know what's worse, dad giving up or you deciding to hide it. You couldn't tell us? Wait, let me guess, you didn't think it was a big deal?"

"I didn't say that."

"You don't say much of anything. Your complacency is hazardous to the people around you." She awkwardly laughed. "Our dad wants to die, and you're letting him."

"You can't put this on me. Dad's a grown man."

"He listens to you. You shouldn't be okay with this. Just because Dad said he's fine with dying doesn't mean you should too. When are you going to grow a backbone and stop just going with the flow? Your father is dying!"

"Jesus Christ, Vanessa, I get it. Our father has cancer. Get off my back."

"Stage 3 cancer. This is serious."

"Let's not do this right now, guys," Eve said. "All this yelling can't be good for dad."

"He has lung cancer, Eve, not heart problems," Vanessa said, going back into the kitchen. "I guess these dirty dishes told

Hendrix they're fine chilling in the sink!" She slammed dishes into the sink as she washed them.

I went back outside and sat in the iron chair beside my dad. He expanded his cigarette. Without the courage to toss it to the ground, I stared at it and then at him as he threw it back into his mouth. There it was, the inhaling, the exhaling, the smiling. He looked satisfied.

Why was he so satisfied?

"It's nice not being on the other side of all that," my dad said.

"You do know you're her father, right? You don't have to take that."

"Neither do you."

"Why do you let her talk to you like that?"

"Why do you let her talk to you like that?"

"Dad, I'm serious."

"And I'm joking? Vanessa has always been temperamental. Like Eve, she's sensitive-they get that from your mother-but instead of crying, she wants to slap somebody. If I had the strength, I would put her over my knee. Since I don't, I let her get it all out. She's grieving; yelling is her way of coping. It's nice to see one of my children is upset that their old man is wasting away."

"Dad, don't do that. You know I care."

He laughed, pitching me on my side. "It was a joke. I know you would cry the most when your old man finally goes home to the Lord. Don't think I don't hear you at night."

"Doing"

"Hardening my towels."

"Really, dad?"

"You have alotta pent-up aggression and stress with no lady to let it out on or in, whatever you're into, son. If it means you turn my face towels into dinner plates, I say, 'cumming never hurt nobody."

"Dad!"

"I'm teasing. I'm talking about crying. I hear you crying."

"It's rough. Mom is gone, and now I'm slowly losing you. It's hard to take it all in."

"You can't lose me."

"I already feel like I am."

I crossed my arms and looked down at a line of ants moving across the porch.

Neither of us spoke. The world froze for a second. We avoided eye contact in the silence, where Vanessa and Eve didn't yell; where no sprinklers went off as they usually did around that time; where no cars sped by like it wasn't a residential area. His inhaling broke the silence. The woven chair cracked under Dad's weight as he readjusted himself. Smoke moved into my field of vision.

Even with lung cancer, he can't give up smoking, I thought.

"Remember that time you tried to sneak out the house to go to some party?" he asked, holding his cigarette between his fingers.

"You mean Joseph Powell's party."

"Joseph Powell. You kept saying that like I was supposed to know who he was."

"He threw the best parties, allegedly. I was almost in the car."

"If it wasn't for that damn mustang."

"That damn mustang, the bane of my existence."

"I woke up when I heard the crash. I looked out the window and saw you standing there, looking like I caught you masturbating, and I just about lost my mind."

"You beat my ass." I laughed.

"You were lucky you were alive to get beat."

"I guess I never thought about how close I was to seeing mom. I don't remember much after I saw the headlights hit that corner." I laughed. "I do remember Eve, though. What was she yelling again?"

"Don't beat my twin."

"That's it. 'Don't beat my twin. If you beat him, you have to beat me." I laughed, and then he joined.

"That girl is so dramatic."

"Always has been and always will be."

"All I could think about was your mother. Why did she leave me? Did she think I could do this alone? So many questions ran through my head when I saw you standing outside that car. You had this miserable look on your face, like a puppy that got separated from its litter."

"She didn't choose to get in a car accident. Just like she didn't choose to die."

He took another drag. When he exhaled, he let all of his stress go. His face confirmed his trouble. His concern. His fingers still wrapped around his cigarette, which hung from his mouth.

"What's wrong?" I asked.

He took the cigarette from his mouth and glanced at me before shifting his eyes to the ground.

"Nothing. This ain't nothing but more of the same."

"Well, I know for a fact that you're not fine, so can we stop dancing? What's up?"

"Hendrix, I need to tell you something."

"Okay."

"Before I tell you, you have to promise you won't get upset, and most importantly, you have to promise you won't tell your sisters."

"O-okay."

"I have to hear you say it."

"Okay. Okay. I promise."

"No!" He stared. "You have to look me in my eyes and promise me you won't get upset or tell your sisters! Say those words."

"Alright. I promise I won't get upset or tell Eve or Vanessa. Just tell me already."

He took a drag and then a deep sigh. His eyes fixated on the ground.

"Your mother isn't dead." He sputtered. A coldness of indifference lingered in his voice.

"Huh?"

"Your mother isn't dead."

A heavyweight sat on my chest. My mind went from having endless thoughts to nothing and back in seconds.

I chuckled.

"Say that again. It sounded like you said mom is still alive."

"Hendrix." He looked me in the depths of my eyes, straight into my soul. "Your mother is alive."

"What the fuck do you mean Mom isn't dead?"

He shushed me. "Hendrix, bring it down. This is our little secret, okay? Your sisters can't know. At least not yet."

My head spun so fast I almost fell from the chair. My eyes watered. "Her ashes are on the mantle."

"Those aren't your mother's ashes. They're Mojos."

"Our dog?"

"It's not my proudest decision."

I laughed. "Nice joke. I have no idea why you felt the need to make the joke, but you got me." I wiped the tears from my eyes with the back of my hand, laughing.

"I'm not joking."

A sharp pain went through my chest. The tears I managed to hold in ran down my face. "Dad, don't tell me this."

"I'm sorry, Hendrix."

"What the hell, dad?"

"I know. I know. One day I woke up, and she was gone. She took everything she could and just left."

"Dad."

"I know. I called her friends and her family, and everyone said they had no idea where she was. I knew they knew. I cried and begged, and they stuck to their guns. I panicked, son."

"Dad."

"Hendrix, I know. But I was thirty years old with twin two-year-olds and a seven-year-old. I kept asking myself, 'what do I do?' I couldn't think straight, and then Vanessa came up to me, crying, asking where your mother was, and I just said the first thing that came to my mind."

"That she died?"

"It sounded much better than your mother walked out on you."

"It's really not. Do you know how many nights we sat up crying? I once heard Vanessa cussing out God for taking mom away."

"You think I don't feel like shit because I do. It's just everything was happening so fast. I never had the chance."

"But you did. You had over twenty years to say something. You choose silence."

"If you decide I'm the world's worst father, I get it. If you decide you want nothing to do with me, I get that too."

"I'm not going anywhere, dad."

"Go ahead. Think whatever you want about me, but let me tell you something. Remember this moment. Remember this conversation when your children look at you like you're some type of superhero. I want you to remember this conversation word for word and then come see me if I'm lucky to see that day. Come and find me, and let me know if it's easy to look your child in the eyes and tell them you can't fly. You think I wanted this? But how do you look at your children and tell them their mother-the person that held them in her womb for nine months-didn't want them? I panicked. Eventually, the crying stopped, and you kids stopped asking about her as much. I couldn't break your hearts again. I couldn't put you through that pain again."

"Why are you telling me all this now?"

"Because I might not live to see tomorrow. I would feel like a dick taking something like that to the grave."

"So you felt the need to tell me of all people? You couldn't tell your doctor? A therapist? A random lady in the bread aisle? Why did it have to be me?"

"Because you can take it. That's not something you tell any old body. You're my son. My boy. Who else would I tell? Imagine if I told Vanessa that. Cancer would be the least of my worries. Now imagine if I told Eve."

"She would drop dead."

"She would drop dead in her $400 boots. We would never hear the end of it. They're like their mother; they can't deal with stress. You're a rock, just like your old man. Nothing breaks you. You're strong--stronger than they could ever be."

"Is that where I'm supposed to thank you?"

"I don't expect that, but I do expect you to break the news to your sisters when I'm gone."

"Or I never tell them."

"That too, but don't be an asshole, Hendrix." He smiled at me, a coy look in his eyes. Then he started coughing. He leaned forward, covering his mouth, and his cigarette dropped to the ground. He couldn't stop; he just kept letting out coughs that sounded like barks.

Eve and Vanessa rushed outside. When they saw the cigarette on the ground and smelt the smoke, they lost it. Vanessa screamed; Eve cried.

"What the hell is this?" Vanessa asked. "Dad, are you smoking again?" She rubbed her forehead as she grimaced. "So you just want to die, huh? You have lung cancer! In what world do you think this shit is okay?"

Dad sighed with a look of guilt, and as he opened his mouth to speak, I stood.

"It's not dad's cigarette," I said. "It's mine, okay?" I lowered my head. "It's mine."

Vanessa slapped me.

Chapter 2
Victoria

I carried Martin into the house since he had left the house without shoes. My mother-in-law opened the door, and Daniel ran inside, making as much noise as he possibly could. He ran around the living room, hopping on and bouncing off the couch. The yelling never stopped with Daniel.

"Daniel," I said. "What's up with you tonight? You're just a little ball of energy, I see." I put Martin down. "Don't leave this house again without putting shoes on, okay?"

"I tried to switch my shoes after we came back from the store," he said. "But Grandma said we were late picking you up. I didn't want you to wait too long."

"That's very nice of you, but don't do it again."

"Okay."

My mother-in-law picked up Daniel.

"Come on, you little Tasmanian," she said. "It's bath time. You too, Martin. Both of ya smell like outside."

Martin stuck out his lips and complained about having to take a bath with Daniel. She gave him this stern look; he followed her upstairs, dragging his feet and pouting.

Hershey was in the kitchen. I watched him from the archway as he checked on the food in the oven. The kitchen light shone off his dark skin and bald head. His tank top and shorts, which stopped mid-thigh, showed off all his muscles. A tingle coursed down my spine. If we were alone, I would have taken him down and made love to him right there; me on the island, with my legs wrapped around him, as he thrust inside me. But we weren't alone, so I was happily admiring all of him.

"Hey, hey, sexy man," I said, leaning against the wall.

He turned around. His gapped tooth smile and "The sexiest chef you'll know" apron always made my heart skip a beat or two.

"Hey, hey, kiddo," he said, walking over and taking me in his arms for a kiss.

"I need another one of those."

We planted a juicy kiss on my lips.

He asked for another; I kissed him. He embraced me tighter. I wrapped my arms around his neck, and nothing felt more right. If the world came crashing down, I knew he would protect me.

He squeezed my ass with force and stroked my neck with his tongue. *Jesus.*

"I want you right now," he whispered and bit my ear.

I giggled like a little girl. Hershey always made me feel like one again. I didn't just love him. I was still a little girl with a crush. Throughout my day, I would tell him how much I loved him through text. Whenever I thought about him, which was almost every second, I imagined him moving his massive hands all over my body.

"I want you," I said.

"I want you, kiddo."

"I want you so bad."

"You already have me."

"Yeah?"

"Yeah."

"Tell me that I'm all yours."

"No problem. I'm all yours."

"Tell me you love me."

"I love you, baby. You know that no matter what, I love you and only you."

"I know."

He put his forehead to mine and kissed me. In the brief moment where our lips no longer touched, it felt like days had passed since I felt them.

"So, how much time do you think we have before those little rascals ruin the moment?" He asked.

"Five minutes-maybe." I giggled. "Daniel is the wild card."

"I can work with five minutes."

"I want at least thirty later."

He removed his apron and pulled down his pants just enough to expose his half-erect dick. "Get on your knees."

After a glance at the stairs, I slowly pulled him into my mouth. My mouth watered as I felt him grow. I held the base when he was fully erect and sucked him nice and slow, just like he liked. His moans heightened my arousal, and I was dripping wet. Saliva built up in my mouth, but I didn't swallow it. I let it cover his dick and drip to the floor. Trying to fight back groans and moans, he shot his warm cum into my mouth. I opened wide to see him admire how much he filled my mouth.

"Good girl," he said.

I swallowed it all and giggled playfully, watching him come down from bliss.

I wiped up the spit as he, pulling up his pants, waddled to check on the food in the oven. On my hands and knees, I looked up at him, smiling at his heavy breaths.

I got up, walked to him, switching my hips, wrapped my arms around his burly figure, and rested my head on the back of his shoulder. He kissed the top of my head before removing garlic bread, on a cookie sheet, from the oven to the stove. The edges of the bread were black.

"Oops," I said.

"No big deal. We can scrape the black off."

As I washed my hands, Martin and Daniel raced downstairs. The thumping of their little feet cast over the screaming and yelling. The madness ended when they plopped down at the kitchen table.

My Mother-in-law dragged her feet behind them.

"Let me guess," Martin said and sighed. "We're having spaghetti...again?"

"If it bothers you so much, Martin, you can have some cereal," Hershey said.

Martin's eyes lit up. "Can I?"

"You're going to eat this spaghetti and be happy."

"We always eat spaghetti when you cook."

"That's because you need your carbs. How else will you two get that unwavering energy?"

Daniel shrieked something that no one understood. The second time he yelled out like a mad man, we made out what he said: "sa-ghetti."

He always had so much energy—the complete opposite of Martin. Up until Martin turned five, Hershey and I had feared he might have been on the spectrum. He rarely spoke and barely did anything. We would take him to the park, but nothing. He never played. Even as a baby, he didn't cry or laugh much.

Daniel, on the other hand, kept us on our toes most days—and nights.

Daniel screeched as if he attempted to sing a song he didn't know the words to while eating.

"Daniel," Hershey said. "I appreciate the zeal, but it's rarely this serious. Bring it down, buddy. You can sing without all the theatrics."

Daniel sang louder.

"Daniel, I'm serious. Calm it down and eat your food."

Daniel giggled. The singing stopped for him to dance.

He tried to use his fork and somehow touched everything and anything except the noodles. It didn't take long for him to use his hands. Even so, he dropped noodles on the table and over himself. He wiped his face with his hands, smearing sauce further across his mouth and cheeks.

"Aren't you just a little monster," I said.

From the bottom of his gut, he gave his best impression of a monster roaring, his hands flailing above his head, slanging noodles and sauce across the table. He grabbed a handful of noodles, grinding them in his hands, and shoved them into his mouth. Most of the noodles fell into his lap.

"Honey," I said, "let me help." I was sitting across from him, and I reached for his fork.

"No, I'm a big boy. I can feed myself."

"Yes, you can, baby. Mommy just wants to help."

"Big boys still can get fed by their mommies," my mother-in-law said.

"Nu-uh," Daniel said.

"Yes-huh. I feed your daddy all the time. Isn't that right, Hershey?"

"Fed," Hershey said. "She fed me all the time. As in when I was a child. Grandma tends to forget that I'm not a baby anymore."

My mother-in-law tried to feed Hershey spaghetti. He stared at her, visibly unamused. After some time, he sighed and rolled his eyes, and then he opened wide. Martin and Daniel laughed and repeatedly said, "Grandma fed daddy." Hershey closed his eyes, trying his best to refrain from yelling. His nostrils flared.

"Martin. Daniel," he yelled, hitting his hand against the table. "Stop playing around and eat your dinner! Do you hear me?"

Martin and Daniel finished their dinner without uttering another word. My mother-in-law took them upstairs for bed after. Hershey and I ate in silence. It was best not to say anything to him. Whenever he took a drink, he slammed the cup down.

He looked silly—something I would have said if I wanted to fight.

"You don't have to be so angry," I said. "It's okay to be fed by your mother. It doesn't make you any less of a man."

"Please don't start with me right now, Victoria. I'm not in the mood."

"What can I do to get you in the mood?" I rubbed his thigh with my other hand. "I think we have another five minutes to spare."

He snatched his hand away. "I'm not in the mood for this right now. Let it go."

After two bites of my burnt piece of garlic bread, I looked at him. "Why are you so mad? It was just a joke."

"I don't like being the butt of a joke. You know that. My mother knows that. I go to work every day and work my ass off to provide for my family. The last thing I want is my children-my sons-to think of me as a joke! I am a man!"

"And they don't think of you as anything short of a man. Just calm down. It's not that serious." I held his hand. "Those boys idolize you. They think their daddy can do no wrong. It's almost like you're a superhero to them. You'll always be. They don't have to see you leap over the tallest building or stop a speeding bullet for their eyes to light up every time you walk through that door. Nothing can change that, even being fed by your mother." I kissed his cheek and moved back slightly to keep our faces almost against one another. "But if that's embarrassing, I guess mama won't give you dessert tonight."

He smiled. "Oh, I'm getting that dessert."

"Only if you're good."

"Shit, you must not know me. I'm always good."

"Oh yeah?"

"I stay good, girl. Now, give me my dessert."

He picked me up and laid me on the couch in the family room. He lay atop me, passionately kissing me with his tongue deep in my mouth. The weight of his body, supported by mine, sent a shiver through me.

I felt his warmth and took in his scent with every breath. My hands explored every inch of him.

He was ready- I could feel him, hard and bulging, against my stomach. Hearing his mother walk downstairs, I hopped up and straightened my shirt. Hershey stayed on the couch, looking towards the entrance of the kitchen. We smiled at his mother as she emerged from the archway.

"I'm about to get going," she said. "Daniel went right to sleep, but Martin is still up, so you have to control those urges for a few more minutes." She grabbed her purse from the floor beside the couch.

"See you tomorrow, mom," Hershey said.

He was halfway up when his mother said, "Boy, I've seen that thing for years, and I don't want to see it no mo. I'll let myself out."

"Good night," I said.

She kissed me goodnight and left.

The thought of his mother openly acknowledging his erection nearly sent me into a fit of side-splitting laughter. As the laugh pressed through my lips, his furrowing eyebrows and eyes narrowing in anger stopped me in my tracks, and I awkwardly coughed to spare the argument.

I straddled his lap, slowly grinding. Rubbing his head, I kissed him on the lips against his resistance. He tried to put up a front. His frown said one thing; his hardening said another. A smirk peaked through his grimace.

He wrapped his arms around my waist and buried his face into my breast.

"Take off your jeans," he demanded.

I stood and turned around. Before taking off my jeans, I did a little dance as I looked over my shoulder at him, biting down on my bottom lip.

He smacked my ass, drawing out a moan. He pulled off his shorts; he was fully erect.

"Sit down," he said.

I slid my panties to the side and sank onto him, feeling him stretch me. He tried to take control. Tried. I worked my hips with purpose and leaned forward into his ear.

"Are you still mad?" I asked.

His head moved back to the top of the couch, and his eyes closed, enjoying the ride.

"I'm cumming," he said right before shoving one of the many pillows on the couch over his face.

His gasps turned into laughter.

When I stood up, cum dripped onto his legs. I repositioned my panties, stepped into my jeans, having to wiggle to get them back on, and dropped beside him with my legs across his lap. His decent size nut soaked through my panties.

His breathing slowly went back to normal. I listened as I stared down at my ring, twisting it around my finger.

"What's on your mind?" He asked. He put his hand on my chin, and when I looked up, he kissed me on the lips.

"Just thinking about the day I'll be Ms. Downing."

"It's in the works, baby. I want it to be special, something out of a fairytale. We've been together a long time; you don't deserve just any old proposal. I appreciate your patience, baby."

"I don't make it a point to rush a man. That's the perfect way to scare him off."

"You make it sound like we won't get married."

I kept staring at my ring, twisting it around and around.

"Victoria." He grabbed hold of my hand, squeezing. "You do know I'm going to marry you, right?"

"Do you know what day Thursday is?"

"Thursday? Like this Thursday?"

"Yeah, as in tomorrow is Wednesday, and the day after that is Thursday."

"Well, unless you're trying to trip me up, Thursday is our anniversary." He kissed me. "How could I forget the day my life changed forever?"

Squeezing his hand with just as much passion, I smiled and blushed. "It's hard to fathom that it has been nine years and two kids later."

"No way in hell has it been that long."

"Do the math, Mr. Accountant. I was a sophomore in high school. What would that have made you? A sophomore in college?"

"Don't say that so loud. It always makes me feel like a pedophile. The last thing I expected was the girl, wandering around campus looking for the Physical Science building, to be in high school. I didn't even know a program like that existed. By the time I figured out how old you were, I was already in love."

Butterflies fluttered in my stomach. It was the same feeling I had when he approached me to ask if I needed help. Back then, he always wore his glasses.

I straddled him and wrapped my arms around his neck. Kissing his chest, I tasted a mixture of sweat and cologne.

"You make me feel like that little girl again," I said.

"That doesn't make me sound any less creepy."

"You know what I mean."

"Mmhm." He caressed one breast while licking the other. "Whatever you say, with your sexy self."

"Touch me like you did when I was just that little girl looking for her class."

He stopped doing everything. "Seriously, Victoria, you can phrase that any other way. I feel dirty."

"Sorry, it's the love talking."

"Is that what love sounds like because it just sounds like you've lost your mind?"

"You have to lose your mind to fall in love. Putting your complete trust and emotional well-being in the hands of someone is an absolutely insane yet beautiful thing we can do as people."

"Yesterday, some woman jumped into the bear exhibit at the zoo because they invited her. Now that's crazy. I'll give my heart to five women before I try to befriend a bear." He turned and looked into my eyes, and I looked away.

"When you fall in love, you give that person your heart. If they wanted to, they could destroy you. It's crazy to put that much trust in someone."

I knew he was looking at me, trying to sort out his thoughts to say something. He caressed my cheek, and I looked up at him, gently resting my hand on the back of his. My body wouldn't stop shaking.

"I love you, Victoria," he said. "If that makes me crazy, then so be it."

I repositioned myself to sit beside him with my back against the arms of the couch, my knees pulled into my chest, and my feet touching his thighs. Looking past him, I stared at a picture of Martin and Daniel hanging on the wall. *My babies.*

After calling my name several times without getting an answer, he leaned in for a kiss. I hid my mouth behind my knees.

He stared at me.

"Thursday," he said, "I'm going to cook you dinner and pamper you like the queen you are, kiddo. Want to know why? Because you are my one." He kissed me. "My only." He kissed me again. "And my forever. I like being crazy."

Hendrix

For the first time in my life, a dark cloud lingered over my life, and even if the sun shone around me, it still rained.

I watched my dad in a coughing spell. From how he leaned forward with a hand over his mouth and the dryness of each cough, the hacking had no end in sight.

A few minutes prior, our waitress, a woman who wore far too much makeup, sat down our drinks; my dad had ordered coffee and a glass of water while I ordered cranberry juice and water. Maybe five minutes after that, she took our orders.

Sips of water couldn't help the coughing. He held the glass with both hands, shaking, barely able to drink. I thought about how smoking wasn't helping. Being at IHOP at 9:35 in the morning wasn't helping. I knew I wasn't helping.

The few people in the restaurant glanced over at the two-person booth that barely fit us.

Like Vanessa and Eve, they probably think he's dying, I thought. He is dying, Hendrix. He's dying, and if I'm being honest, you're letting him die. What the hell is wrong with you? Why are you allowing him to smoke? All you have to do is say something, but your contentment is his death. You aren't saying anything. You're just letting him die. He trusts you because, for some reason, you won't nag him. Maybe he needs to be nagged. If you did, you might be with his doctor right now, getting the help he needs, not pancakes. Maybe Vanessa was right. Maybe I am irresponsible. No responsible person would sit back and stay quiet as their father smokes himself, one carton at a time, to death. What the hell is wrong with me?

The coughing stopped, and he drank coffee upright in his seat so fast that when he took the cup from his lips, he gasped for air with a grin. He looked around at everything except me-the other individuals in the restaurant, the waiters and waitresses passing by, the passing cars outside, my glass of cranberry juice.

"Vanessa and Eve are going to lose it when they find out," I said. "On you, on me, on IHOP. I'm not trying to get slapped again."

"That's why we're going to do everything in our power to make sure they don't find out. We don't want them to lose anything. Next time, Vanessa might knock you into next week."

"You make that sound so easy."

"It sounds hard because you're making it hard."

"You know, one of the things I respect about you: you're unwavering cool. It may not sound like a big deal to you, but I'm living in a house of cards right now. When they come crashing down, you'll either not care or be gone."

"Look it here, Hendrix. I asked you to hold onto our little secret; I'll admit that. But I want you to know something, son. I held onto that secret for as long as I did because it was the right thing to do. You or my conscience can't convince me otherwise."

I chuckled. "I can't with you. You're indescribably unbelievable."

"If you want to tell them, go ahead."

"Why is that on me? It's your secret, dad. You tell them."

"It is my secret to tell. To keep. I'm not asking you to agree or understand. Son, you have a fight in you that you don't realize most of the time. Your sisters, they don't have it in them yet. I tell them about your mother, and the next time they'll see their old man is when I'm resting under palm trees."

I shivered. "You and these palm trees."

"I don't need you to cover for me, you hear me? I'm a grown man who doesn't need protecting. I'm trying to protect them from themselves. They aren't you."

"Yeah. They have a backbone."

"You're pretty steady yourself, son. Want to know what your problem is? You don't throw it in our faces in rage. You have more finesse."

"You're still expecting me to carry a lot on my shoulders."

"I expected to be in bed right now, and yet, here I am, sitting in an IHOP booth. I expected to be a millionaire, but all I managed to accumulate in my life was debt. I expected to live a nice, healthy life, but here I am, son, living God's plan. I have expected many things in my life that never came true, Hendrix. I wouldn't have loved you any less if you told me no. I never expect things to go the way I expect them."

The cigarettes on his breath reminded me of death.

"I'm letting you die."

"No. Hell no, I'm not letting you do that. Listen to me and listen to me good. My journey ends on God's say. If it comes prematurely, that's on me. Not you. If anything, I'm killing myself. You're just respecting my right to do so."

"I just don't understand why you're giving up. What happened to all that fight I got from you? It just up and disappeared?"

"Hendrix-"

"You would always tell me to fight no matter what-for myself, my goals, my family. Why can't you take your own advice? Cause if you did, you could beat this, dad."

"Hendrix-"

"If anyone was going to beat cancer, it's you. It's not too late. All you have to do is fight."

He placed his warm hand atop mine and looked into my eyes. "I've been fighting my entire life, son. You can only get knocked on your ass so many times before you throw in the towel. You can call that giving up, like how you could call me a coward. Say what you want. Just never think for a second that I'm not happy." He paused, looking down and nodding. "You and your sisters are grown now. I can finally be tired."

The waitress returned with four plates, one in each hand, and balanced two on her forearms. She set the plates in front of us, asking if we needed anything else and when we said "no," she told us to enjoy and walked away.

Dad and I ate in silence. I kept my head down the entire time, watching him cough under his breath. My throat tightened, my eyes watered, and I felt a growing desire to storm out.

Eve sent a text message, asking if the treatment had started.

I should tell her now, I thought. You should tell her everything.

I started and stopped the message continuously. When I typed the entire message, confessing, I deleted everything and started from scratch. Everything felt unbelievable, unsendable, surreal.

I looked up to meet dad's gaze. His fork, holding pancakes covered in syrup, almost pressed to his closed mouth. My thumb lingered over the send button; my eyes traveled from him to the phone and back. I should've sent the message. Still, I deleted the message and sat my phone down.

"Let me guess," he said, eating pancakes. "Your sisters?"

"Sister. Eve. She's asking about your treatment. Your fictional treatment to fight your very real cancer."

"Looks like you're suffering from a classic case of guilt. You told her?"

"Told her what? That you aren't doing chemo? Instead, you and I are eating pancakes at IHOP? Absolutely." I rolled my eyes. "C'mon, dad, you know if I told Eve, Vanessa would've already been here raising hell."

"Vanessa doesn't play."

"That she doesn't."

He laughed, which turned into coughing, relieved by a sip of water. "You and Eve used to be so scared of her. This one time, I left you two with her to do God knows what. You were crying crocodile tears before I could put on my shoes."

"I saw her float once."

"You saw what?"

"I saw her float."

"She isn't that bad."

"No, dad. One time I literally saw her floating. When she locks in and focuses, she commits to being a bitch."

He swatted my hand. "A joke has its limits, Hendrix. Now, you don't have to love everything she does or says because Lord knows she's a handful, but difficult or not, she's your sister. I don't ever want to hear you call her out of her name again. Do you hear me, boy?"

"Yeah. I'm sorry."

"Good. Now, text your sister. Tell her the treatment is about to begin."

Against my better judgment, I sent the message word for word, and Eve immediately replied with a sad face and a heart.

While I had my phone in my hand, I looked through my student email account, seeing a message from one of my instructors. She stressed the importance of having the book-I didn't have mine yet.

"For the life of me, I don't understand this generation's obsession with their phones," my dad said. "You kids are so scared that you'll miss out on something that you miss out on everything. Look up sometimes. You'll notice the world is passing you by." He shook his head and ate some hash browns. His teeth scraped the fork and made this sharp and dull sound.

I cringed. "It's for school."

"I can't believe in a couple of weeks I'll see my baby boy walk across that stage….If the Lord blesses me with a couple more weeks, that is. Feel any different?"

"If only I were lucky. You want to know the scary part?"

"Which is?"

"Life. For the past few years, I always knew what was next. Now, I don't. I hope it's a good-paying job. Then, I have to find a place to stay, because I can't live with you forever. Then there's bills and loans. What if things don't work out? I don't find that good-paying job that I love? I can't even find a job? What if I can't pay my bills? There's so many 'what ifs?' I'm losing my mind!"

"What did I tell you about those 'what ifs?' You ask yourself one, and fifteen more hypothetical situations will follow. You'll end up falling deeper and deeper into the madness as you try to make sense of something that's supposed to be a mystery. I won't tell you life isn't scary, but son, things tend to work out for people like you. Hold on. That's all you have to do, no matter how crazy life becomes."

"It would be nice if the world slowed down for a second. It's moving too fast for me."

"My sentiments exactly. I've been asking Father Time to throw me a bone since I was 25. One minute I was drinking beers with my friends, chasing every skirt that looked way better when hiked up."

"Aye. Come on, Dad. All that is unnecessary."

"The next, I'm 58 at IHOP with my son." He sighed. "Life is something else."

"Don't sound so upset about it. I might start thinking I was a mistake."

"Of course, you weren't a mistake. Vanessa was, but your mother and I intended to have you and Eve. Well, maybe not both of you; we wanted a daughter, so maybe in a way, you're a mistake, but I love you both nevertheless."

I sat my phone on the table and ate the rest of my scrambled eggs before moving to the hash browns.

My dad laughed at me.

"What's so funny?" I asked.

"Your particular eating habits."

"I didn't know my eating habits bothered you so much."

"Oh, they don't bother me. Bother would imply I care; I don't. I would say your eating habits amuse me more than anything else. For God's sake, you eat your fries before you even touch your hamburger."

"So?"

"So it just ain't natural."

"Let me get this straight; you're saying that from the moment burgers and fries became a thing, people just naturally ate them together? And not only did they naturally eat their burgers and fries together, they, without socialization, but also alternated eating them? Fries, burger. Fries and then burger."

"Exactly. The human way."

I laughed. "Whatever you say." I ate some hash browns.

"Call me crazy, but I don't think I can fully trust someone who doesn't alternate eating their burger and fries."

"What's up with people judging everybody on personal preferences?"

"Son." He put his hand on mine. "Has someone else been judging you for eating your French fries before eating your burger? If so, tell them it's just food; it's not that serious."

"No." I moved my hand. My arms were on the table, and I leaned forward. "So there's this girl."

"About time. Jesus! Son, don't get upset, but I convinced myself that Trinity turned you a little fuddy-duddy. How long has it been since you two broke up? Two, three years?"

"Four years."

He mouthed, "Four years." He scrunched up his face, showing his teeth, and groaned.

I ventured back to the days where I cried in my dad's lap after she broke up with me. At the time, I tried to keep my head up, and for the most part, I did. I only cried when I was in the shower. But one day, as my dad and I watched T.V., her absence in my life further stretched the void she left. I expected him to demand that I stop crying. To my surprise, he patted my back and promised everything would be okay.

My dad made an engrossed noise.

"Can we focus?" I asked. "Nobody cares about Trinity."

"What's her name?"

"Victoria."

"Is Victoria cute?"

I rolled my eyes and sighed. "It's not like that."

"Oh, it's not like that. Then what is it like?"

"Cordial. We were talking about music, and she tried to convince me that you can tell a lot about someone based on their taste in music."

"She isn't wrong. You know how the saying goes: you can tell a lot about someone within the first few minutes of meeting them."

"Yeah."

"The same goes for music. If I met someone, and within the first few minutes, they turned on Elvis, I would end all relations right then and there."

"What's wrong with Elvis?"

"Ask the Negros he stole from."

"I'll do that."

"I know good or bad is all subjective, but damn, Hendrix, would you let someone who eats shit suggest a restaurant? And I'm not talking figuratively. Literally. They eat literal shit."

"Of course, I wouldn't, but they might have my ear with anything else."

That's when he gave me this look that I'd never seen before; he was never that serious or at least hadn't been since being diagnosed. "Would you really want to take suggestions from someone who thinks eating human waste is a good idea?"

The sound of dishes clattering together came from the kitchen. Individuals sitting at tables and booths scraped their utensils against plates and bowls as they conversed. More people were there now, and chatter filled the room.

With what I assumed were their two grandchildren, an older couple sat in the booth behind me. The kids in the seat wouldn't sit still, and I felt every fidget. Their names were Madison and Melissa. Their grandparents called them enough for everyone to remember.

When my dad finished eating, he occasionally looked at the family behind me as he sipped his coffee. He had a somber look on his face.

"So this girl you mentioned," he said.

"Before you ask, let me go ahead and disappoint you. Victoria's just a friend."

"Everybody starts as friends. Nothing good ol' charm won't change."

"It's not like that. She's married."

"Then why the hell are we talking about her?"

"For the sake of conversation."

"Son, I hate to sound like one of those nagging mothers, but when are you going to give me some grandchildren? I don't know how much time I have left in this world, and I would love to be able to hold some grandchildren before I go."

"I'm twenty-five years old with no career or a place of my own. You aren't getting any grandchildren over here. You better go talk to Eve or Vanessa."

"You're in that curious stage in life, son. Go out, have some fun, make some mistakes. Whatever happens, happens."

"Take that energy over to your daughters."

"Vanessa is waiting for the perfect man to show up at her doorstep, and Eve has her entire life planned out to a T. Did you know Eve wants to be in her career for at least four years and be married for at least two before she even considers having children? Four years. She's living like that well can't dry up. She barely started her current job and still doesn't have a man. I'll be rotting in the ground before either even consider kids."

So once again, dad is looking at you, Hendrix, I said to myself.

. . .

I was already in the car, checking my email on my phone, when my dad got in, coughing.

Victoria had sent an email to the entire class, asking if anyone could send her the notes for tomorrow's lecture since she wouldn't be able to attend. I replied, teasing her about missing class the first week, but I promised to send the notes. I ended the email with the chorus of "4 Leaf Clover" by Erykah Badu but changed all the mentions of love with "my notes." I put my phone down and slid the keys into the ignition. My phone vibrating stopped me from starting the car. Victoria had already responded.

Quite a few emojis were in the message-smiling and laughing faces mostly. She thanked me and expressed her love for my version of the song. She and I exchanged emails every few seconds like text messages, though the more I read over them, it became blatantly obvious to me we talked about nothing. The conversation died after I asked her if she thought more about my taste in music and if it would classify me as "so fresh and so clean."

My dad, by now, had his coughing under control.

"That's the look of a man crushing," he said.

"You're the oldest kid I've ever seen."

"I've crushed on a lot of women in my day, so I know what it looks like when cupid shoots an arrow in a man's ass."

"Looks like the Love Doctor needs to find a new field because I don't like Victoria. Can't a man be platonically invested in a woman?"

"Sure he can, but ain't nobody smiling that hard over a platonic friendship."

"Then, that man didn't have a true friend."

I'm not crushing, I thought. I've done my fair share of crushing-most of it hopeless-and this wasn't one of the times. If it were, I would cuddle my pillow while Ginuwine, Miguel, The Temptations, and Luther Vandross lulled me to sleep. If I were crushing, butterflies would flutter in my stomach, my heart would race, and every second of every day, I would have her on my mind. But I don't like her, so there are no butterflies, and my heart doesn't seem to be racing.

My dad teased me for the first half of the car ride, and I ignored him, so eventually, he stopped. We rode in silence until he played a mixed CD that's been in my player since he gave it to me years ago. Anytime I needed to think back to the days where my dad was okay, I listened.

He sang along to the first track: The Ohio Players' "Sweet Sticky Thing."

"I used to sing this to your mom all the time," he said.

"That's sweet."

"She hated it." Laying his head back on the headrest, he smiled as he drifted down memory lane.

Love is a strange thing most comparable to addiction, I thought. It eats away at us, and most of the time, we never want it to stop. Look at him, sitting there smiling like mom didn't walk out on him. She doesn't love you, dad-she never did. Well, she might have loved you, but she eventually fell out of love. She left you. More importantly, she left us.

Sadly, the woman who carried me for nine months and rocked me asleep when I was a child, the woman who called me her "Prince," meant nothing to me. I felt nothing when I thought about her, even when I envisioned her in a casket.

"When was the last time you saw her?" I asked.

"The night she gave up." He stopped smiling. "She was coming from you and Eve's room. That day both of you came down with a bad bug. She said she was going to get a snack. I went to bed, and when I woke up, she was gone."

"You had to know something was up. Your wife decided to walk away from her family. There's no way she blindsided you with something like that. Did anything seem different? Did she act differently? Did she say anything?"

"By all appearances, she seemed happy. That morning we had a nice little quickie before you kids woke up."

I thought of how sweaty and disheveled my parents looked in a photo on dad's nightstand.

"Thanks for the image."

"But sex doesn't mean shit."

"So, you never heard from her again?"

"Not from her directly. Every now and then, I'll get a call from a bill collector asking for her. She remembers the number to give to a bill collector but not to call her children."

I thought back to all the times where dad sat on the porch, yelling at someone on the phone that "this isn't her number. She's dead to me." Me, Eve, and Vanessa would watch him from inside as he paced across the porch, chain-smoking and rubbing his head.

I changed the song; The Temptations "Since I Lost My Baby" played. He skipped the song. As soon as "What's a Telephone Bill" played, he switched it to another. He kept changing the music, not letting one track play for more than a second, until eventually, he ejected the CD.

"Turn this shit off," he said, slamming back into his seat. "Matter of fact, nobody's trying to hear this shit at all." He looked as if he was going to snap it in half, and he tried. I stopped him before he could.

"Dad!"

He snatched away and threw a cigarette, sticking up from his front pocket, into his mouth. My stomach burned as I watched him spark up with a lighter lying in the passenger door. From the first exhale, the anger, frustration, and sadness left his face.

Say something, I told myself. Do something.

I didn't. I kept driving, watching him blow smoke out the window. The coughing didn't take long to follow.

"I need to go to the store," he said.

I turned into a nearby grocery store parking lot and parked in between a silver Accent and white Ford Fiesta. A woman placed the bags of groceries into the trunk as her husband or boyfriend held their daughter up in the air while making funny noises.

My dad stopped and turned to me on his way out of the car.

"Are you coming in?" He asked.
"I'd rather wait in the car."

Chapter 3
Victoria

I read through the list of ingredients in different bread brands, interrupted by someone an aisle over, falling into a nasty-sounding coughing fit. From the dry coughs, it sounded like they smoked a carton a day. The depth of my shock in the hoarse coughing could only be matched by my disbelief at the excessive amounts of sugar in the bread.

Martin stood right behind me, more invested in his Nintendo Switch than the outside, and I almost fell over him. I put a loaf of bread in the basket, simultaneously rubbing Martin's head.

"Is that a man or woman, mommy?" He asked.

"They're human. That's all that matters."

"I just want to know."

"The only thing you need to know is that smoking is bad for you."

"I won't smoke if I'll sound like that."

"You will and more."

We walked down the aisle and turned onto the next.

A man stood in front of a glass case, browsing the collection of alcohol, with a box of powdered donuts tucked under his arm. He hunched forward in another coughing fit. The dry, hacking cough made my chest hurt. Like Hershey, he was dark and bald. Unlike Hershey, his body was giving out on him, he didn't have a goatee, but he did have a grey beard. The stomach-churning smell of smoke excreting from the man burned my lungs.

"It's a man," Martin said. "The person coughing is a man."

I shushed him.

It took me a minute to find the specific white wine. As I reached for the bottle, the man, coughing, reached out for me like he needed help. His coughing stopped, and his hands were still outstretched toward me.

"That's a precious ring you have there," he said. "Where, huh…where did you get it?"

"It's my wedding ring."

"If it's not too intrusive to ask, do you know where the lucky man bought it?"

"The pawnshop off Rosecrans."

"The one that has the commercials?"

"That's the one. You know what they say: One woman's trash is another woman's treasure."

"I get an old pair of heels, but what type of woman would give up such a beautiful ring?"

"Sometimes, you have to separate yourself from bad memories."

He stared at the ring, resisting the desire to reach out and grab my hand to get a closer look.

"Would you like to see it?" I asked.

He looked at me, his eyes swelling with tears. "You wouldn't mind?"

"Of course not." I handed him the ring.

His thin and bruised hands trembled as he stared at the ring sitting in the palm of his hands.

"I gave my wife this exact ring," he said. "It took me quite a few paychecks to save up for this thing. I'm pretty sure it was way more than what your husband paid. I feel cheated."

"You have great taste."

"That's what she told me."

Overwhelming guilt overcame me by how he looked at me like he and his wife divorced, and I wore the ring he worked so hard to buy. It was unique enough that I shopped for rings for months and never saw anything like it. This was his wife's ring. I was sure of it.

"So, how long have you been married?" I asked.

"We were married for five years." He paused. "She passed away."

"I'm sorry to hear that."

"Don't go feeling sorry for me. That was many moons ago. I've done my share of crying. Time for this old man to suck it up and move on with his life. That's what she would've wanted."

"Do you still have the ring?"

He waited so long to reply that Martin looked up from his video game. "It hasn't left her jewelry box since."

I sighed in relief.

"Thank you so much." He returned the ring and turned back to the shelves of alcohol.

Hendrix turned onto the aisle, more annoyed than relieved.

"Dad," he said.

The man turned to Hendrix then back to me. A childish smile crept across his face, almost like he did something he wanted to hide.

"Is this your son?" Hendrix's father asked. "Sorry to be presumptuous."

"My oldest."

"Oh, the synergy of parent-children relationships. Ain't it something how, in a world of kids calling for their mom and dad, we know exactly when it's our kids screaming for us?"

"Look who it is," Hendrix said, walking over and then smiled. "Looks like you met my dad. Hopefully, he didn't bother you too much."

"Not at all," I said.

"That's good. He's known to be a piece of work."

"Somehow, I ended up being the child," his father said, "Good to know."

"Dad, Victoria. Victoria, my dad."

"A pleasure," his father said, shaking my hand.

"Likewise," I said.

His father went back to admiring the case of alcohol.

"Is this your son?" Hendrix asked.

"This is my eldest, Martin."

Martin nodded at Hendrix, with his eyes glued to his video game.

"Sorry. I promise there's a kid with manners in there under that dead gaze."

"He's fine," Hendrix said, positioning himself to see the Switch's screen. "You didn't say he was playing Smash Bros."

"I'm not quite sure what that means."

Martin blows air from his mouth and rolls his eyes.

"You know Smash Bros, mom," Martin said. "I only play it all the time."

"It's the best game ever," Hendrix said.

Martin smiled. "On me."

"Who's your main?"

"Definitely K Rool and Captain Falcon."

"Oh man, that Falcon punch. I used to play that game all the time."

"It just came out."

"I'm talking about the original. Back when you couldn't even wavedash."

For the first time on his own accord, Martin paused the game and looked up from his game. His eyes and smile widened.

"No way," Martin asked.

"Yeah, man. We all couldn't grow up privileged."

"Did you play Smash 4?"

"Not as much as I liked. I was always so tired after work and school. Ugh. Don't grow up."

"I won't."

They rambled on about smash orbs, Pokéballs, hammers, and a bunch of jibberish that made it increasingly difficult to follow. I gave up on discerning their foreign language when Hendrix referred to Baby Link and Pit as his "mains."

Whatever that meant.

"Were you good?" Martin asked.

"I'm decent. Now, Brawl. I was the man back then. If I were a man of less class, I would flex on you by sharing how many tournaments I won."

"Mommy, mommy," Martin said, reaching up and tapping my arm, bouncing.

"Honey, calm down. I'm right here."

"Mommy. He loves Smash Bros!"

"I heard."

"Mommy, can he come over and play? If he does, we need to get chips, cookies, and soda. Mom!"

Hendrix laughed. "As awesome as that sounds, I have to take a rain check."

"What does that mean?"

"He can't come and play, honey," I said.

"Fine. But can we still get some chips, cookies, and soda?"

"You have to take a rain check on those as well. No junk food."

He poked out his lips. "But mom."

"Why do you need junk food when you can have apples?" Hendrix asked, kneeling in front of Martin.

"Eew gross. Nobody wants to eat an apple unless it's apple pie."

"Something tells me you never had a green apple in your life."

"I've had every apple before, and they're all gross."

"What do I hear with my ears? Do you know that tingling feeling in your mouth when you're sucking on a jolly rancher?"

"I love that feeling."

"Well, the same thing happens when you bite into a green apple, only difference is your teeth will thank you later."

"Nu-uh."

"Would the guy who loves the greatest game ever lie to you? Trust me; I have good taste. You should try one and see for yourself." He stood and turned to me. "Gotta go, but I'll catch you later." He looked down at Martin. "Keep getting good."

"Okay. Bet."

By this time, a manager handed Hendrix's father a bottle of Hennessy from the case before rearranging cases of beer. His father, walking down the aisle, stopped when Hendrix called out. As they walked from the aisle, I swore his father asked about chemotherapy symptoms.

"Mom," Martin said.

"Yes." I never broke my stare at Hendrix and his father.

"Can we buy some green apples?"

. . .

Standing on the stone bench in front of the school, I watched for Hershey's silver Chrysler 200. It was 7:30 pm, and class just ended. Dozens of my fellow students, who hurried from their classes, walked through the parking lot, while others got into cars parked at the pick-up area, or like me, waited. I called Hershey; he didn't answer.

Butterflies fluttered in my stomach. Everyone who saw the girlish smile on my face probably thought I was crazy. They would have been right: I was crazy-crazy in love.

Thinking back to the day Hershey and I met, I remembered it like it was yesterday. I had wandered around campus for the Physical Science building when Hershey strutted towards me in suit and tie.

Individuals walked across the school's lawn behind me, going wherever it was they were going, and their shoes squeaked in the grass. Footsteps moved closer from behind. When they stopped, a shadow shrouded me.

It was Hendrix. I heard him curse. I turned around and laughed as he struggled to untangle his earphone cords.

"You really need to invest in wireless headphones," I said.

He looked up. "Who are you telling?"

"So, are you going home, or are you trying to waste time again?"

"Are you asking me to keep you company?"

"If I want something, I ask. I don't have time for all the mind games."

"You and two other women in the world." He checked his phone. "I'm headed home. Traffic probably died down."

It took him a while, but he finally untangled the headphones. We said our "goodbyes," and he walked to the parking lot.

Something told me Hershey was going to be late. He was always late, anniversary or not.

I called him. He didn't answer once again, so I had to leave a message and send a text. Still no response. Then I called his mother; she didn't answer either. Knowing my kids, she was probably busy chasing after Daniel.

Why did I let Hershey convince me to go to class?

. . .

8:07 pm crept up on me, and I still sat outside a college campus in a black dress with a slit so far up everyone, even a mile away, could see my entire broken vintage hand mirror tattoo across the front of my thigh and breast pushed up to my chin. I must have looked stupid. Although no one looked at me directly, I knew that people stared whenever I looked at my phone to text Hershey. Their eyes burned through my skin. The butterflies no longer fluttered as I thought of Hershey. I thought of a hundred things I would do to him, none of them good or sexy.

I had no idea what I was going to do or how I was going to get home. The only two people I could depend on weren't answering. Were they dead in a ditch somewhere? Were my kids alright? Did they finally realize what my parents knew years ago?

A figure I immediately recognized as Hendrix by the hair and bounce in his step made its way from the parking lot to the bookstore. Although the darkness and distance made it hard to tell, something about him always stood out.

I hurried to the bookstore, feeling the eyes of everyone staring as I passed. I stood just inside the door, looking for Hendrix, spotting him walk from the refrigerated section with a bottle of water. He waved at me and walked over.

"I thought you left," I said.

"I did, but then my sister called, yelling about something, so going home isn't the best option right now."

"So, you just came back to school? You scholar you."

"You don't get a 4.0 GPA by slacking off. It takes hard work and dedication, and if it takes sitting in your car at school while listening to podcasts, so be it."

I laughed and shrugged. "Whatever works."

"I figured you would've been long gone by now." He gave his approval of my dress with a nod. "You look like you have places to go and one person in particular to see."

"I thought I did."

"You thought?"

"When it's your anniversary, you would assume you and your husband have plans, but obviously, I'm just a dreamer."

"He forgot? Oh, man, I'm sorry."

I looked past Hendrix, at a couple holding hands and kissing in front of an espresso machine, and back to him to see the concern on his face. It was that or pity. "No! I made that sound terrible. My husband didn't forget our anniversary. I married a good man, Hendrix. I resent the implication."

"Sorry. You made it seem like." He cleared his throat. "The way you were looking, I just assumed. Jesus, Hendrix. Sorry, I misread this entire conversation."

"It's not your fault." I rubbed my face, sighing. "I completely overreacted. He's running a little late from work, that's all. He'll be here soon."

"I can take you home if that's easier for him."

Against my better judgment, I said, "Oh, no. It's fine."

"Cool. Hey. Um. I should pay for this and get going. Vanessa can't yell at no one. Well, she could and has."

"Sorry. I feel like I made things awkward."

"Never that. I should get home before my sisters lose their minds. It was nice chatting with you. Enjoy your anniversary. Tell my buddy shielding before he hits the ground can break his fall."

"Is that English?"

"It's a Smash Bros thing."

I smiled at the thought of Martin, either crying in rage or screaming in joy, as he played his game. "Of course, it is."

"See you later, Victoria."

I waved him goodbye.

As he stood in line, I browsed around with no intention of buying anything, making sure to keep my eyes on him, and when he left, I hurried from the bookstore. I never realized how fast he walked until then. He was already stepping off the curb when I got outside.

For a moment, I nearly laughed at the picture of me asking another man for a ride-and on my anniversary. He walked with a bounce in his step, arms swinging, and head nodding to the music blasting in his headphones.

He was so strange. Why would he sit in his car for hours instead of going home or anywhere else other than a poorly lit parking lot?

Losing sight of him in the dark, I had one realization: Hershey wasn't coming anytime soon, and the only chance I had of getting home was probably driving away.

Taking a deep breath, I ran towards the parking lot, called out Hendrix's name until he emerged from the darkness in a hurry.

"Victoria," he said, breathing heavily. "Are you okay? Did something happen? What's going on?"

"Do you want to keep me company?"

He looked deep into my eyes until I looked down. "As long as your husband isn't the jealous type. The last thing I want is an angry husband trying to throw hands because he thinks I'm hitting on his wife."

I laughed. "You don't need to worry about that. He has me forever-he knows that."

We went back to the bench where I sat before, and this time I didn't feel like people stared. I sat down, but Hendrix stood, bouncing.

I wanted to ask him for a ride home. Damn pride. It kept my lips from uttering the words. I went from convincing myself Hershey would come to accepting he wouldn't. I called myself stupid, knowing Hendrix wouldn't wait with me all night. For some strange reason, all I could say was, "I'm sorry about your mother."

"What about her?"

"She died."

"How do you know about my mom?"

"Your dad."

"Oh yeah, you did meet my dad. You know, he wouldn't stop talking about you or your ring."

"He said your mother had the same ring."

"Is that right?" He stared off, and it wasn't at the cars.

"You didn't notice this was the same ring your mother had?"

"How did you know you were in love?"

"Huh?"

He looked at me again. "How did you know you were in love?"

I stammered. Every time I thought I had my thoughts together, I fumbled over my words as soon as I spoke. Then, I couldn't even stutter; nothing came out.

Hendrix laughed.

"Say no more," he said. "I guess it's true what they say… words can't describe love. When you're in love, you just know."

"Exactly."

"That's a shame. I would've loved to hear the story. I bet it would have been the words straight out of a romance novel."

"Why so curious?"

"What can I say? I'm a sucker for a good romance."

I laughed.

"Laugh, all you want. I'm not ashamed to say nothing warms the spirit like a tale of unbreakable love." He checked his phone. "Are you sure you don't need a ride?"

"What time is it?"

"8:44."

"I'll take that ride if it's not too much of a hassle."

"Come on now." He nudged me. "If it were a hassle, I wouldn't have asked."

. . .

His car smelt like the banana lying at my feet. As he drove, he sang along to Marvin Gaye, "I want you." His voice cracked and went out as he attempted to croon a falsetto.

"I would like to think if I were in love, this song would play nonstop in my head," he said. "Or I would hope." He sang some more. "Come on. You know this."

"No." I laughed. "I'm alright."

"You don't like this song?"

"Come on, of course, I like this song."

"Then why aren't you singing?"

I laughed. "Because, unlike you, I'm ashamed of my terrible singing."

"You say that like it's a bad thing. I'm not afraid to laugh at myself."

"Even if other people are laughing at you?"

"Who cares what other people think? Besides, it's hard to care about people laughing at you when my laughter drowns the world out. If me having fun bothers people so much, then they're living wrong."

"You're better than me."

"I'm happy."

"-And you think I'm not?"

He raised his right hand in the air like he was under arrest. "I'm just saying, why would I care what someone else thinks or feels? That's how you end up unhappy."

"So what you want me to believe is you never worry about what other people think or feel about you?"

"That's human nature. I can't stop the feelings from creeping up on me, but I don't let them bring me down. I let them come and go. It's hard to worry about someone else when I'm focused on me, myself, and I. We're all messed up. That's what makes us beautiful. I'll be damned if I let someone just as messed up as me tell me I'm not drop-dead gorgeous."

His awful singing pulled me into the moment. I sounded just as bad as he did. For some reason, he looked at me as if I was the greatest singer he had ever heard. I stopped singing, and for the rest of the ride, my body faced the door. When we pulled up to the house, I thanked him and hurried outside before he could reply.

The light in the hall upstairs peaked through the window. Hershey's 2014 Camaro Z/28 was in the driveway. As soon as I opened the door, the smell of steak hit me, and my stomach rumbled. I walked into the kitchen. Two empty plates, browned from the remains of a meal, a half-drunk bottle of white wine, and two glasses, sat on the table. I flopped down into a chair and put my head on the table, sighing.

Footsteps came downstairs and closer to the kitchen. I told myself it was a woman, and my heart stopped when I heard heels clicking against our tile floor. I looked up at a woman who shook in place. She looked to be everything I wasn't: in perfect shape, clear-skinned, young, happy.

"Shit," she said.

Hershey strutted down in his boxers and stopped himself from wrapping his arms around her waist when he and I locked eyes. His brain worked in overdrive to find a bullshit excuse.

"You don't have to say anything, Hershey," I said and sipped from the wine bottle. "I already knew about the women. They call the house; they stop by; for Christ's sake, I clean their makeup off your shirts."

He chuckled in guilt. "Baby, listen." He paused. "You have to give me something. Victoria. Something other than this."

"I'm giving you everything you give me."

"You're internalizing. You walked in on your husband with another woman. It's okay to be pissed."

"I'm passed being mad, Hershey. I don't want to be mad at you."

"I don't want you to be mad at me either."

"I love you. I love you so much."

He ran over and embraced me, kissing my neck. "I love you too, baby."

"But I'm done. I can't let you do this to me anymore. At first, I convinced myself I was staying for the kids, but I wasn't. I was staying for myself. You have a way of making me feel loved and unwanted at the same time."

I pushed him away and hurried outside. He followed, but despite how much I wanted him to, he didn't beg or plead for me to stay. Life slapped me across the face with a cold, hard realization.

I was just another woman. I was just the one desperate enough to want a family and life with a man who didn't want to be kept.

Hendrix, still in his car, in front of the house, ended up meeting me halfway down the driveway.

"Hey, are you okay?" He asked.

I turned to him—years of disappointment built in my eyes.

"It's okay," he said. "Whatever is going on, it's going to be okay."

"Who the hell is this?" Hershey asked. "So you can go around being a fucking slut, but I'm a bad guy for fucking other women. Real classy, Victoria."

I wanted to explain how I never thought of another man touching me or how he was the only man I could ever want. I tried to tell him that I saw my hopes and dreams when I thought of him, but as I turned around, Hendrix grabbed my hand and pulled me back.

"What are you doing?" I asked.

"I have no idea."

He placed his hand on my cheek and, in a brief moment, admired me in every way that Hershey didn't and then kissed me. My lips never puckered to kiss back. After a second, he still had his lips to mine, and I didn't push him away, too taken back by the force he embraced me. It was like he thought he would lose me if he let go.

I couldn't move from confusion and anger.

Hershey screamed and cursed at the top of his lungs. Bitch. Slut. Whore.

His whore stood beside my husband, in the threshold of my house.

To the sight, I wrapped my arms around Hendrix's neck and kissed him.

Chapter 4
Hendrix

Damn, I thought. What were you thinking? You kissed her. You fucking kissed somebody's wife---somebody's mother.

I sped down the street, aimlessly driving through the city.

Victoria, in the passenger seat, sang along to whatever song played on her phone. She was smiling. I wanted to ask why she smiled at a time like this. As soon as I opened my mouth to speak, I convinced myself it wasn't the right time. So I didn't say anything, content in occasionally glancing over whenever I stopped at a red light or stop sign. The guilt ate at my heart and brain, so I cracked and apologized. She didn't say anything, forcing me to keep apologizing until she finally said something: "You shouldn't have kissed me."

"Seeing you cry set my soul on fire. I didn't like the way he was talking to you, Victoria. It was like you were the one caught naked with another man. That doesn't justify anything, but how the hell can he talk to you like you aren't one of the most beautiful women in this world. Since he couldn't see that on his own, I figured I'd make him."

She turned her body to me. "Do you really think I'm beautiful?"

I winced. "I really need to stop talking."

"You can be honest with me. Do you really think I'm beautiful?"

"After everything I said, you want to focus on that?"

"You said what you said. Now own it."

"I don't know too much about you, so I'm talking strictly physical when I say this." I took a minute to myself. "You are-- to me-- the closest thing to fucking perfect."

"What would make me perfect?"

"To be my girl. And for the record, I'm not asking or insinuating." The silence hurt. "When I find someone special, I want it to be said, I see her differently than every other woman. That sounded more romantic in my head."

"There is no such thing as perfection."

"Well, someone needs to tell my eyes that because they don't see a flaw in you. Oh my God, Hendrix, stop doing stuff. Stop talking. Stop kissing other people's wives. Just chill!"

She didn't say or do anything, so neither did I. I just kept driving, and she kept smiling. Eventually, that smile turned into a frown.

"I just ruined everything," she said. "He's going to leave me. I can fix this. If I call him, we can talk things out." She pulled her phone from her purse but threw it to the floor before she called. "Shit. Shit. Shit. Why did you kiss him, Victoria? You're going to lose everything. He won't let you see Martin and Daniel again. You're going to lose your kids."

What can you say? All of this is your fault. Just shut up.

I pulled into the drive-thru of a McDonald's, which shared a shopping center with a Lowes and KFC.

"Want anything?" I asked.

She didn't answer-I didn't expect her to. I ordered two happy meals and an ice cream sundae. The man taking my order asked whether the happy meals were for a boy or girl. I got one for each. The toys were a pink horse and an orange triceratops.

My attempt to pull into a parking space ended with me crookedly in two. My stomach cramped too much to eat. I took a deep breath, closed my eyes, and for some reason, used the toys to reenact how her night was supposed to go. The horse, who I named Starlight, came home, and her husband, the triceratops, named Stomps, greeted her at the door with a kiss. I had voices for them and everything. I played the role of the narrator and examined how they got their names. Starlight was born under the stars, and Stomps was always mad, so he stomped around 24/7. I continued by noting that Stomps was never angry when with Starlight. He was only upset when he couldn't be next to her. When Starlight got home, Stomps took her to a restaurant that only served the finest of grass. That night they had one for the history books, and when they went home, they made love.

I opened my eyes to see her blank expression. I raised Stomps as if he was talking to her.

"Victoria," I said in Stomp's voice. "I know we met a few days ago, so maybe I'm jumping the gun, and if I am, so what, because I think you're a wonderful person. You're a beautiful person. And again, I could be completely off base here, but until you prove me otherwise, I say you're amazing. That man back at that house is an idiot. I'm wont even call him your husband because he doesn't deserve the honor. If I had the chance of calling you mine, no other woman in this world would exist. You would have my eyes, my heart, and everything else I could give. I would do everything I could to make you happy." I had to take a second to gather my thoughts. "You didn't ruin anything."

She remained quiet. She barely blinked. The worst part: her face still lacked any discernible expression.

I held Starlight up.

"Please say something, Victoria," I said in Starlight's voice.

"Give Hendrix something," I said in Stomps' voice. "He's dying out here."

She cried, but it wasn't in heartbreak or sadness because she smiled. She exploded from her seat to wrap her arms around me.

"Thank you," she said.

Her tears rolled down my neck. I embraced her tightly. I didn't want to let her go, and she didn't want me to either because every time I loosened my embrace, she squeezed tighter.

"I'm so stupid," she said. Her voice muffled from her face pressed against my neck.

"I don't see anybody stupid in this car."

"I don't know why I love him."

"Sometimes, we don't get a choice on who we love. It just happens."

"He doesn't love me. He never did. I'm so stupid."

"Stop doing this to yourself. There's one stupid person here, and it isn't you. Only idiots would cheat on a woman like you just to settle for a hamburger."

"What?"

I pulled a hamburger from one of the rolled-up bags at her feet and held it beside her face. "Victoria or hamburger. Hamburger or Victoria. Call me crazy, but I'm taking Victoria any day."

"You're a dork." She smiled. "A sweet, adorable dork."

"I'm just a man with southernplayalistic taste."

We stared into one another's eyes with goofy smiles.

The lights hanging above the car failed to keep shadows from plastering over much of her face. I turned on the light in the car for a better view.

Her curly hair hung over her face. Her eyes, which always seemed to shine, sparkled and glistened more intently under the light in the car. In them, I saw my reflection. Damn, she was gorgeous.

She turned away from me, put her feet in the seat, and lay her cheek on her arms.

Her face pointed towards the door.

A breeze came in and circulated through the car. The unique smell of McDonald's overtook the fresh air and became more potent as she ate the French fries, one by one. She took a sip of her soda and went back to eating the fries. Once she finished, she picked up and stared at a hamburger; laughing, she placed it back into the bag. She kept her head forward the entire time, almost like I didn't exist.

"Has anyone ever told you that you're strange?" She asked.

"I've heard it a few times. Never let it bother me, though."

"Of course, you don't. By the way, I don't mean that in a bad way. You're just different."

"I don't get it. What's so strange about me?"

"For starters, we're in the parking lot of a Mcdonald's, eating Happy Meals. What happened to the good old fashion hug?"

"I tried that, remember? I ended up kissing you."

"Did you? As I remember it, you went straight for the kiss."

"If you could have been inside my head, you would have seen a man struggling."

"That brings me to example number 2: The kiss."

I shifted in my seat. "I already explained that. At that moment, I thought it was the best thing to do so, he who will be nameless, got a taste of his own medicine. No more, no less. Was it the smartest thing to do? Probably not. You can't say it didn't work, though."

"So that's the only reason you kissed me? To make Hershey jealous?"

"Whoa, we won't say that name. Not up in here."

"So you kissed me to make him jealous?"

"That I did."

"Is that right?"

"Hmm." We had a good laugh when I hit my right blinker. "Do you want to hear something funny?"

"Only if it's funny."

"I think it is. Then again, I'm a weirdo."

"You're building yourself up quite a bit here, Hendrix. Don't disappoint."

"When I was younger, I swore I saw my sister, Vanessa, levitate."

She laughed. "What?"

"I know it sounds crazy; just hear me out. In my mind, she was levitating through the hall. I've been terrified of her ever since, which is crazy to think about because we were kids back then. I wouldn't play with her. Shoot, I barely talked to her. Eve, the glorified middle child, would, but you couldn't pay me to play with the girl I saw flying through the hall. I didn't have any friends, so I ended up playing alone. My toys made it easier, though."

"I knew Stomps and Starlight came a little too natural."

"Every toy had a name-even if it already had one. Buzz Lightyear? Nah, his name was Augustus. They weren't toys to me; they were people, little plastic people with lives and emotions. People who depended on me to tell their story because no one else could. Since I was the only one who could tell the story, I put on entire productions. Legit TV shows. I had music and everything- even commercials. One year my dad messed up and bought me a camcorder for Christmas. It was a wrap at that point."

"So, is this you trying to prove you aren't strange?"

"Maybe I need to shut up before I dig myself too big a hole to climb out of."

"I like it. I want to hear more."

"That's it."

"No, that's not it. You have to tell me what inspired you to make your return as a writer, director, and actor today of all nights."

"Desperation. You were freaking out, and I didn't know what to do. I'd rather see you smile than cry."

"It worked."

"Mission complete."

She took a sip of her drink. "Do you want to know a secret?"

"I always want to know a secret."

She twisted her ring around her finger and then took it off. She held the ring, opening and closing her hand in a deafening silence that I thought she forgot she asked a question. Sniffing, she ran her arm across her eyes.

"I'm not married," she said. "I was never married."

"He's an idiot."

"I would say that if I wasn't the one who wasted nine years of my life."

"Nine years? How old are you again?"

She laughed. "It's kinda a funny story."

She looked at me, with her arms around her legs and her cheek lying across her knees.

The cars on the nearby street passed by the plaza. Their revving engines echoed; it was so loud it sounded like they were still there even when they long passed. I listened to my running engine. For whatever reason, the sound kept me at ease. I admired the third-quarter moon from my window and turned back to Victoria, who held her eyes closed. As I looked back to the moon, I noticed a man, hunched forward, walking through the Mcdonald's parking lot and smoking. The night and distance hid his face, and even so, he looked identical to my dad in my mind.

Why do people smoke cigarettes? Alcohol gets you drunk, drugs get you high, but what's the point of a cigarette? Addiction? What type of person would smoke a cigarette, knowing there are only two outcomes: Addiction or cancer?

A stabbing feeling shot through my stomach and settled in my chest, twisting and turning, deeper and deeper, when Victoria said, "Your father."

"What about him?"

"He loved your mother."

"More than I'll ever understand."

"You can tell by how miserable he looks when he talks about her."

"That's the scary thing about love: the person we cannot live without wields destruction in their hands."

"She didn't choose to die."

"Yeah….Yeah. I was talking in general." I winced. "My mom made a lot of choices; dying wasn't one of them."

"Why is love so painful?"

"It's not. We just make it painful."

"Being in love is a cycle of pain and joy. For as much joy we'll feel with the person we want to spend the rest of our life with, we'll feel equally as much pain."

"Okay. And?"

"If we're going to accept happiness, we have to live through the pain."

"I respectfully call bullshit."

"What about it is bullshit?"

"Everything! You make love seem like it's a system of checks and balances. Like for every good moment, there has to be a bad one to keep you humble. It shouldn't be like that. It can't be like that. Say what you want. There should be a disparity in love. There should be so much love that the pain should be something you can easily work through."

"Not everything is going to be a walk in the park. You want something? You better be ready to fight with every fiber of your being, cause if you aren't, you might as well save everybody the time."

"Cool. It shouldn't be hard either. If you're telling me I have to be just as miserable as I am happy, then I'd rather stay single for the rest of my life because that right there is so bullshit. No way you believe that's what love is."

"Well, I don't know what to tell you, Hendrix, because I do!" Tears swelled. "That's exactly what love is, and until you get into a committed relationship where you dream together and bring kids into this world, you can't tell me shit about love and what it's supposed to be like!"

"I get that, but-"

"-but this is real life, not one of your little romance novels."

"Maybe you're right." I looked out my window. "But hear me out. If we weren't so quick to give up our dreams, maybe we would be happier. Or maybe I'm just a dreamer."

Silence. The silence drowned out everything, eating away at me.

She pulled her hair back, holding it with one hand, and tied it with a hair tie around her wrist.

"I like that you're a dreamer," she said.

For the rest of the night, her head lay on my shoulder. We talked about everything, from music to our families. Her hair smelt like vanilla, and it took everything in me not to run my fingers through it.

She explained how she and Hershey met when she was sixteen, and not even a year later, she was pregnant. Since Hershey was four years older, they kept their relationship a secret. She lied to her parents and told them her boyfriend ghosted her, and they helped raise Martin, although they never approved of her having a child out of wedlock. When she got pregnant again, they kicked her out, and not long after, they disowned her; she hadn't spoken to them since. Just mentioning Hershey brought tears to her eyes, and she held them in until she repeated his promise that day: "I'm your family now...for eternity."

That's when I held her, keeping her in my arms while she dozed off several times throughout our night together.

. . .

With all the windows rolled down, the wind felt like a brick to my face. The speakers cranked up, the streetlights and the utility poles went in and out of focus in the rearview mirror, which rattled to a random Trap song Spotify recommended.

Without blinking, I stared at the road ahead. My eyes drooped downward, and just as I was about to fall asleep, they snapped back open. Why do our bodies decide to do the most when it's most inconvenient?

At home, my dad sat on the porch in his wicker chair, enjoying a cigarette. I parked behind Eve's car. Before I could step out of the car, dad stood at the passenger door. He gave his disappointed "dad look" with his arms crossed.

I stepped out into the night air.

"Boy," he said. "Do you have any idea what time it is?"

"No." I had a goofy smile on my face. It had been plastered over my face since I took Victoria home.

"You been drinking? Boy, are you out of your rabbit ass mind?"

"I haven't had a sip of alcohol."

"Then you must be high, cause boy, look at you. Hendrix, if you're on that shit-"

"I'm happy, dad. Just happy."

He stopped glaring and uncrossed his arms. Now, we both smiled like dorks. "My boy went out on a date."

I smiled harder. "It's not like that."

"My baby boy is not a baby anymore."

"If I had a date, I would've told you."

"Then, you skipped right over the courting." He winked. "You were out boning?"

"Dad, I would appreciate it if you never say 'boning' to me again."

"Ain't nobody coming home at 3 in the morning, smiling from ear to ear unless they grabbed something to eat with a special somebody or ate out that special somebody."

"I'm just happy, dad. Victoria and I got the chance to hang out a little. That's all."

I don't know why I'm so happy, I thought.

My dad wanted me to join him on the porch. Although I wanted to collapse in my bed and feel the coldness of my pillow against my cheek, I sat with him as he smoked. As soon as I sat down, my eyes closed on their own. What felt like minutes later, I snapped awake; coming to, I tried my best to focus and, more importantly, stay awake. He stared, inhaling, and exhaling.

He leaned forward, putting his weight on his arms, which were on his legs, and crossed at the wrists. His nose and forehead scrunched up, and his mouth opened a little. The way he looked at me, there was no way he thought of me as a son in that moment. He went to talk and decided a sigh and a shake of his head better fit the situation. The wheezing was getting worse, at least it seemed like it.

"You're mad," I said.

"And she's married, Hendrix."

"It wasn't like that, Dad. If it were, I'd tell you. We were catching a vibe, you know, as friends."

"No, Hendrix, I don't know anything about catching a vibe." He stood with his free hand balled into a fist so fast the chair slid back and slammed against the wall. "I don't make it a habit of canoodling with married women."

"Nobody was canoodling."

"She took vows, Hendrix."

I brushed him off with a laugh.

"Boy, laugh one more time. I want you to. I bet you won't fix your mouth to do it again."

"It's not that serious. You're working yourself up over nothing."

"You were out until three in the morning with a married woman, and your smile...your smile tells me it wasn't as innocent as you're letting off."

"Nothing happened."

"Okay, nothing happened, but something could have happened, Hendrix. You were out with a married woman until three in the morning. You were the serpent in the Eden that is their marriage!"

The only thing I could think to do was shake my head.

He was out of breath and wheezing. He sat and leaned back in the wicker chair, never taking his eyes off me. I had never seen my dad look so disgusted, not with the situation, but with me. It didn't take long before he got up and stormed down the street.

I followed. The smoke flowing over my dad's shoulder blew into my face, and I coughed, exaggerating, so he got the point.

His coughs outlasted mine long enough to imagine each would be his last. The coughing stopped for Death to watch him struggle through another day.

Dogs jumped against fences and greeted us with barks as we passed their yards. The streetlights I walked under made a buzzing sound. Our shoes scraped against the concrete.

I had slowly eased closer, and after passing dozens of houses, we walked shoulder to shoulder. I might as well not exist to him. Sometimes I would inadvertently make a noise or brush against him without him giving me so much as a grunt or a look of disapproval. I stepped in front of him.

"Alright, I'm sorry," I said. "I'm sorry for being the snake in their Eden. I messed up."

He stepped into the street and walked past me. "I don't want you to be sorry. I want you to be smarter."

"Then teach me." I grabbed his arm. "Be my father and teach me how to be smarter because obviously, I don't know how."

"I need you to understand just how stupid you were."

I closed my eyes and ground my teeth. My head hurt. "You're talking in riddles. Can you stop storming off like a child and tell me what's on your mind?"

He turned around and stared me down as a man, not his son. "I knew you were going to sneak out to that party."

I rolled my eyes. "Well, maybe if you said that about seven years ago, you would still have your truck."

"Hendrix, I'm your father. I know you better than you think you know yourself. You have this smile that always lets me know you're doing something you have no business doing. The same smile you had when you stepped out of that car. What happened tonight? And I swear to the Good Lord if you say 'nothing."

"You want to know what I did? Fine. I kissed her."

"Hendrix-"

"It's not what you think it is."

"Then what was it, because from the outside looking in, it seems like you're a mistress. You defiled the sanctity of marriage! That girl took vows, and you helped her break those vows!"

"Her husband broke them first!"

"Two wrongs, Hendrix. You know the saying."

"It was their anniversary."

"That somehow makes it better?"

"Her husband was supposed to pick her up after class, but he never came, so I took her home. She found him in bed with another woman. You should've heard the way he talked to her, dad-- like she wasn't shit. So as I saw it: Fuck em. He needed to see how it felt, dad. He needed to realize what it would feel like to lose a great woman."

"So you're the love child of Batman and Cupid now? You're a vigilante fighting against all those who stand in the way of love?"

"What?"

"I don't care if that man has seven mistresses. That's between him and his wife. Not you!"

I was itching to reveal Victoria's secret. He had worked himself up so much that I thought it would be best to let it go. He was breathing heavily, gasping as he inhaled. Shaking. Dying.

On the walk back home, I apologized periodically to his silence. I couldn't decide which hurt worse: Him ignoring me or his wheezing.

In my room, bags of clothes lay at the foot of my bed, filled with designer clothes. Eve, in bed, slept with the covers over her head. I lay down on an inflatable mattress and immediately fell asleep.

Victoria

The ground under my feet extended with every step, and before I made it halfway to the front door, my heart raced, beads of sweat layered my skin, and I gasped for air that thinned with each inhale.

My head spun with so many thoughts; Hendrix's kiss, Starlight and Stomps, Hershey, Martin, and Daniel. When I made it to the door, I stood there, gasping, without the courage to reach for my keys. If I stayed outside, then maybe I never had to live the consequences of last night.

With any luck, Hershey would apologize for creeping, accept my apology for kissing Hendrix, and then we could get on with our lives. It most likely would never happen. But, it sounded like a dream.

Hershey had left the door open, in what I hoped was a peace treaty.

I inhaled and pushed the door open. Exhaling, I stepped inside the home that didn't feel like mine anymore. Hershey said as much without a word from the way he glared at me from the couch.

"Who is he, Victoria?" He asked, standing.

"A friend-"

"Don't give me that bullshit! Friends don't kiss friends! Who the fuck is he, Victoria?"

"Excuse me, Hershey, I'm not the one who got caught cheating-"

"This isn't about me. This is about you kissing that man, Victoria, and for what? To prove a point that you can just as easily hurt me?"

Matching his energy felt like a lost cause. That's exactly what he wanted. "You're a dog."

"I just might be, but every day I get up and work my ass off, so you and those kids never have to worry about having a roof over your heads or food in your mouths. So if this dog strays a little too far from home for your liking, install a doggy door and rub my head when I finally come home because it's a luxury I can afford."

"Thank you so much for taking care of your family, Hershey. I don't know what we would do without you. Is that what you want to hear, or should I fall on my knees and worship the ground you walk on?"

"I provide for my family, Victoria. I put a roof over your head, food in your mouth, and clothes on your back. I put money in your pocket so you can have all the shit you don't need and barely wanted. I do all of that out of love for you and those boys. And I never once put my hands on you, so if I'm a dog, you should be glad you found a domesticated one."

"Oh, trust me, I heard your eloquent analogy the first time."

"You are something else. How you think--how you do shit. If I was the dog you want me to be and any less of the man my mother raised me to be, I would tell you about yourself."

"Tell me about myself, Hershey. Please do. I would love to hear it."

"You're out here being a slut."

"A slut, huh? You're going to call the mother of your children a slut? Good to know how you feel."

"You didn't give me much to work with, Victoria. Because the only people I know who do what you did leave their family at home so they can flaunt around the city until 3 in the morning, doing God knows what-are sluts. Do you know how upset your children were?"

"Don't try to guilt-trip me, Hershey."

"Our children, your sons, kept asking where their mother was, and I had to lie. I had to tell them you had to take care of some business. I had to cover for you while you were out fucking another man, throwing away everything we've built!"

"Stop it."

"Where did you meet him?"

"Stop it."

"School? Did you meet him at school? Is that why you were so adamant about going back? So you could meet men? I should've known."

"Hershey, please, can you just stop?"

"No, you stop. That's what you should have told yourself when you decided you wanted to fuck someone else." He rushed and sized me up like I was a man out in the streets. His heavy breathing from his nose pushed my hair. "Was he bigger?"

"You're crazy."

"Was he bigger?" He slammed his hand into the front door.

"I didn't have sex with him."

"Stop lying."

"I'm not lying. We didn't have sex."

"You just love him."

"I don't know him, Hershey. He's a guy from one of my classes."

"You're going to lie to my face, huh?"

He went upstairs and came back, holding Daniel; Martin followed. Martin and Daniel were yawning and rubbing their eyes.

"Where are we going?" Martin asked through a yawn.

"Your mom is home."

"Mommy," they both yelled when they saw me.

Daniel just about leaped to the ground, and Martin ran to me but neither moved nor made a sound when Hershey yelled.

He glared at me.

"Are you going to lie to them?" He asked.

I broke down crying, unable to take in air to speak, while he kept demanding me to tell Daniel and Martin what happened.

Your father is a liar and a cheater. For the last six years, he tried his best to tear this family apart with his infidelity, and I had to turn a blind eye for you-for us. I fought the tears, anger, and the little pride I had left to continue to love him, so you didn't have to grow up in a broken home. When he never came home at night, he wasn't on a business trip. Instead, he chose women over his family. Martin, when your father learned I was pregnant with you, he left until you were one year old. He doesn't love us.

I wanted to say every word, and I was ready to tear him apart. Daniel and Martin's little eyes stopped me in my tracks. I couldn't bring myself to bad mouth their father.

Martin and Daniel kept asking what happened, I kept crying, and Hershey kept yelling. Since I couldn't talk because I was still trying to catch my breath, Hershey told them I wouldn't be home for a few days. He didn't tell them why, no matter how many times they asked. Then he made them go upstairs.

Martin cried.

Hershey stared at me.

"I don't think I can be with someone who can't respect herself," he said.

. . .

A half-hour later, I stood on the curb, waiting for Hershey's mother. Four black plastic bags, tearing from most of my belongings stuffed inside, lay at my feet. Clothes that I didn't have a bag for draped over my shoulder. Tears poured down my face, and his words knocked the air from my chest each time I replayed them.

By the time Hershey's mother arrived, I sobbed. She held me in her arms until the pain was easier to manage. We threw all my bags and clothes in the backseat of her car and drove to her house.

I stared at the ring on my finger, twisting it around and around. I could hear Martin and Daniel crying as they called out my name for me to stay. Their voices deepened, and eventually, they sounded like men, but they no longer asked for me. Instead, they cursed my name like their father. No matter how much I gasped, I needed more air. Tears and snot dripped into my mouth, and I could taste the salt.

Hershey's mother put her hand on and massaged my knee. She didn't say anything; she just sighed.

Reaching into my purse for a tissue, my hand grazed something plastic and rough to the touch.

Whatever it was, I pulled it out. Starlight. I smiled, holding back laughter.

I lay my head back onto the headrest as I stared out the window. After a while, I couldn't hold in my laughter. Hershey's mother put her hand back on my knee and said, "let it out."

I put my feet into the seat and held Stomps and Starlight on my knees. Looking at them brought me back to the previous night.

"Are those the boys'?" She asked.

"They're mine."

"Hmph."

"Weird, I know."

"I guess we all like our fair share of non-traditional things."

"A friend bought them for me."

"What an odd thing to buy as a gift. You seem quite amused by those toys. You look downright happy if I was to go out on a limb."

"Let's stick with amused."

"I'm going to stay out on my limb."

I turned to meet her gaze. "I don't know why."

"You're smiling like a kid in a candy shop."

Hendrix talking as Stomps and Starlight drowned out her voice. I closed my eyes and listened as I envisioned Stomps and Starlight act out his every word. Before long, I fell asleep and dreamt about Hendrix. I heard him singing, his voice cracking and going out. He asked me to sing along, and just as I started, Hershey's mother woke me with a shake. I jerked forward, knocking the toys and my phone onto the floor.

I still had a giant smile on my face. Hendrix still sang.

She led me inside by the hand to the guest room. There, creepy wooden dolls sat on the shelves. Their painted-on eyes followed you around the room. She left and closed the door. I sat on the edge of the bed, still in my dress from last night, and through the space between the door and floor, I saw her walking. Her footsteps echoed down the hall and away from the room.

I took my bags into the boy's room; it had two beds. One had race car sheets. The other had sheets with animals and a pile of teddy bears.

I closed the door and changed into shorts and a T-Shirt with a faded image of a cartoon Panda. Then I lay down in the bed with the race car sheets—the pillow smelt like Martin. I nuzzled my face into the pillow.

I listened to Hershey's mother talking as I fell asleep, her voice muffled by distance and the wall.

. . .

In the morning, the sun shined through the slightly opened blinds, warming the side of my face.

I woke up, not knowing where I was or what had happened. My first reaction was to jump out of bed. Everything started coming back to me: the woman, the kiss, Stomps and Starlight, Hershey, and Martin and Daniel. Martin and Daniel's crying echoed in my head. I dropped to the edge of the bed, leaning forward, with my head down, and listened to Hershey's mother argue on the phone.

She was talking with Hershey. She said his name in almost every sentence. When I had called her earlier, I didn't expect her to come, like I didn't expect to hear her coming to my defense. She saw me as everything that Hershey didn't. To her, I was beautiful, hardworking, strong, perseverant, intelligent.

Her conversation ended. Soon after, she walked into the room and sat beside me, tapping the cordless phone on her knee.

"No one ever wants to sleep in that room," she said. "The dolls aren't that creepy."

"They're terrifying."

"I guess I'm used to the creepy." We didn't speak, and she broke the silence with a brief hmm. "Hershey told me everything."

"Oh, God."

"He said you kissed another man. He said you left with the same man and didn't come home until 3 in the morning. The 3 in the morning part cuts him deep."

"There is a lot more to it than that."

"I know he conveniently left out the point about him chasing behind fire trucks."

I turned my body to her. "You knew?"

"Honey, please. It wasn't like it was some big secret."

Her words cut deep. "The whore baths."

"You would think he would know dousing himself in cologne wouldn't mask the smell of sex."

"Cheap cologne at that."

"Ain't nothing wrong with saving a dollar or two. I'm just happy you finally realized that Hershey isn't worth a quarter."

"He isn't that bad."

"Try to trade Hershey for a piece of bubble gum, and the Candyman would pay you to take him back."

"If Hershey isn't worth that much, I would hate to know what you think of me."

"I think the world of you."

"He's your son, and I'm just-"

"A woman that endured the most in the name of love. Now, I will admit it, you willingly choosing to deal with Hershey's bullshit lets me know you ain't got no damn sense." She cackled and slapped my thigh; she only did so when she thought something was hilarious. "But it's sweet in a dumb way. Think of this as a new beginning. You have the chance to start over. Take it, girl. Take it and enjoy the fruits of life instead of worrying about Hershey's ass dragging you through the mud."

"Yeah." I lay back down.

She got up and walked to the door. "Don't get too comfortable. The kids will be here soon."

I sat upright. "Why are you doing all this for me? Hershey's your son."

"Hershey is my son, and he'll always have my love. Supporting all his foolishness ain't love. He still got me. You got me too."

"Thanks."

"I figured he would look at his father to see what was to come, and I pray he figures it out one day. It goes to show you, no matter how much you invest in your children, sometimes we cannot help them from themselves."

"We can try."

"Lord knows that's all we can do. I ain't have many choices in the man Hershey became. I do, however, have the chance to try to right his wrongs. You're my daughter, and ain't nothing Hershey or the world can do to stop me from loving you."

She left, closing the door.

I jumped up and hurried to the bathroom for a quick shower. I did my hair and put on this white sundress that was Hershey's favorite-he brought it during a vacation to San Francisco. I was in the bathroom, getting ready when they arrived. I heard the car doors close and Daniel yelling about being at "Nan-Nan's" house.

His screams drowned out everyone and only grew in volume as they came inside.

Through the walls, I heard them talking. Hershey's mother uttered something that sounded like my name. No matter how intently I listened, the walls kept the conversation to a muffle. I pulled back the shower curtain and placed my ear to the wall, listening, straining to hear the conversation on the other side.

The doorknob jiggled, and the door proceeded to creep open. Hershey stood there, rolling his eyes at me. My ears and hands were still on the wall, listening to the mutters, and I tried my best to play it off.

"I should've figured by the way she defended you," he said.

"We need to talk."

"I'm not in the mood to talk right now."

"Do you hear those kids? We owe it to them to try again."

"I owe them my love and support. That's it, and as long as there's air in my lungs, they'll have it."

"What about your promise to me? What happened to you loving me forever?"

"We are still a family, but you have to let that dream go, Victoria."

"Hershey, nothing happened. He kissed me. That's it."

"Nothing good happens at three in the morning."

"I had nowhere else to go. He took me to McDonald's. Hershey, you're the only man I could want in this world."

"It's too late, Victoria."

"It doesn't have to be. That's what I'm saying. We can work through this like we always have."

"You hurt me, Victoria. There's no coming back from what you did."

"Martin and Daniel need their mother."

"They'll always have you." He started walking down the hall, and I followed.

"Fuck you."

He snapped around, making me flinch. "No, because if that's what you were doing last night, this wouldn't be happening right now."

"I want to see my children, Hershey."

"You must be crazy."

"Those are my kids." He put his arm against the wall, blocking me from passing.

"Move."

"You aren't seeing those kids. I don't care if they don't see their grandmother until she's in her grave because as long as you're here, my kids aren't stepping foot in this damn house again."

"Then I'll take you to court."

He laughed hysterically. "With what money? I paid for everything. The mortgage. The bills. The dress you're wearing. Let's say you can even get a lawyer; what do you offer? You have no job-let alone skills. No house. No car. You can't take care of those kids, Victoria. It's best if you pick a battle you can win." He snapped, laughing. "You know what? I'll see you in court. Until then, have a blessed day, Victoria."

It felt like dull knives stabbed into my chest and stomach. My blood boiled as I glared at the man, who was supposed to love me, as he walked into the kitchen. His mother shouted as he demanded Daniel and Martin to get up. The dull stabbing sensation twisted deeper into my chest and stomach at the idea of Martin and Daniel seeing me. In an attempt not to break down in front of them, I hid in the bathroom as Hershey's mother tried to talk sense into him. He slammed the door; the pictures and mirrors hanging on the walls rattled.

"What's wrong, daddy?" Martin asked.

"Get in the goddamn car," Hershey said.

Hershey's mother walked into the hall and stared at me.

"I told you," she said. "He ain't worth a quarter."

I told her everything Hershey said, and her face scrunched in anger. She took me back into the boy's room.

My phone vibrated from a video Hendrix sent with the caption of "Because… don't forget to smile." He played with two action figures in the video, bouncing them up and down as he said, "good morning."

The stabbing feeling in my stomach and chest eased each time the video replayed. My hands must have had a mind of their own.

Hendrix

Two hours later, my phone's alarm went off, nearly giving me a heart attack. I turned off the alarm and shuffled from my room to the bathroom.

Eve, already fully dressed, moisturized her hair in the bathroom mirror, running her fingers across her scalp.

The bathroom had two sections; a door separated the sink from the toilet and shower. I used the bathroom, and when I came out, she was back in my room. She and I alternated between the bathroom and my room as we got ready for the day. We didn't say anything to one another, past grumbling, "Good morning."

We ended up going downstairs at the same time. Dad sipped coffee at the kitchen table. The steam could've knocked the wrinkles out of his shirt.

"Good morning, Eve," he said and smiled.

"Morning, dad."

"Good morning, son." He never looked at me.

"Morning."

I made lunch for the day, which was leftover roast beef and rice from two nights ago. For breakfast, I ate yogurt, toast, and some fruit at the counter. I kept my back to my dad. For some reason, it felt better that way.

"Are you two mad at each other?" Eve asked.

"If I had a problem with my son," dad said, "he would know."

"So, are you mad at him?"

"Not that I know of."

"Hendrix, what did you do?"

"Nothing," I said.

"It doesn't look like nothing."

They sat at the table, discussing plans for their day: breakfast and then car shopping, for Eve, of course.

Vanessa came downstairs and rolled her eyes at the conversation. She and I exchanged a mocking laugh at Eve's expense. That prompted her to come to me.

"Don't worry about taking dad to his appointment today," she said. "Eve and I got it."

"Hendrix and I have a system," dad said. "No need to mess with the program now."

"Are you sure that's a good idea?" Eve asked. "For Hendrix's safety."

"I'll be fine," I said. "You heard the man, no need to mess with the system."

Vanessa held back a few curse words. "Are you sure?"

"It's going to have to," dad said, "because that's what's happening."

"There you have it," Vanessa said, rolling her eyes.

"What can I say? It's male bonding," I said. "Dad, I'll be back around 12:15 pm."

Victoria

Before class, Hershey's mother and I drove to this Toy Store in the same plaza as a Baptist church. All the other businesses had relocated a few years back, leaving just those two.

The store was twice as long as it was wide. If I stood on the glass counter, which divided the store into two aisles, I could touch the shelves along the walls. The crowds during the holidays had to be a nightmare.

Only one employee worked. He was the only person there, and he waved as we entered. We both took an aisle and searched the shelves jam-packed with toys and collectibles for the perfect gift.

"What about this?" Hershey's mother said, raising a Tyrannosaurus rex standing a foot tall.

"No, it can't be a dinosaur."

"Why not?"

"Because he already gave me a dinosaur. It has to be something different to show I put some thought into it."

"It would help if you knew what he liked."

"Music. Romance novels." I shrugged. "I don't know."

"Those aren't the only things he likes."

"Am I forgetting something?"

"A certain Victoria of your persuasion."

"I walked right into that joke." I ran my finger across the edge of the glass counter, looking at clear containers of Legos and army men. "We're just friends."

"You know what I think?"

"That he likes me, I know. But he doesn't."

"Mmmhmm. What about this?" She held up an alien toy in packaging that saw better days. I shook my head, and she put it back. "I'm sure there's a chance he doesn't like you. I'll give you that. But I know for sure you like him."

"Now, I know you like to hear yourself talk. I don't like Hendrix."

"Nice name. And a seemingly nice guy. How old is he? Since you don't want him, no need for a good man to go to waste."

The only reply I could think to give was an unamused look.

"If you don't like the boy, then why are we here?"

"To buy him a gift."

"Why does a platonic friend you just met need a gift?"

"Because he got me one."

"Why are we putting this much effort into buying him a gift?"

"To say thank you. Last night he was talking about how he loved playing with toys as a kid, and I figured this would be the perfect 'thank you."

"So, he was a normal child?"

"I know it sounds weird. You have to trust me on this. He'll appreciate this more than going out for lunch."

"I'm sure he'll happily take the date."

"Very funny."

"If he'll appreciate the toy, then let's just get him the alien."

"It can't just be anything. It has to mean something."

"And you want me to believe you two aren't crushing?"

"I can only speak for myself when I say nobody is crushing on anybody else. I'm still in love with Hershey."

She raised a Batman action figure. "A man in black always did it for me."

"Eh," I said, shaking my head. "Batman is kinda cliché."

"I think you should give this Hendrix guy a chance."

"Okay. That's wildly inappropriate."

"Because I'm Hershey's mother? As my son, I wouldn't replace him for the world. As a husband, that boy isn't worth a pot to piss in."

"That still doesn't change the fact that I've been single for all of five minutes. I'm not ready for another relationship."

She walked around the middle counter and into my aisle. "A loveless nine-year relationship, might I add. Your heart has been yearning for affection for years now. Poor thing, you were just too caught up in what you perceived as love to notice."

I squeezed past her and ventured deeper into the store. I picked up some of the toys and made them bounce up and down. None of the toys spoke to me. I couldn't imagine Hendrix giving any of them voices. All the board games were at the back of the store, and I turned onto the second aisle, looking across the top shelf at a plush of a character I saw in the game Martin always played.

The tag read Link. The adorable look in its eyes let me know I found the right gift. I held it to my chest as I made my way to Hershey's mother, who browsed through the board games. She turned to me.

"Looks like you found the right something," she said.

"I did."

"What is it?"

I held out the plush, and we both examined it. "Link."

"What is Link?"

"He looks like an elf. I heard him talking about how much he likes this Link guy, so I can't go wrong with this, right?"

"You better hope he likes it. We can't have this relationship starting off on the wrong foot."

"The relationship can't start off on the wrong foot since this is strictly platonic."

"Mmmhmm."

"We don't like each other."

"Say what you want, but nothing will change the fact that we're at a toy store looking for a gift for a man you supposedly don't like. It's not like you're getting him a soda or a bag of chips. You're going to buy this thing-whatever it is-to make a lasting impression. You can say whatever you like, dear, but you're crushing."

"For the last time, I'm simply showing my appreciation."

"Then give him a hug or the classic, 'thank you.' You want to show him more than your appreciation, but you can't give him the goodies just yet, so you're looking for something in between. And do you know what shows appreciation more than saying 'thank you,' but less than the goodies? Link."

. . .

With Link tucked away in my purse, I hurried to class with a stride in my step, nervous to see Hendrix's reaction, anxious that he'd misinterpret my intentions.

He wasn't there yet, which was weird because he always beat me to class.

Our classmates entered and went directly to the desks they had been sitting in for the past week. As they conversed, their voices echoed. It was so loud that I couldn't think, and I put on my headphones to keep the noise down.

I kept my eyes on the door, waiting for Hendrix to walk into the classroom with his headphones on. I had Link sitting in his chair. I couldn't wait to see his face when he noticed. As time crept to 6 pm, my smile softened. He wasn't there yet, and when our professor started the lecture, my smile had faded completely. As Link sat there, I thought about what the gift said—what it implied. I stuffed Link back into my purse and took notes as our professor continued last week's lecture.

I considered myself fortunate that he didn't show because I would have looked silly. Hershey's mother was right; it was flirting. Hendrix was a friend, and I had no intention of being with him. Being how I didn't like him romantically, it was best not to gift him the plush in the slight chance that he earnestly saw me as more than a friend. It would have spared us both from the awkward moment of him confessing his affection. And worse, me rejecting him.

Our professor had closed the door when she came in. Now, like myself, everyone looked towards the door as it opened. I thought it was Hendrix.

It was a guy who always came late and left early and always carried a notebook, no pen. He plopped down into Hendrix's seat, leaned back in a stretch to ask to borrow a pen. I was just about to say I didn't have an extra pen when I realized I had two on the edge of my desk. I handed him a pen without taking my eyes off the professor.

The lecture was always a chore to get through. The professor had a magical way of making exciting material feel bland. She expected us to read the lecture notes before class, which I always did. During the class itself, she stood behind a podium and read the notes word for word.

The lack of sleep caught up to me, and I dozed off. My eyes snapped open when someone walked inside.

Hendrix stammered in. Usually, he had a giant smile on his face. Now, he forced an uninspired smile without showing his teeth, and his eyes glanced at me in a way I wondered if we were the same people from last night. The guy that took his spot had already left by this point, and Hendrix sat in front of me.

Hendrix

Dad was right, I thought. I should have kept my lips to myself. I could have everything but that. I probably made things ten times worse between her and her husband.

I felt the need to move during class to avoid her staring daggers into my back.

After class, we gave each other one of those awkward stares, where we both looked guilty and tried to avoid eye contact.

I wondered what happened after I took her back home. There was no way she and her husband could act as if nothing happened. She caught him in bed with another woman; he watched us kiss. I wondered if true love was forgiving one another no matter the mistake. I wondered if there was a fine line between true love and stupidity and how we knew if we crossed it.

She still wore her wedding ring. There wasn't anything to say.

. . .

I sat across from my dad in a booth at In N Out, listening to him graze on his double-double without onions. I ate my fries as I read for class. The textbook sat on my lap, propped against the edge of the table. The words went in and immediately out, forcing me to read a page twice to retain the information. So many thoughts ran rampant through my head, and I couldn't focus on one before thinking about another. I thought about Victoria and how she looked disappointed two days ago at school. I thought about our kiss. As soon as I relived our lips touching, my parents came to mind. Then I thought about school.

I had eight more weeks before I graduated. Life would start at that point, and I had no idea what happened next.

I looked up from the book at my dad. He was almost done with his burger.

"How did you know you wanted to drive garbage trucks for a career?" I asked.

"You make it sound like kids grow up dreaming of working in waste management. It's far from a terrible job, but it's not one you plan for-you kinda just wake up one day knuckle deep in someone else's trash. Without the education, I had to take whatever paid the bills."

"You always came home looking so drained."

"When you work twelve hours days, you tend to look tired."

"Nah, you weren't tired. You looked physically and mentally drained. It was like it knocked the life out of you, and every day, you looked more and more unhappy."

"That's because I hated that job."

"Then why didn't you just quit?"

"I had three little musketeers to feed and more bills than I hope you will never understand. I had a lot on the line."

"I couldn't imagine working a job that I hate, let alone doing it for years."

"Most people hate their job. Here's a harsh reality for you, son. Sometimes responsibilities kick you right in the gut, and no matter how much you want to hit that snooze button, you don't cause you can't. You put on a smile and act like you have the greatest job in the world."

I cringed.

It was no telling the look on my face, but I knew it was bad because my dad put his greasy hands on mine.

You'll be alright, son," he said.

"I hope."

"Look at me, son."

I took my eyes from nothingness to him. "I know, dad, we got this."

"Hendrix, right now, you're in a transitional stage in your life. Your eyes are on the prize. You know exactly what's going to come next. It's just the life you're worried about isn't thinking about you yet, son."

"In other words, suck it up."

"Not what I'm saying, but kinda."

"Save the speech, okay? You're not going to convince me I'm wrong for worrying about my life."

"You're right. You're right. It's your life. Let's be real, you're a broke college student who lives at home with his father." Before his words drowned me in thoughts, he diverted my attention with a tap on my arm. "Son, you're twenty-five years old. Go out in the world, see what it holds for you. This is the time where you learn about yourself and this thing called life. Stop jumping stages, Hendrix. You're where you need to be, and even if you cannot see them, blessings are coming your way."

Life is like a carousel, I thought.

As a child, my dad would put me on the horse. Even before the ride started, as all the other kids hurried to their favorite horses and adults trailed behind, getting whatever was available, I would close my eyes as I clenched onto the pole for dear life. My dad would be off to the side, shouting my name, followed by words of encouragement. Before the music began, I knew everything was fine, and I would kinda get excited about the ride. Once the music started and the carousel crept to a start, I broke out in a sweat, my heart faltered, and my eyes popped open. I would look to my dad, who still cheered me on as he snapped pictures, and I knew my face told him how much I wanted to get off. Still, he kept shouting my name. All the other kids screamed and yelled in excitement, to my relief, drowning out my cries.

The faces of the onlookers and those passing by smiling and laughing kept vanishing as we went around. The music seemed to get louder and slower until I only heard the screaming kids and onlookers like my dad in the crowd. Then, the music got louder, distorted, and slowed down to a muffle. Everything blurred together. The music got louder, and so did my cries. Then, the ride would stop. Gradually, the music lowered, and children hollering and the chatter from the crowd roared. Faces in the crowd slowly cleared, the carousel slowed to a stop, and Dad emerged from the crowd first, his thumbs up in support. I always knew what would happen if I got on the carousel, and every time, I always agreed to get on.

Life is like a carousel, but unlike one, it doesn't end, I thought. There are no animatronics horses to sit on, and if there were, you have to buy them, so for the most part, you're paying to run around in circles. Nobody is looking on from a crowd because they either don't care or are also on the ride. Not too many people are laughing, and those who are, only do so on good days. Why would they? The music changes by the day, and the ride only spins at sickening speeds. No matter how much your feet blister or you cramp up, you have to keep running towards an unknown goal. The music goes in and out, and sometimes if you listen hard enough, you can hear laughter; it comes from nowhere and everywhere at once. It's from no one but everyone.

Back at In N Out, the room spun.

Life is moving too fast, I said to myself. Life is moving too fast. What happens after this? School is almost over, and the real world is waiting. I can't hide from life anymore.

On my tenth birthday, while my family packed into my dad's blue 2-Door Honda Civic, our neighbor came up and asked me, "How does it feel to be ten, big guy?" I shrugged. She told me to enjoy my youth because I would wake up wishing to be a kid again one day.

My chest felt empty.

The room spun faster, forcing me to hold onto the table with a vice grip. The laughter from the patrons enjoying their meals and conversations deepened to a point it sounded like growls.

My throat tightened.

When dad touched my hand, I jumped.

"Anybody home?" He asked.

"What if things don't happen as planned?"

"You're jumping stages, Hendrix."

"Dad-"

"Why do you insist on being miserable?"

"And why do you hate being a father sometimes?"

"Hendrix-"

"I didn't mean it like that…I just need you to listen. No proverbs. No Dr. Phil moment. Just listen."

"I'm not going to watch my son drown, Hendrix. If that makes me a bad father, so be it."

"I didn't mean it like that."

"Let me ask you this, what's worse: falling into some shit and getting up or wallowing around in it like a pig?"

"Neither if I had the choice."

"Look, son. You're a brilliant, hard-working young man. Stop stressing yourself out. Everything will work out in the end. You have to trust me on this. You'll change the world, and I'll be right there, shouting your name."

"Remember when we used to go to the fair?"

"Before you kids got too cool to hang out with your old man."

"And what do you call this?"

"This right here? This is just sad. You need some friends, son." He winked. "Tell me about the fair."

"I hated the carrousel."

"You don't say." He chuckled. "I saw the fear of God in your eyes. You would think you were riding that horse to the gates of hell. And yet, every time you saw one, you asked to get on."

I laughed. "You always looked so happy watching. I couldn't take that away from you."

"It wasn't that serious for me."

"Well, if I knew that at the time, I definitely wouldn't have gotten on. I was so stupid."

"I called it facing your fears." He winked.

He squeezed down on my hand. The force squeezed a smile out of me. He let go, and I took a bite of my burger; it was a little cold.

Dad went to refill his drink.

He could drop dead right now, in the middle of In n Out, I thought. Don't die on me just yet, dad.

I held my eyes open wide, fighting back the tears. He came back and said the very words I was thinking: "I'm going to miss these talks."

"Can you not say stuff like that?"

"I'm just saying, it's nice conversing with my children and not having them nag me or hold their hands out. The only thing you ask of me is company and advice. I like that. Keep it up."

I winced from the throbbing in my head. "My head is killing me."

"That's because you need to eat." He nodded to my burger.

I finished eating, and in the car, I noticed it was 6:13 pm.

"I'm late for class," I said.

"Then, get to class."

"I have to take you back home."

"That's out of the way. By the time you take me home and come back, you might as well stay home. I'll drop you off." He winked.

...

This guy, who always came to class late and left early, decided to take my seat. Before I looked back across the room, seeing quite a few people staring, I connected eyes with Victoria; she looked amazing. My natural response was to smile. She smiled back, which took me completely off guard. I found a seat in the back of the class, mid-lecture.

Word for word. Our professor stood behind a podium and read the notes she posted online, word for word. The same notes she has displayed on the board. The same notes I read before class per her request. The same notes I was paying thousands of dollars for.

Memories, thoughts, and images of dad pulled my focus from the lecture on Michel Foucault and his theory of Panopticism to a world, where the classroom spun, and everyone turned in their seats looking and laughing at me while I nearly fell as I fought through the dizziness and hurried from the classroom. Outside, I leaned against the wall beside the door and gasped for air. The fresh air couldn't calm the burning in my chest and throat. I closed my eyes, fighting away the images of my dad lying in a casket while Vanessa and Eve lost it when our mom revealed herself at his funeral.

The door squeaked open and closed. I tried my best to hide the fact my world was falling apart; my mind had other plans. Just as I pushed myself off the wall, someone took me into their arms.

Lavender and vanilla.

Victoria.

As long as my eyes stayed closed, I didn't have to acknowledge how hard I cried or try to prove my masculinity. I kept them closed.

She held me so tight in her arms until I got myself together. She gazed at me without speaking, took me by the hand, and led me around campus.

I didn't say anything at first-too embarrassed from the moment before. I figured if I didn't speak, then I didn't have to live in a world where I hated my life.

Before I knew it, I blurted out everything wrong in my life. She never said anything during my ramblings until I almost forgot she was there until I took in the smell of lavender and vanilla.

Then, she replied, giving the same cliché reply when you want to comfort someone but don't know what to say. Somewhere in her response, she used the word "Stages."

I took a step back. An eternity filled the small distance between her and I. That's why I never let go of her hand or resisted as she took me back into her arms.

"My dad is dying," I whispered, with tears rolling down my face.

"He's alive. Don't rush him to the grave."

"Victoria, that man is a pack away from coughing up a lung, and I keep giving him a light. The way I see it, I've pushed him into a grave; he's burying himself."

"You have to stop doing this to yourself. He's a grown man. You're not putting the cigarette in his mouth. He's going to do what he wants to do regardless if you say something or not."

"That's the problem. I choose the wrong times to be quiet."

"You're trying to be supportive. Lord knows he needs a friend right now."

"I'm not his friend. I'm his son."

"Again, you're trying to be his support system. It sounds like he doesn't have anyone else. He knows he can turn to you. Cherish that connection. Not too many have it."

"Then maybe he needs to know I think he's a coward."

"He's not."

"He's giving up, Victoria."

"He has a lot to deal with right now."

"I do too! Why doesn't he care I still need him? I can't do this without him."

"You have to stop thinking like this."

"Two years ago, in the middle of winter, the water heater went out. I saw that man change it himself. He went to the store and came back an hour later with a water heater. Less than an hour later, hot showers. What do I do when he's gone? I can't change a water heater. I can barely hang a picture straight."

She held me tighter, and I felt her trembling and tears soaking into my shirt.

We stood on the front lawn of the school, under the branches of a tree. I stepped back, our hands still interlocked. We stared into each other's eyes. The light-post didn't give much light, and the tree blocked the moonlight, making it difficult to see her completely. I saw just enough to make me smile.

She wore her hair in a ponytail. A twig hung from a strand of hair just above her hairline.

I stared as tears rolled down her face. She smiled.

"What?" She asked, in a whisper.

"Nothing."

"It's always nothing with you. What's with the smile?"

"You need to get those eyes checked cause I'm not smiling."

"Oh, okay. Well, your lips are doing this weird thing. You might want to get that checked out cause you look pretty silly." She laughed, wiping the tears from her eyes. "It's like you had a stroke."

"Next time I'm at the hospital, I'll have a doctor check it out."

"No, whatever it is, keep it."

"Yeah?"

"I like it. I would feel inclined to say you have a nice smile. If you were smiling, that is."

"So do you."

She blushed.

I know my deal," I said. "But why are you crying?"

"I thought about something sad."

"But, you're smiling."

"I'm a ball of emotions right now. Don't mind me."

"I'm right there with you."

She extended her arms for a hug. "If you need one."

"Since you're offering."

She wrapped her arms around my neck and lay her head on my shoulders. We held each other in desperation.

And I didn't want her to.

"You'll always have me, Hendrix," she whispered. "You'll always have me. No matter what happens, you aren't alone."

We took our arms from around each other.

"We barely know each other," I said. "That's a big promise."

"Then let's get to know each other."

"I'll like that."

We walked around campus, telling one another our life stories, and then some-I purposely avoided talking about my mother.

The conversation switched to relationships, and she pried for details. It wasn't as important to me as it was for her. She wouldn't stop asking and always brought the subject back to relationships every time I casually changed it. I took a deep breath and told her about my ex. She looked surprised that I dated my ex for four years. I told her how we started dating when we were seventeen, and like most relationships, the honeymoon phase had me walking on sunshine. I went on, telling her things about the relationship that I never shared with anyone. A look of hurt and empathy lingered in her eyes the entire rant.

"The entire relationship?" She asked.

"She was with a guy the night I made it official."

"Shit." She winced. "Sorry."

It was now her time to talk my ears off. Of everything, she spoke the most about Martin and Daniel. About how they got their names to their random quirks. She named Daniel after Hershey's younger brother, who died in a car accident, and Martin after her father.

As we talked, no one else mattered. No one else existed. We stood on an empty campus, where the moon shined down on us and only us. The wind blew to give me the chance to smell her and her hair.

When she laughed, it didn't feel like it was at me, instead, we laughed together. Typically, as I walked across campus, I smelt the wet grass, and these flowers that everyone on campus agreed smelt like cum. Lavender and vanilla masked every smell. She was my world.

The clock tower chimed, and we didn't think anything of it. We just continued walking. In the brief moment of silence, where we both goofily smiled, my mind had enough time to venture back to my mom.

Was she that afraid of commitment? I thought. Was she that unhappy that she left her three children without saying a word? Dad can be a piece of work, but what did Vanessa, Eve, and I do for her to leave us? All we did was need her—want her. What happened to that unconditional love from a mother? Why didn't she come back?

"So was being practically married worth it?" I asked. "Was all the love worth all the heartbreak?"

"Hershey and I were never married." She extended her hand in the air to examine the ring. "Surprise."

"You told me...the other night."

"Oh, that says a lot about you, Hendrix. You're so easy to talk to." She winked.

"Are you two back together?"

"That's probably never gonna happen. I like wearing it though. I guess it was my way of holding onto hope that Hershey loves me."

"Damn. I don't know what else to say except 'sorry.'"

"I stopped feeling sorry for myself a long time ago."

"Just because you stopped doesn't mean I have to follow your lead."

"You should, Hendrix. You'll stress yourself out for nothing." She twisted the ring. "Hershey did enough apologizing. I've heard those words so much that I don't think they mean the same thing anymore."

"You can't let one asshole make you this cynical. Besides, if a word loses its meaning by how frequently it's used, everything would be meaningless."

"Who says everything isn't meaningless?"

"Your sons, every time they call you mom, mommy, mama. What's the saying? A mother's job is never over. 'Mom, I'm hungry.' 'Mom, my stomach hurts.' 'Can you buy me this toy, mom?' 'Mommy, please.' I guess being a mother is meaningless just because your little boys can't get enough of you."

"Alright, alright, everything isn't meaningless. But it doesn't change the fact I'm tired of hearing people say they're sorry." She paused. "I'm tired of hearing Hershey say he's sorry. So don't be sorry. You didn't do anything wrong. You did everything right."

"Once again, these lips show women the light. They're like disciples of Jesus himself."

"Women, huh? Sounds like you're quite the ladies' man."

"I've kissed my fair share of women. Not as many as you may think, of course. I'm not easy."

"Who says I'm putting that much thought into your love life?"

"You."

"Get over yourself, Hendrix."

"Correct me if I'm wrong, but you're the one who brought up my love life. You want to know how many lucky ladies got to kiss these lips."

"I didn't say that."

"You don't have to say it. I can see it in your eyes. You want to know how many women got to experience these lips- other than yourself, of course. Ain't that cute."

"I'm just trying to make sure I don't wake up with any surprises."

"I'm not sure if we're still joking, but in all seriousness, you don't have to worry about that. I haven't kissed too many women because, like yourself, I wasted a lot of my time in a terrible relationship."

"I wouldn't exactly call mine a waste of time. As shitty as he is, Hershey gave me two blessings. I guess the Lord giveth and the Lord taketh away."

"That means what, exactly?"

"He kicked me out of the house." She pushed out a deep breath. "He says I can't see them again."

I almost apologized. Before I uttered the words that would have surely set her off, Victoria shrugged and said, "I'm done crying."

"He'll be back. You know that, right?"

"What makes you think that?"

"Because you're amazing."

"Next time, you don't have to take the scenic route to a compliment."

"I'm serious. You are!"

"How could someone cheat on you?"

"The same way someone could cheat on you, I'm guessing. Some people are so precious, not everyone has the skills to handle them."

"Or maybe we're so nice that people decide to use us."

"Maybe. I don't know. I like to be a little more optimistic."

"Go ahead and share some of that optimism."

"I like to think we haven't found the right people yet."

"Maybe the right person doesn't exist."

"Maybe, just maybe, that person does exist, and we aren't looking in the right places."

"Maybe."

It was then we realized that we had yet to let each other's hand go. We squeezed with the same force as before-if not tighter.

The clock tower chimed for a second time. We glanced up at its face illuminating the campus.

8 pm. We realized classes already ended hit us at the same time.

We ran back to class, afraid that our professor locked our belongings inside.

The door was open, and another class was in session. Our bags sat on the table in front of the class. We hurried in and out of the class, never looking directly at anyone. On our way out, the professor stopped the lecture to joke about our "long bathroom break." Everyone laughed. Outside, Victoria burst into laughter.

She spotted her mother-in-law's car in the drop-off zone.

"My ride is here," she said. "I probably shouldn't keep her waiting any longer."

"Probably not. My guess is she's been there a while."

"You have that effect, Hendrix. Time flies when I'm with you." She let go of my hand. "I'll text you when I get home."

As she walked away, I checked my phone. It was dead.

"Victoria," I said.

She turned around. "Hendrix."

"Do you think your ride will mind making a pitstop? Phones dead. Can't call my dad."

We walked to the car and hopped inside. I sat behind her. I spent most of the ride trying to convince Victoria's mother-in-law that I wasn't hungry.

She didn't take "no" for an answer.

It took about twenty minutes to get to Victoria's mother-in-law's house. Rocks and peddles made up the front yard. The smell of a home-cooked meal in the oven greeted me at the door. She could throw down in the kitchen if the food tasted as it smelt.

"You two, go and wash your hands," her mother-in-law said, pointing down the hall.

I nodded. Walking to the bathroom, I heard a loud swat and a groan. I looked over my shoulder and saw Victoria jerk forward, holding her butt, her face scrunched in disbelief.

We shared the bathroom sink to wash our hands, where our hands touched once or twice. We looked at one another in the mirror. Although she was smiling, she looked uncomfortable.

"I guess I should get hungry," I said.

"I guess so." She dried her hands with paper towel and hurried to the kitchen.

Two plates, with lasagna, salad, and a breadstick, sat on the table across from one another. Victoria's mother-in-law placed a pitcher of homemade iced tea on the table, then two glasses from the cabinet.

"You can eat," she said. "I'll be out of your hair in a moment."

Once she made herself a plate, she went upstairs without saying a word.

I stared at my plate, trying to prepare myself mentally for the heaviness of the meal. I looked up at Victoria; she stared at me. The lights under the hanging cabinets dimly lit the kitchen.

"This isn't how I pictured my night ending," she said.

I took a bite of a breadstick. "I'm not mad at it."

"Is this awkward to you?"

"Not really. We've kissed, and I met your son already. It's about time we started to take things slow." I watched her poke at her lasagna with her fork. "You're thinking way too much into this."

"I guess."

"By any chance, do you have any spare blankets?"

"Why do you need blankets?" The way she looked at me made me laugh.

"You'll see and love it."

Victoria

Almost every blanket and sheet in the house draped across the boy's room. Two nights ago, I never, in a million years, imagined I would kiss someone other than Hershey. I sure as hell never imagined that the same man would have made us a blanket fort.

I stood in the hall, outside the bedroom door, watching him crawl inside the fort with his plate in hand. Inside, he reached for mine, and I reluctantly gave it to him, and like that, he disappeared back into the fort.

"I thought you were joking," I said. "But you were serious. You really made a fort."

He stuck his head out. "I never play about my blanket forts." He extended his hand. "Come on in. You're letting all the cold air out."

I took his hand. Looking at the childish grin on his face and feeling how firm he held my hand, I felt at ease. I crawled inside as I giggled like a little girl.

His head barely cleared the bedsheets when he sat up straight.

"So, we're here," I said, "inside a blanket fort."

"It kinda has a club vibe."

"What? Dark and cramp?"

To the melodies of the most ratchet song—so ratchet I presumed it a parody—he scarfed down his food. Every few bits, he hiccupped, holding his chest as the food went down; I thought he was choking. Right after, he went right back to eating like he hadn't in days.

I thought it was interesting that he didn't touch his lasagna or salad until he finished his breadstick. But it was just weird that he was eating his lasagna before his salad. I covered my mouth to hide my laughter.

"Not you too," he said.

"What?"

"You know exactly what I'm talking about."

"What are you talking about?"

He stared with a deadpan look. "You find it weird I'm eating my salad last."

I burst into laughter. "Why are you eating your salad last? It's not like the greens are going to wash away the carbs. I can't get over how weird you are."

"I take offense to that. I don't think I am weird at all."

"But weird is good. You aren't afraid to be yourself in a world that tells us who to be."

"Do you consider yourself weird?"

"I'm sitting inside this fort with you, aren't I?"

"You are. I can't take that away from you. A lesser man would call you out for your hesitation to join this beautiful palace of the highest thread count."

"You got me there."

"Come on, you gotta give me something. Show me how weird you are. Show me how spontaneous you can be."

He kept insisting, with his head tilted to the side and a mischievous grin. After the third or fourth time, he stopped, but the smirk stayed on his face while gazing at me, hopelessly. His gaze was as vibrant and welcoming as the other day.

My only desire was to feel his lips against mine a second time. My heart slammed intensely against my chest, throbbing harder by the second. My breath thinned. Then he called me a name that he never used before: Vita.

"Hmm?" I asked.

"Vita."

My desire to feel his lips turned into a longing after I kissed him. Our lips barely stayed together before he moved his head back. His eyes stayed locked onto me, going from wanting me to confusion. I kissed him again, still without force to our kiss; our lips rested upon one another's. I moved my head back, and he came closer, gently running his bottom lip across mine. No longer restraining ourselves, we kissed with passion, desire, and lust. I held his face, and he firmly grabbed my thighs.

Time didn't exist in the moment.

He stopped kissing. I took a deep breath that smelt like sauce, moved my face closer to his so I could feel the warmth of his breath on my lips. I opened my eyes. He kept his eyes closed, and just when I thought the moment was over, he moved his tongue into my mouth. Like our hands, our tongues couldn't refrain from touching each other.

When we finally stopped kissing, we kept our lips inches apart.

"Vita?" I asked, breathing heavily.

"Vita."

"Where did you get that from?"

"There's a Playstation Vita on the dresser. I always thought the name was cute, so I said to myself, 'Hi self. Victoria is cute. The name is cute. Why not give the cute name to the cute girl?"

"You're such a weirdo."

"From what I heard, being a dork is a good thing."

I caressed his cheek. "It is."

"Oh, by the way, I meant to say 'beautiful.' You aren't cute. You're beautiful."

. . .

The sun glared down on the back of our necks, and our clothes, soaked in sweat, stuck to us. One cloud looked like it waded through the sky, and Hendrix swore that it looked like a mouth, but I didn't see it. In true Southern California fashion, the mid of November felt like a summer day.

We finished our fourth lap around the park, filled with screaming kids as they swung on the swings, hung from the monkey bars, went down the slide, or ran around aimlessly. It was the same park I took Daniel to let him burn off some energy, and he spent most of his time rolling around in the grass. On Saturdays, we took Martin.

Today was Saturday, and I wasn't with my boys.

Maybe Hendrix could read my mind, or maybe my face told just how distraught I was. Whatever the reason, he let go of my hand, put his arm around my waist, and pulled me closer.

"We got this," he said. "Even if it is us vs. the world. We got this."

He sounded so positive. It was always like he knew something I didn't. Like most times where he amused me, he smiled.

We walked down the street before we came to a McDonald's three blocks down. As we passed, I saw a We're Hiring sign in the window.

At that moment, I heard Hershey's words, and they cut just as deep the second time.

"Are you going to apply?" Hendrix asked.

"You think I should?"

"That depends. Do you mind smelling like French fries all day?"

"I need the money."

"There's your answer." He groaned, biting down on his lip. "I'm kinda in the mood for french fries now."

Hendrix

It was almost midnight when I made it home. For the past few days, I drove around the city after class, going nowhere in particular, in hopes of getting back home as late as possible. My dad wasn't sitting in his wicker chair on the porch, and there was no lingering smell of smoke. The air was still, and even at night, there was an essence of summer. A moth flew wildly across the porch, hitting and bouncing off the wall beside the light, which detected me as I came up the lawn. From the outside, it looked like every light inside the house was off. The sight of the palm tree arching over my house drained the little energy I had. Walking felt involuntary. I went inside and stopped, noticing my family at the kitchen table. They sat there, hunched forward, long-faced... worried.

"You didn't come home for dinner," Eve said. She got up and sat my backpack on the floor from over my shoulder.

"Sorry," I said, walking into the kitchen. "I didn't know you were cooking dinner."

"She didn't," Vanessa said. "I did, and we told you this morning."

"Now that I don't remember."

"You have been having quite the memory lapses lately."

"Not to mention, you haven't been looking well," Eve said.

"Well," I said, "I'm sorry to worry everybody, but I'm fine. Everybody can go to bed now."

"You know we don't believe that, right?"

"You don't have to believe me."

"I wish I could. You can take all that somewhere else, Hendrix. You don't look fine. You don't seem fine."

I rested my hand on Eve's cheek. We stared deep into one another's eyes, and she squinted in an attempt to read my mind. "I'm good. I promise." As she smiled in relief, I squeezed her nose and ran away before she could hit me. "You moved away and took our magic twin bond with you. You, of all people, shouldn't have to ask how I'm feeling."

"Our magic twin bond would be fine if you weren't a little jerk."

I opened the refrigerator, letting the cold air brush against my face, and pulled out containers of leftovers from that night's dinner.

The smell of food didn't overtake the house for hours, as it usually did. There wasn't even a smell coming from the containers, which I found odd.

Eve rushed over and moved me aside by hitting me with her hips to fix me a plate of Turkey wings, yellow rice, and yams. She used the fork to tear pieces of turkey from the bone.

"Come sit down, Hendrix," Vanessa said.

I sat beside dad. He stared down with his elbow on the table and his head in his hands.

Eve microwaved my meal and sat next to Vanessa on the other side of the table. Afterward, they stared at me as I used my fork to sort the turkey pieces from the rice.

My thoughts drowned out dad wheezing.

"You need to stop eating so fast," Eve said. "When acid reflux has you up all night, I'm not bringing you tums."

"I'll be fine."

"Of course, you'll be fine. You were fine yesterday. You're fine now. You'll be fine tomorrow. You do know we'll love and support you even if you aren't fine, right? If life slaps you across the face, Vanessa and I will slap it back because you're our brother, and we love you. Don't let pride leave you miserable, alone, and with your chest on fire."

"Okay."

They wanted a long, drawn-out response about how I felt so much, they kept watching me. Their stares went from concern to eagerness while they still waited for me to say something.

"What?" I asked.

"Do you like the food?" Eve asked. "It's like dad made it, right?"

"You're slowly morphing into dad in the kitchen."

"I'm slowly morphing into dad in the kitchen," Vanessa said.

"Vanessa made a bet with dad. She said you wouldn't be able to tell the difference," Eve said to me and looked to our dad.

"See, Dad, I told you. You better look out. You have some competition."

"I guess so," dad said, without looking up.

I looked at our dad. "What's wrong with you?"

"You know what's wrong with him," Vanessa said. "He's worried about Hendrix. What else?"

"We're all worried about Hendrix," Eve said.

"The difference is, dad can't afford to be this stressed out."

"He isn't a child," I said. I ate the last pieces of turkey from my plate and moved on to the rice.

"Want to know what's worse than being treated like a child? Being terminally ill."

"Can you not say that?" Eve asked, covering her ears. "No one is dying."

"Grow up. This is real life we're talking about, Eve. We can't sit around and act like none of this is happening."

"Why do you have to be so insensitive?"

"Why are you so sensitive?"

"Okay. Okay. I'm sensitive. Can we stop arguing now before we stress dad out more?"

"He's already stressed out because of your twin!"

"Vanessa," dad said, standing. The base in his voice startled Eve and made me look up from my plate. "Being unnecessarily extra won't get us anywhere, sweetheart."

"Can you stop protecting him? He isn't a baby."

"All of you are my babies."

Vanessa, shaking her head and sighing, stood and walked towards the back door. Halfway, she glared at me from over her shoulder.

"Can you just stop being difficult and tell us what's wrong with you?" She asked. "Nobody can help you if you don't tell us what's wrong. If it's because of dad, I get it. Eve and I aren't okay, either. We can get through this together."

"I'm not upset about dad," I said.

"Then what's wrong?" Eve asked. "I know when there's something wrong. I'm your twin, remember?"

"Eve-"

"You're fine, I know." Eve sighed. "Look me into my eyes and tell me you're fine."

I kept my eyes down.

"Hendrix, look me in my eyes."

"Alright," dad said. "Alright. I let this go on for too long. But we're done. Vanessa. Eve. Drop it. Now."

"I'm not dropping it," Vanessa said, "because you're going to keep working yourself up over Hendrix. He's acting like a goddamn baby. He needs to grow the fuck up and realize that there are more important things than his problems!"

"Okay, now I'm stressed and pissed off. If your brother says he's fine, drop it. Why are we pressing the issue?"

"And I'm stressed too. I have been working my ass off, cooking and cleaning because you can't, and Hendrix won't, but he has the nerve to be walking around like the world is against him!"

"Who says anything is wrong with him?"

"He looks like shit, dad! You know it. I know it. Eve knows it. For the last week, he hasn't been eating, he hasn't been sleeping, his memory has been shit, and he has barely said a word to anyone-you said so yourself. He comes home after school and sits in his room all night. Does that scream, okay?"

"And when I come into the room, he leaves," Eve said.

If I ate any more, I would have thrown up from fullness. I still had enough yams and rice for a meal. I looked around to catch their gaze.

The air turned on, and the vents made a popping sound. The breeze went through me, and I shivered. I kept grinding my fork into the plate, and occasionally, I looked up to see if they were still looking. They glared. Vanessa looked upset, while Eve looked concerned.

"Let's have a talk outside," dad said, pulling me out by the elbow.

We walked outside, and I sat in the iron chair, crossing my arms.

"Is it your mother?" He asked.

"It's everything."

"You gotta be more specific than that."

"Pick something. You, your health, the smoking, school, life, mom."

"What about her?"

"She isn't dead!"

"Hendrix, bring it down."

I shot up from the chair, throwing my arms in the air and screaming. All my thoughts and emotions came out together, and I struggled to speak.

"Calm down, son."

"Why did you tell me that? It's like you wanted to mess with my head."

"I wasn't trying to mess with your head, son." He reached out and grabbed my hand; I snatched away.

"Come on, dad."

"I'm sorry. I'm sorry."

"Some things you should take to your grave. I didn't need to know my mom was still alive."

"You're right. You're right. I shouldn't've forced you to carry my burden. I'll tell them."

"It's not even that, dad. Keeping the secret isn't what's killing me-it's the secret itself." I winced. "Dad, our mom-your wife- is still alive. She never died. Dad, we had a funeral and everything. I try to wrap my head around it, and I just can't. Mom left us. Why the hell didn't she give us a chance?"

"She didn't deserve you."

"But, I deserved a mother!"

When he pulled me into his arms, I couldn't hold the tears in any longer. "You did. All of you did."

"I can't lose you too, dad."

"You have me."

"But I won't."

"You'll always have me." He held me tighter. "You'll always have me." His voice cracked.

His week-old beard, black with patches of white, scraped my face. He let go and gently tapped my right arm with a fist. He slapped my left arm. Then my right arm again.

"Come on," he said, "give me a smile."

For whatever reason, I laughed. Then he joined along, but his wheezing stopped me immediately.

I pushed past him, purposely bumping shoulders, and walked towards my car. I patted myself down, searching for my keys. Since they were inside, I walked down the street. He followed. The spark wheel rotating and him inhaling and then exhaling sounded like a score in a horror movie.

"You're more like me than I'm willing to admit," he said. "A nice little walk always calms us down." He inhaled.

I turned around, snatched the cigarette from his mouth, and took a puff. Bringing in too much smoke, I choked. After a few seconds, I still coughed, which turned into gagging—gagging into vomiting. After throwing up the only meal I had eaten on our neighbor's lawn, I dry heaved. The ground seemed to move under my feet, and I leaned forward with my hands on my knees. Each breath burned and irritated my throat.

"That is hands down the worst thing I ever tasted," I said and then coughed.

"Smoking is a disgusting habit for disgusting people."

"How do you smoke those things?"

"I lost free will a long time ago. The first time was horrible. That didn't stop you, old man. Curiosity brought me right back onto the road of addiction."

"You make it look so relaxing."

"It is, once your lungs are a little black."

"I think I'll stick to my walks."

"Those are nice too. A man like myself needs to inhale and exhale." He pulled a cigarette from a carton in his pants pocket, lit up, and inhaled in love. Smoke trailed behind him.

"And all it does is kill you," I said to myself.

The smell churned my stomach and pulled more of my dinner into my throat. He was halfway down the street when I no longer had the urge to vomit and had the strength to stand upright. Under the streetlights, the smoke looked like clouds, radiating and captivating.

"Dad," I said.

He stopped to let me catch up. "Son."

"Tell me about her."

"You know what I know. I may have lied about your mother dying, but she's the woman I described through and through."

"I get that, but how was she with me? What was she like? Was she ticklish? Did she put sugar on her grits? Who the hell is she?"

He thought long and hard before he spoke. With his eyes closed, he took a drag and let the smoke drift from his slightly opened lips. The smoke, burning my throat and nose, made it harder to breathe.

He smiled. It wasn't long before that smile turned into a frown and then laughter. After, he grunted. He went to speak but laughed again just as he put the cigarette to his lips and inhaled. Smoke wildly burst from his mouth. When he found his words, he went on forever about her, finally having the chance to talk about the woman who left him all alone with three kids and a cigarette addiction.

He told me things I never knew about my mom. She was an esthetician who moved from New Hampshire to California on her 18th birthday with more hopes than dreams. Piss her off, and she would think about it every day for a week, not before cursing you out in the politest way possible. If it were up to her, she would have never listened to a Jimi Hendrix song. Like me, she was musically ambitious yet far from inclined; that never stopped her from singing original songs when working around the house. Dad couldn't remember any of them.

Dad went on about her obsession with ice cream when she was pregnant with Eve and me. On Eve and I's first birthday, mom let us try ice cream for the first time, and I spat up across her brand new dress. He wouldn't stop talking about ice cream. My mom only ate it in a cone; they went to an ice cream parlor on their first date; the day she left us, I ate ice cream without throwing up for the first time and had it every day until high school.

"Demons could have crawled from the depths of Hell, and everything was A-Okay as long as you had your ice cream," he said. "You had to have your ice cream. If you couldn't, oh boy, you cried crocodile tears. That's all you wanted. Breakfast, lunch, and dinner. Rainbow sherbet in a cone. It was like she was your ice cream. That's one habit I wouldn't mind having. Obesity and diabetes don't sound as bad as cancer."

"Yeah."

"I could've sworn you saw her leave."

"I would've remembered my mom leaving me."

"You could've blocked it from your memory for a good reason. You wouldn't stop asking for ice cream, especially the morning after. You woke up, begging me to get you some. So I did."

He rambled, but I listened to everything he said. According to him, whenever I cried, mom sat in the laundry room because the rumbling sounds of the washer and dryer calmed me down.

There were owls out. Sometimes they would sit on the windowsills, hooting.

The neighborhood was like a maze. Many of the streets were dead-ends or cul-de-sacs. When I was younger, back before technology ruined our sense of fun, Eve, Vanessa, and I, along with all the other kids in the neighborhood, would watch cars backtrack, looking for a particular address.

Dad, yawning, dragging his feet across the concrete, and slurring his words, went back home around 1:30 in the morning. Not long after, I followed behind him.

Eve sat in bed, with her back against the wall, munching popcorn from a bowl.

"We used to make so many forts in here," she said.

"Dad hated Fortlandia."

"Really?"

"Oh yeah. If you paid attention, you could tell how much he hated us using his good sheets. It was all in the cabinet slamming. If he slammed a cabinet, he was pissed. That and smoking."

"It's not easy raising three kids on your own. He had every right to be stressed."

"Yeah."

"Remember that time we refused to take down our fort? We had it up for like four days before dad took it down when we were at school."

The floor in the hall creaked from the weight of footsteps. I glanced over my shoulder at Vanessa walking down the hall, scratching her head.

"I smell popcorn," Vanessa said.

"Please spare me from all these calories," Eve said.

"What's the password?" I asked, looking at Vanessa from over my shoulder.

"The sweetest strawberries picked on Wednesdays," she said.

I let her in, and she sat beside Eve. She ate one popcorn at a time.

"I can't believe you remember the password to the fortress of Edrix," Eve said.

"Like you two made it easy to forget. I couldn't come in here without saying it. Trust me; it's permanently imprinted in my brain. It might just be the last thing I think about before I die. Thanks, by the way."

"Thank Hendrix. That was his genius at work."

Vanessa looked at me. "How did you come up with such a ridiculous password?"

"Does it matter 15 years later?"

"Has it been that long?"

"Eve and I were ten."

"Can we stop walking down memory lane? I'm starting to feel old."

"Scary, right? Our childhood is drifting further and further away, and the crazy thing is, we don't even notice."

"It seems like yesterday I was standing outside that door and saying that silly password for the first time."

"I remember making it up."

"So, are you going to share with the world how you came up with it?"

"I saw it on a show. Well, kind of. It was a documentary about a woman who lost her vision. The lady was talking about everything that she still does with her husband. One of them was picking strawberries every Wednesday morning. I assumed they would be sweet."

"The sweetest strawberries picked on Wednesdays," Eve said and smiled.

"The password is so ridiculous," Vanessa said.

"It's better than 'The pizza place on Parkway pleasantly pleases Peter," I said.

They, scrunching up their faces and looking off, tried to repeat the saying. They messed up and started over. Vanessa said it correctly first, but she spoke slowly. Her efforts to say it faster only ended with her getting tongue twisted.

"That's a stupid password," Eve said.

"The pizza place on Parkway pleasantly pleases Peter," I said.

"I'm glad you went with the other one."

"The pizza place on Parkway pleasantly pleases Peter."

"Okay, I get it. You can say the password, and I can't. No need to rub it in."

"Hey, Eve," Vanessa said. "The pizza place on Parkway pleasantly pleases Peter."

Eve threw popcorn at us; she missed me-not even coming close. I ate it from off the ground, and grinning, winked at her.

"Thanks," I said.

"Now that's the Hen-Hen I like to see," Eve said.

"Can you not call me that?"

"But that's your name."

"That's not my name."

"Aww, you don't like your name? Stop acting like this is brand new. It's been your name for years."

"And I hated every minute of it."

Vanessa threw popcorn at me.

"What's wrong, Hen-Hen?" She asked.

"How did we go from the pizza place on Parkway that pleasantly pleases Peter to this?"

Vanessa shrugged and then got up and went downstairs. She came back with three bottles of water, one tucked under her arms. I stopped her at the door. She rolled her eyes at my sheepish grin.

"What's the password?" Eve asked.

"The sweetest strawberries picked on Wednesdays," Vanessa said. She handed me a bottle of water. Then she sat back on the bed, giving one to Eve.

"It's nice that she can still enjoy life after everything that happened."

"Who?" Vanessa asked.

"The woman in the documentary."

"You aren't wrong. There's worse things than being blind."

"It's more than nice; it's beautiful."

I thought back to the look of satisfaction on the woman's face after saying she still picked strawberries on Wednesdays. Everyone with a heart who had watched the documentary probably smiled and called her strong.

In the alternative universe that featured our dad in the documentary, viewers, looking for a feel-good story, shook their heads at his selfishness and poor decision-making. He lived his best life at the cost of his health and family.

"I wish I could go back," Eve said. "It was so much easier back then."

"I'll be right here in the present day," Vanessa said.

"What? You wouldn't kill to be a kid again. Us three in the backseat of the truck on our way to Toys-R-Us."

"I'm not too big on living in the past."

"I don't want to live in the past. I just want to visit."

"Be careful not to get lost. You'll start asking 'what ifs' and 'maybes.' Those are never good."

"What if mom never died?"

"That's the shit I'm talking about--That right there. A what-if isn't going to dig mom from that grave."

"But, hear me out, what if she never died?"

"Stop being stupid." She spoke sternly.

Eve watched Vanessa eat popcorn. The owls hooting and Vanessa eating made the only sounds. When the owls weren't hooting, and Vanessa wasn't chewing, it was dead quiet. Eve moved the bowl as Vanessa, looking forward, reached inside.

"Why do you have to be so rude?" Eve asked.

"I'm not trying to be rude. I'm trying to save you from yourself. Stop worrying about something you can't change. Mom died. Why are we wondering about life if she didn't?"

"The point is to dream."

"Excuse me if I don't concern myself with something that has no bearing on life whatsoever."

They went back and forth about the purpose of dreaming. Eve thought dreaming was healthy for the soul, and Vanessa believed it was detrimental.

They are both right, I thought.

Since dad told me the truth about our mother, I saw her in my dreams every night, holding me so tight in her arms as she rubbed my head and kissed my cheeks like I was a child. Daydreams carried me through the day. The more she appeared in my dreams, speaking in a voice that was not her own, the more energy drained from my body. The dreams never stopped. I saw and heard her when I brushed my teeth, ate, showered. Everything. She clung to my life and made it her own.

I stood over them, took the bowl from Eve, and handed it to Vanessa.

"Life is all about balance," I said. "You can't do that, and you'll fall. Dreaming is equally as important as air or water. It's essential to our sanity. Life has its ways of knocking you to the ground and punching you while you're trying to get up. Sometimes dreaming helps the dirt taste like cake."

"If that doesn't sound like something dad would say," Vanessa said.

"He probably got it from dad," Eve said and laughed. "There is no way he made that up himself."

"Aww," I said. "You two are just jealous."

"Jealous of what? You? Please."

"That's right, jealous. You can't stand seeing me flaming you with the quotables. It's eating you up inside."

"Whatever. Did you make that up?"

"I did. Right on the spot."

"Oh, God. You're becoming Dad."

"Is that a bad thing?"

"No, it's not, Hen-Hen."

Vanessa left again, hurrying down the stairs, and came back with three cups and a bottle of cinnamon whiskey. She uttered both passwords, pushing me to the side. They drank cup after cup like water. I couldn't bring myself to drink, too afraid of losing myself in the process.

They kept asking and nudging the bottle closer. That never changed my answer. It wasn't long until they could barely hold their glazed-over eyes open as they swayed from side to side. Eve fell across Vanessa's lap. Vanessa nearly fell forward off the bed several times. Luckily, she caught herself.

Eve ate popcorn as Vanessa drummed on her head. They slurred their words, and I couldn't understand what they were trying to say, but it had to be a joke because they laughed. Their laughter turned into silence as they dozed off mid-conversation.

Vanessa was still sitting up.

I sat the bowl of popcorn on the nightstand and laid them down in bed. Afterward, I lay on the inflatable bed and tried my best to fall asleep. Eventually, I did.

The dreams about my mom woke me up.

. . .

When I ventured downstairs for a late-night snack, I stifled my fear at the sight of Vanessa standing in front of the refrigerator in pitch black. Her demeanor, calm and unbothered, settled on the same certainty she had the night before she moved away for college. Before I could acknowledge her with a *hey* or a smile, she slid over a pint of chocolate chip ice cream as she asked about graduation and if I planned to attend grad school or find a job. The day before, the Harper residence experienced the typical ups and downs of a dysfunctional family, where we took it as a personal challenge to bicker and fight. Thinking back on it all kept my mind in a fog, and before I knew it, I asked, "so, are you going back home?"

"Damn. Tell me how you really feel."

"Not like that. You asked about my career plans, and then I thought about yours. This is coming from a place of concern, really. Vanessa, you've been here for a minute. Do you still have a job?"

"I graduated high school with an associate's degree, finished undergrad with a 4.0 GPA, completed both my grad and Ph.D. programs before thirty, and rarely, if ever, took a day off work. I think I put in the work to afford bereavement." She gingerly brushed the countertops with her fingertips, and in the low visibility, she resembled our mom with her downside turned lips and square-shaped face. "Besides, what do I look like leaving my dad and my annoying little twins?"

"Yeah."

Plagued by guilt and a fear of never living up to Vanessa, I hobbled to the kitchen table and gorged on ice cream fast enough to cause a brain freeze.

Vanessa tapped my shoulder with a firm slap, which turned into a massage when I glanced up with the fakest of smiles.

"I know I act like I'm mom sometimes-"

"You aren't mom. You're far from it."

Her eyes glazed over to fond and untainted memories of my mother that I would never have. With her voice jumping in volume and adoration every second, Vanessa shared untold stories about our mother, and right there, when she had so much love for the mom who eventually abandoned us, I understood why dad chose to lie over the years.

If only dad let me live in that lie.

Victoria

The Manager at McDonald's had called back that Monday morning. Tuesday afternoon, I sat across from her, our knees touching in the tucked-away office for an interview. She hired me on Thursday.

For the last three days, I worked the register.

There weren't any lines, just a mass of people standing around, blocking the doors, restrooms, soda fountains, and unoccupied tables.

Customers, waiting to order, somehow knew who was next up. Those who already ordered looked up from their receipts every time Samantha brought bags to the counter and back down when they didn't hear their number. No matter how many customers we served, the lines grew. That was the lunch rush.

Everyone who wasn't on the registers hurried back and forth across the kitchen, preparing orders. Sunder, Tyson, and I were just as stressed. The manager occasionally walked by, demanding we take orders faster.

How?

After the lunch and dinner rush, we stayed consistent. During slow periods, I cleaned tables and picked up trash to keep busy.

Towards the end of my shift, the guy that always came to class late and left early walked in with who I assumed was his little sister.

"Oh, hey," he said, looking at my nametag, "Victoria. You're in my class, right?"

After awkward small talk, he ordered a number one-large-and a happy meal. He decided to wait for his food by the soda fountain. The entire time, he talked on his phone. When Samantha called his number, his sister nearly knocked the tray off the counter as she reached for her happy meal box.

"Hey," he said, taking the box, "Chill."

"I want my toy," his sister said.

"You'll get it after you eat. Cool?"

She crossed her arms and stuck out her lips. "Cool."

"Cool."

He nodded to me. "See you in class, Victoria."

They sat at a table along the wall, beside the main entrance. The girl could have bested Hendrix in an eating contest.

I was pleasantly surprised when Hendrix walked inside with his head down and feet barely lifting off the ground.

We hadn't spent much time together since the interview. Work and school took up most of my time throughout the day. It all worked out perfectly since Hendrix hadn't been feeling well the last week. And he looked it.

He had heavy bags under his eyes, and he reeked of smoke. If he told me he hadn't slept in three days, I would've believed him. My manager, Barry, was cashing out Tyson at the register next to me, so I couldn't ask Hendrix anything except, "Welcome to McDonald's. May I take your order?"

He ordered a large M&M Mcflurry and a small drink. I got his order, and he sat in the booth in the back corner.

"I'm going to clean up a little," I said to Barry.

"Make those floors shine," Barry said.

Hendrix

The lights from the parking lot shined through the windows covered in handprint smudges. I massaged my forehead with my fingers in an attempt to calm my pounding headache. Staring directly into the lights made the pain worse. I ate my McFlurry, and after each bite, I held the spoon in my mouth, imagining it like a cigarette, holding it with two fingers, inhaling, exhaling, occasionally, taking it from my mouth.

But I wasn't smoking, and I held the ice cream in my mouth to savor the taste. The coldness on my teeth made me shiver. I heard two individuals conversing, and footsteps moved toward my table. In the reflection of the mirror, I saw Vita holding a bucket.

"You have that look in your eye," Victoria said. "What's wrong?"

"Tired... that's all."

"It's 3 in the morning. You can always go to sleep."

"I'm not sleepy. I'm just tired."

"I get off in an hour. Hang tight, and we can talk then."

She wiped down the tables and chairs as I watched anytime her back was to me.

I went to fill my cup. My shoes stuck to the floor as I walked. The lemonade looked and tasted like water, so I settled for unsweetened iced tea. I ordered another McFlurry from Vita. Since her manager wasn't around, she refused to charge me for the McFlurry.

Back in my booth, I dreaded the thought of having to wake up for work in a few hours. I wondered how many times I could call out before my boss called my bluff or believed I was actually dying. Closing my eyes, I tried to keep myself from thinking.

Vita returned to the table, holding a bag under her arm and another McFlurry, and slid beside me. The sadness that clenched my heart loosened enough for the pain to ease. We kissed; her lips tasted like lip balm. She smelt like French fries.

"Ask me what's in the bag," she said. Not letting me answer, she slid the bag to me, smiling, and watched as I unfolded it and reached inside. There were two toys-one for a boy and the other for a girl. I ripped the plastic with my teeth. The boy toy was a pterodactyl, and the girl toy was a unicorn.

I smiled.

"That's the reaction I was looking for," she said.

"I needed that."

"I could tell." She nudged me. "I was thinking; maybe we could name them Skyler and Majestic."

"Skyler and Majestic, the two BFFs that live with Stomps and Starlight. They were all friends in college. Since they got along so well, they decided to rent a place. Their house has everything you could want: central air conditioning, prime real estate, a pool, a garden. Sounds like the life."

"How do you come up with this stuff?"

I shrugged with the spoon in my mouth. "Survival."

Lost for words, she churned the spoon through her ice cream. "Let's see what's so good about these things."

"You never had a McFlurry?"

"I make it a point not to eat fast food. I hadn't been to a McDonald's for years before you took me."

"Now, the clown owns your soul. He owns all of us, him and The Mouse."

"All for minimum wage and free food that I don't eat. One of the managers calls me weird every time he sees me with my lunch bag."

"Don't forget smelling like grease."

"Oh, thanks." She scooted to the edge of the seat, and I lay my head on her shoulder. Her hair, dragging across my face, tickled. "Don't touch me. I thought I smelt like grease."

"You do, but unlike you, I don't mind fast food. You're my little chicken nugget. I'll be whatever dipping sauce you like."

She turned her head and looked at me, furrowing her eyebrows. Right as I smiled, she pushed me by the forehead and swung her legs from the booth to leave. She sat with her back to me, but her head turned enough so I could see her face. I embraced her from behind before she could stand.

"You don't want to be my little chicken nugget?" I asked in a weird voice, trying to get her to laugh, and seeing her suck in her lips to fight back a smile, I knew she was going to break. I kissed her neck. "I'll dip you in buffalo sauce any day of the week, girl. I'll chew on you for as long as I can to savor the flavor. I'll serve you up on the finest of China and wash you down with the finest of wines because you fancy, girl."

She burst into laughter, going from loud and frequent to quiet and sporadic, and back after, she made a noise that sounded like a car starting. She turned her head, so our cheeks touched, and wiggled to get her body closer to mine.

"I'm your chicken nugget Vita," she said.

"Yes, you are."

"I rather you not think of me as greasy and looking like this."

"I don't see anything wrong with how you look."

"I look and feel disgusting."

"You're beautiful as always, and you feel just right."

"Sweet. I give you points for the effort, but compliments aren't going to change my mind."

"I'm not trying to change your mind. I just want you to know how I feel."

"Do you want me to know your every thought or only the ones about me?"

"I want you to know every little thought I have."

"That's a little sudden, isn't it?"

"Possibly, I guess. What's romance if you aren't willing to die?"

"That's sweet in a morbid way."

"Or it could be the dumbest thing I have ever said in my life."

"What makes you say that?"

"Like you said, it's a little too soon to be talking like this."

"Then why did you say anything?"

"Because holding you right now feels so surreal. It's like a dream."

"You're such a dork."

"I am." I shrugged. "Sometimes, I can't help it."

"I like being in your arms."

I only heard some of what she said.

In my mind, she was no longer in my arms. Oh no. I sat inside our fort, watching her crawl towards me with a look of confusion. The light from the ceiling fan shining through the sheets created a green hue around us. I saw us kissing on the front lawn as Hershey carried on like a fool. I saw us spending all day in the house, her laying on my bare chest, occasionally kissing it as I wrapped my fingers around her hair. I saw us dancing, going out for dinner, and vacationing on beaches. I saw our lives together as we grew as a couple and people.

For however long it all lasts, I thought. I could wake up tomorrow, and this could be a memory of what could have been. Being with Victoria feels like a dream, but we know that at some point, dreams can turn into nightmares, and eventually, they end. You're so stupid. You're walking straight into heartbreak because this probably won't last. Realistically, it won't last. You two come from different worlds. She's a mother. You, you're an of-age child hoping to figure the world out. Not that I want it to end, though. I'm being honest with myself. I know how relationships like this work. One day, the excitement will wane, and we'll be left with ourselves, our true selves. The good, the bad, and the ugly. That's when it will all come crashing down.

Hendrix, I said to myself, you know this is a dream, but then, maybe you aren't silly. If this dream turns into a nightmare, don't beat yourself up for enjoying it. Not everyone can say they lived a dream.

I refused to let her go or loosen my embrace.

"You're lost in your thoughts again," she said. "Want to tell me what's on your mind?"

"This girl I know."

"Is that right? Good thoughts, I hope."

"The best."

Chapter 5
Victoria

The sun barely cleared the houses in the distance, leaving the sky an orange hue. The clouds, well above the sun, resembled smoke.

I stared into the sky from atop my mother-in-law's car, my feet swinging in and out of the open passenger window. The vibrations from the running engine traveled through my body. Under the lights atop long steel poles in the parking lot, the exposed skin on the back of his arms, his opening and closing hands, neck, and throat, glistened and popped. Leaning against the car, in-between my legs, he tilted his head back, and I leaned forward to give him a peck on the lips. He nuzzled the side of his face into my thigh. There was a tingling pulsation in the exact spot his lips brushed against, not taking long to spread throughout the rest of my body. It left me flushed, warm, and trembling. I gently closed my thighs around his head. I wanted him there for the foreseeable future.

Pushing himself off the car, he turned to me and took my hands.

"Vita," he said. "My Vita. We should probably get home."

"Together." Gazing deeply at him for a flirtatious staring contest, I undressed him with my eyes. "We should get some sleep."

With our hands still together, I caressed his cheek with the back of my hand, and letting go, he interlocked our fingers. He kissed my hand and smirked as a wave drifted through me.

"I want to stay here with you," he said.

"That would be perfect."

"But I guess we have to go back to the real world at some point."

I slid off the car. He lifted me off the ground by the waist to kiss me. When my feet touched the ground, my legs, trembling and yearning for his touch, buckled, and I swore I was still in the air. They stayed weightless and weak on the drive home.

My mind spun at the same wild speed as my heart while the entire world moved at a slow.

. . .

The sun was in the sky when I pulled into the driveway. The clouds were white, and the orange tint was gone.

My mother-in-law hurried outside, pulling a bag half her size. It all came back to me then.

"You're late," she said.

"I know, I know. Sorry. I must have lost track of time."

"A part of me thought you were lying in a ditch somewhere."

"Sorry."

"Then, I figured the boy was probably lying in you." She sat her bag at my feet and looked at me from head to toe. "Girl, you look like you need to be touched." She cackled and slapped me on the butt. "Go ahead and put my bag in the trunk."

She hurried back inside. I threw her bag into the trunk and met her back inside, catching a whiff of her perfume as she rushed past, into the bathroom. She rummaged through the drawers and cabinets.

"What time does your flight leave again?" I asked.

"Noon."

I checked the time on my phone. 7:17 am. "Why so in a rush?"

"You say that until it's 11:40, and you're rushing through the terminal to make your flight."

She came from the bathroom and stopped in the hall, holding a toiletry bag in one hand and a surgical mask by the string in the other. "How was work?"

"Not too busy. The day came and went before I knew it."

"Did the boy?"

"Whoa. You really asked me that."

"I'm proud of you, girl. You jumped back on that horse and rode it like a pro."

Her sexual implications aside, she was right. I hopped back into the dating game relatively quicker than I originally thought.

Hendrix taught me. The way he looked at me and spoke with such certainty made it easy to share his optimism. Whenever I began to lose hope, he said or did whatever it took to make me smile and restore my belief. It felt impossible to feel alone or defeated with him around. It was always "us" and "we" when discussing my problems. When we weren't together, he always seemed to send a message or call when I was at my lowest.

My phone, in my pocket, vibrated. Of course, it was a text from Hendrix, reading:

I can't stop thinking about you, Vita, and I never want to not think about you.

He sent another about seeing a girl wearing a Mario shirt made him want to beat Martin in Smash Bros.

My mother-in-law walked past me to the kitchen.

"Let me guess," she said, "the boy."

"Yeah." I followed her into the kitchen, looking down at the messages. "He's weird."

She poured herself a cup of coffee and slowly settled into a seat at the table. "Good weird or bad weird?"

"Both."

"I doubt he's both, honey. What'd he do?"

"He just sent a message saying that he can't stop thinking about me."

"That's not weird."

"I get it, we're in the honeymoon phase, but he can't stop thinking about me? I find that hard to believe."

"Back in my day, we called that cute."

"It is cute," I grunted. "He has this way of making me feel like the most important person in the world. The way he looks at me, talks to me, touches me, he takes my breath away and gives me life at the same time. I don't get it. Why am I so special to him?"

"So he thinks about you a lot and makes you feel like a natural woman. I'm assuming that's the good weird. What's the bad weird?"

"Right after telling me the sweetest thing ever, he sends me another one saying he can't wait to beat Martin at Smash Bros."

"Ooh."

"Right?"

"That is a bad weird. A grown man shouldn't be talking about beating a kid in any way."

"Martin and I ran into him at the store a few weeks back. They hit it off over some video game. That's cool. I'm just confused as to why he's thinking about my son?"

"He gets along with kids. I take back my bad weird. That's a good weird. A really good weird."

I growled.

"It could be bad if you want."

"He always sends me messages like this. A few days ago, he sent me a picture of a park, saying it would be a great place for me to take the boys."

"He understands the importance of mother-son relationships. That's not bad weird. That's not even good weird. That's excellent."

"What happened to the good old messages where he says 'hi' or asks about my day? It's like he knows everything is going to work out and he reminds me every chance he gets."

"At the most, that's not even good weird. It's like he's Oprah."

"Oh my God, I'm dating a black male Oprah. Now you have to consider that as weird."

She shrugged. "It's still a good weird."

"Why is he so weird?"

"That no-good son of mine has completely warped your perception of good and bad. Now, this boy could turn out to be bad weird, but just because he believes in you more than you believe in yourself or that he understands it's not just your heart he needs to win over doesn't mean you should be worried."

"Hershey." I lowered my head, watching the walls grow taller and the floor extended. "Have you heard from him?"

"I have."

"Did he say anything about me?"

"Honey, live your life."

I looked around to take in the room that was ten times the size as it was before. Everything had a place and purpose. The refrigerator, table, sink, the spider in the corner of the windowsill outside. Everything but me. My mother-in-law paid the bills and cooked most of the time. The day she sided with Hershey, I would be on the streets.

"Why are you doing all this for me?"

"We aren't going through this again. Not now." She held my hand. "I don't do charity cases."

She walked into her room and returned with two bags; they were much smaller than before. We put the bags in the truck and headed out.

I offered to drive. It took an hour to arrive at the airport with all the stop-and-go traffic.

A crowd hurried past each other in the crosswalks, weighed down by bags. Some pulled or pushed their luggage by the handles; others hauled theirs over the shoulder.

I pulled to the curb at her terminal. Police directed traffic and shouted at any car if parked too long. She opened the door, and the sound of car engines, the voices of people greeting or saying goodbye to their loved ones, shoes against concrete, horns, and plane engines came in at once.

"I'll call you if anything changes," she said.

"See you Wednesday."

. . .

In the front yard, Martin and Daniel ran laps around Hershey. I noticed them well before they saw me, and when they did, my boys raced towards the car as I pulled into the driveway. They both looked like they had grown.

An emptiness I grew accustomed to filled with uncontrollable joy each time they called out for me. "Mommy." I heard them clearly over the engine and music playing softly. It felt like years since I last listened to their voices or held them in my arms.

I hopped out of the car to meet my boys and squatted for both to fall into my arms. The force of their bodies slamming into mine almost knocked me over.

They wouldn't let go, and neither did I. I squeezed them as tight as I could, and they didn't squirm or resist like they normally would.

A feeling of fullness overtook me. Nothing else in the world seemed necessary, not food, water, or money.

As long as they kept saying "mommy," I had no control over my emotions. It felt like I was in the hospital again when the doctor placed them into my arms. They stepped back, and I admired their faces; all of us smiled. I was the only one sobbing uncontrollably.

I never thought I would ever see them again, I thought.

Martin ate sliced apples from a zip-lock bag. I pulled him back into my arms and then did the same to Daniel. Looking into their eyes, I remembered my purpose.

Hershey stood at the top of the driveway, looking on with a smile. His hands were in the pockets of his gray sweats. I stared at him, smiling, and looked at Daniel when he said, "Where have you been, mommy?"

I didn't know what to say, so I didn't answer.

"Mommy has been with grandma," Hershey said, walking toward us.

"And you didn't come home?"

"Try not to hold it against her too much. Grandma needed help around the house."

"We needed you, too," Martin said. "Dad was always late picking me up for school. I had to start packing an after-school snack."

"That's all you needed me for, huh?" I asked and smiled. "Since I'm not appreciated, I might just stay with grandma."

"No!"

"You gotta come home, mommy," Daniel said.

"Why did you leave without saying anything?"

Hershey grabbed the top of Daniel's head. Daniel, making weird noises, punched at Hershey's arms.

"Mommy wasn't home because daddy was mean," Hershey said, kneeling in front of Daniel.

"Why were you being mean to mommy?" Martin asked.

"When you grow up and find the woman you love, never take her for granted. You hear me, son? Never for a moment think she isn't worth the fight."

Martin nodded.

"I wasn't nice at all." He motioned for Martin, and then he held their hands. "I want you both to remember something. Never be mean to the people you love. Cherish them. Love them. Do everything that you can to make them happy. Okay?"

"Okay," they said.

"Good." He held and caressed my hand. "I'm sorry, Victoria."

"That's not Victoria, daddy," Daniel said. "That's mommy." He cackled as he waved his hands in the air.

"That's not her name," Martin said. "She's our mom, but her name is Victoria."

"Victoria!"

"Alright," Hershey said. "Calm down, Daniel, before you hurt yourself." He looked at me. "Can we talk?"

"If you're looking for your mother, she went to Jackie's. She won't be back until Wednesday."

"Luckily, I didn't come to see her." He twirled his finger around my hair.

"You made it clear that you didn't want to see me."

He looked at the boys, who stared back, and turned to me. "Can we talk inside?"

I scooped up Martin with one arm and spun until I lost my balance, stumbling around, nearly falling over. His laughter was contagious.

"You still haven't lost that tooth?" I asked.

"It's getting looser," he said, wiggling it.

"Oh, that's going to come out soon. Are your hands clean?"

"Kinda."

"What do you mean, 'kinda?'" I tickled him. "If your hands are kinda dirty, then keep them out of your mouth."

I sat him down. I put my hands under Daniel's arms and picked him up, spinning as he cackled and screamed.

"Come on, boys," I said.

We went inside. Hershey followed us like a sad puppet.

"Mommy and Daddy need to talk in the kitchen," Hershey said.

"Are you going to be mean again?" Daniel asked.

"To your mother? Never. I vow to be nice from this moment forward."

"Okay. I believe you, daddy. Don't be mean."

"Martin, take your brother to the room, would you?"

"Come on, Daniel," Martin said, leading Daniel down the hall to their room.

Hershey and I went into the kitchen. He sat down at the table, and I stood in the door, leaning against the wall, with my arms crossed.

"You don't have to stand there," he said.

"I know."

"You don't want to sit down? Get off your feet for a second?"

"I've been sitting all morning." I sighed. "What do you want, Hershey? Believe it or not, I have things to do other than wait at your beck and call."

"I want the chance to have an open conversation with my wife."

"Well, you might want to look somewhere else because you don't have a wife here."

"Okay."

"Okay? That's all you have to say?"

"What do you want from me, Victoria? Do you want me to do backflips, huh? Because if that's what you want, I'll do it. Frontflip. Backflip. I'll do it all if it means you give us a chance again."

"Okay."

He forced a laugh through gritted teeth. "This is awkward." He admired me from head to toe. "I'm digging the uniform."

"Thanks."

"How's work?"

I rolled my eyes. "It's work."

He laughed. "Victoria, a working woman. I can't believe it."

"Well, try not to hurt yourself thinking about it too hard. Just trying to make something out of myself. You know, I think about you every day at work."

"I do love my Big Macs."

"It's weird because I can't stop thinking about you."

"I don't think that's weird at all. I can't stop thinking about you either." He walked to me and held my hand; it was soft and limp.

"I pull my manager aside every day and ask, 'How did someone who has no skills get hired?' And every day, he answers, 'don't flatter yourself. We can teach an idiot to cook french fries."

He extended his hand. "Come here, Victoria."

Against my better judgment, I listened, standing over him as he caressed my arm with the knuckle of his curled index finger. "Yes?"

"Victoria, I was angry."

"Oh, why didn't you say that before? I wouldn't have taken it so personally."

"Victoria, I'm sorry. I was beside myself, and I was just saying anything to hurt you. You hurt me." He paused and grimaced in pain. "I hurt you…a lot. I wanted to come over to apologize--to say I'm sorry for everything I said and did to hurt you. You deserved better. If you ever get tired of living with my mom, you know you're always welcome home with the boys and me. You were right. A mother deserves to be with her children."

"Thank you, Hershey."

"You're welcome."

He let go of my hand and smiled, reaching to put his hand on my cheek, and I moved away, furrowing my brow.

"That was sarcasm," I said.

"Right."

"Do you work today?"

"At noon."

"I want them to stay."

"Until when?"

"Sunday. I want them for the weekend."

"Done."

"Good."

"You can come home anytime."

"We'll stop by later to pick up some things. I don't know if you'll be home."

"It depends on what time you're coming by."

"Noon."

He nodded, looking off to the right. "I'll leave the door unlocked. You know the code for the alarm."

Hershey went into the boy's room and said his goodbyes. Martin and Daniel walked with him to the door. I watched from the archway as they hugged. Hershey turned to me and waved. When I didn't wave back, he forced a toothless smile and left.

...

Martin wiggled his tooth.

From a toy box, stuffed to the brim and barely able to close, I pulled out a nerf gun buried deep into the toy chest and aimed at Martin.

"Hands off the tooth, Martin," I said.

Martin raised his hands over his head, his eyes wide open and dotting from left to right. He knew what he did.

"Calm down, partner," he said. "I don't want any trouble."

"Then, you can't be wiggling that tooth, my friend. Not around these parts." I approached him. "Now, I'm going to lower my weapon on the count of three. Then you're going to go in that bathroom, wash your hands, and then and only then can you wiggle that tooth. You get me?"

"Got it."

"One, two, three."

Martin slowly lowered his hands. Daniel, his hands extended in front of him and fingers wiggling, ran towards Martin, screaming. They wrestled to the ground with Martin, quickly getting the best of Daniel. He straddled Daniel and pinned him to the ground by the wrists. Daniel, who still screamed and laughed, squirmed and kicked. Not long after, his laughs turned to cries.

"Get off, Martin," Daniel said.

"Why are you crying?" Martin asked. "You started it. Stop being a baby."

"I'm crying because you are ugly!"

"Hey," I shouted. "Daniel, no name-calling. Do you hear me?"

"Get off, ugly."

"Daniel, what did I just say? And Martin, get off your brother."

"I'm going to let you go," Martin said. "Don't hit me, Daniel."

As soon as Martin let go, Daniel balled his hands into fists, reached back, and hit Martin across the face. Daniel cackled like a demon baby.

"Ugly!" He screamed.

"Daniel," I shouted. "Get your little self over here right now!"

He broke out in tears and slowly made his way over to me, holding his head down and hands behind his back.

"Why are you crying? You weren't the one who got hit in the face."

"But mommy," he said. "Martin wouldn't get off me."

"Daniel, mommy is talking right now. When mommy talks, you listen. Now, first, apologize to your brother."

"Sorry, Martin."

"No, tell him to his face."

Daniel, flailing his arms, ran to and flung his arms around Martin for a hug. "I'm sorry, Martin."

"It's okay," Martin said, tickling Daniel.

Screaming and laughing, Daniel ran back to me.

"Now, give me a hug," I said. I opened my arms for him to ram his head into my chest. "When you get upset, I want to see you do something other than hitting and using names. Something nicer, you hear me?"

"Mmmkay."

We broke from our embrace. "Remember what Daddy said? You shouldn't be mean to the people you love. You have to cherish and love them, remember? You have to do everything you can to make them happy. Hitting Martin and calling him ugly isn't making him happy."

"Okay, I'll be good."

He climbed over the back of the couch and fell into the cushion. With his legs on the sofa, he put one hand on the floor to hold himself up, and he reached for the remote on the coffee table. He lacked the length. He slid off the couch, grabbed the remote, and climbed back up. Lying on his stomach, he turned on the television and flipped through the channels.

Martin stood in front of me.

"He'll be preoccupied for a while," I said. "Are you okay?"

"He wishes he could hurt me."

"I love you, honey."

"Love you too. I missed you."

"I missed you too, honey."

"Are you and dad still fighting?"

His question hit me hard- a shot to the kidneys. The answer to that question was a lot easier to say in my mind. I fell out of love with their father years ago, and now, I'm dating someone better.

I told myself to stop thinking about Hershey. I was with my boys now.

It had felt like an eternity since I last saw their faces, heard their voices, and had their arms wrapped around me. Time had moved at a soul arching crawl whenever I thought about them. I had a purpose again. If I had to, I would have gladly given up anything in this world, including Hendrix, to be with them forever and see them happy and in good health.

Working had thrown off my sense of time. Often, I forget what day it was. Last week, I went to class on Wednesday, and as Hershey's mother stopped to let me out, I remembered I didn't have class. We had a nice laugh about that. Today was Friday, but I thought it was Saturday. The note Hershey's mother left for me on the kitchen counter about leaving early to get to the airport reminded me it was Friday.

Martin should have been in school. I never let him stay home unless he was sick, and even then, he had to be fighting death itself. I assumed it would build perseverance, and when he got a job after graduating from college, he would work hard without complaining, no matter what. He would be a valuable asset that every company wanted so that he would have his pick at any job, and wherever my boy went, he would work his way up to high-paying positions. He would be the one who would advise kids to stay in school and get good grades so they could be like him. He would make a difference in the world since I couldn't.

He isn't sick, I told myself. He doesn't look sick. He doesn't sound sick. He wasn't sick. Why is Hershey letting him stay home? Does it matter?

He still waited for me to answer. Now, he looked concerned. I kneeled, put my hand on his cheek, and moved my thumb from side to side to feel his smooth skin.

"Don't worry, honey," I said. "Everything's going to be okay."

Was it, I asked myself. I couldn't imagine myself being with Hershey again, cleaning the sheets that reeked of sex and clothes that smelt like another woman. I refused to see myself turning a blind eye to all of the cheating. Hershey had broken his promise. In the literal sense, we were always going to be one- a mother, father, and children. But, that little girl he met years ago grew up.

You're thinking of Hershey again, I told myself. Stop. You have someone better. You know better.

. . .

No one was home.

The alarm beeped as we entered. With Daniel asleep in my arms, I struggled to enter the security code into the control panel.

When I punched in the code, the control panel beeped twice, and a robotic voice indicated the alarm was turned off. I kicked the front door shut.

"Go pack your bag, honey," I said to Martin.

"I thought you and dad weren't fighting anymore."

"We aren't, baby."

"Then why do we have to go back to Grandma's house? Why can't we stay here?"

"Honey, I know all this is confusing, but everything will make sense soon, I promise."

"I want you to come home." His eyes watered with tears. "Why don't you want to come back?"

"There's nothing in this world that I want more than to come back home."

"Then why don't you?"

I sighed. "I can't right now!"

"Yes, you can! Dad said you were coming back today!"

"And I was, but grandma needs me to watch her house while she is visiting."

"So, you're going to come back?"

"Of course. Once Grandma comes back from her trip. You'll stay with me at Grandma's until Sunday. Then, all you have to do is wait three days, and I'll be back home."

His face lit up. "Really?"

"Mommy wouldn't lie to you, honey."

Why did you tell him that? Victoria, fix this right now before he gets out of control. Just tell him the truth. It's only going to hurt him more when you don't come back next week.

My phone rang, and I dug through my purse to find it. One of my managers called. I had the weekend off, and I knew why they called. Someone called off, so they needed me to cover the shift. I let the voicemail pick up, and my phone rang again. They called again.

. . .

Hendrix came to mind first. He was the only person I could call.

I called him when the boys and I got back to my mother-in-law's house. The boys ran to their room, sounding like a stampede. I walked into the kitchen and dropped into a seat at the table. My fingers rhythmically tapped against the table.

"Come on, Hendrix," I said. "Pick up the phone. Pick up."

Just as I thought his voicemail was going to answer, he picked up. "Vita." I barely understood him through the mumbles.

"Are you sleeping?

"I'm up now. What's up?"

"I need a huge favor. It's going to be weird and borderline inappropriate, but my mother-in-law is out of town, and you're the only other person I can call. Don't feel obligated to agree. If you don't want to, I completely understand because it's something that I would never expect you to do, at least not right now-"

"-Vita."

"Yes?"

"We got this."

My stomach fluttered. I sighed. "If you say so."

"What has you all worked up?"

"I need you to watch Daniel and Martin." I cringed. "You're the only person I can trust. Please don't feel like you have to agree. I know this is crazy, but-"

"Are they with you right now?"

"Yeah."

He took a long pause. "Say no more, Vita. Name the time and place, and I'm there."

...

I heard them as I walked up the porch. A beating of a drum and Hendrix singing a song I never heard in my life. Daniel tried to sing along, doing more screaming than harmonizing.

It was midnight. Martin and Daniel should have been in bed five hours ago. Before leaving for work, I gave them specific instructions: Listen, don't talk back, and be in bed by 8 pm. I didn't think Hendrix needed the same talk.

When I walked inside, I fought back a smile, seeing them march across the living room, with buckets, from a fast-food restaurant, on their heads. Daniel had the largest bucket, and he held it with both hands to keep it from falling over his face. Martin drummed on a plastic bucket, and Hendrix pretended to play a toy guitar with buttons instead of strings, with the passion of a rock star. They all wore black shirts. Martin and Daniel marched behind Hendrix and tried to mimic his Michael Jackson-inspired dance moves. Martin danced slowly--always one move behind--and Daniel looked like he made up his own.

A wave of tiredness hit me as I took in the toy chest lying on its side, and every toy Daniel owed scattered across the floor, and for a moment, I saw myself cleaning the entire house for hours before I could get to bed. The music playing from the paused video game pulled me back into reality. Nintendo controllers lay on the back of the couch. Plates of unfinished meals and way too many cups for three people took up the coffee table.

I crossed my arms, and I thought I had a stern look on my face, but when they saw me, they kept singing and dancing around me. Each time Hendrix moved past me, he put his face near mine for some reason. It wasn't for a kiss.

On maybe the tenth time Martin completed his circle, he flashed a toothless smile.

"You lost your tooth," I said.

"Yup. And it's already under my pillow, ready for the Tooth Fairy."

"She'll never come if you don't go to bed."

His eyes lit up. "You're right."

"That's why you should go to bed."

He stopped dancing.

"You too, Daniel," I said.

"Come on. Let's get some sleep," Martin said, pulling Daniel to their room.

Hendrix knew I was upset, or maybe he didn't. No, he did. His smile told me that much.

I stepped closer for a kiss, stopped, and scowled at the mess he and the boys made. Damn. His lips called my name.

I had convinced myself I was happy for years out of convenience. Sadly, I realized how empty I felt until I met Hendrix. He and I weren't in love, but he did something to me that I couldn't explain. I wouldn't dare try because words couldn't capture his spirit. If there were, I wouldn't have known how to convey them.

From the moment we kissed in the fort, I wondered if the boys would like him. After all, my heart wasn't just my own. I had no intention of him meeting them so early—destiny had a different plan.

They like him, I thought. I like him.

I considered myself an idiot for feeling such strong emotions for a man I barely knew.

Before that moment, back when I left Hendrix with the boys, I knew our relationship wouldn't last because Martin and Daniel would hate him, or worse, he would want me without committing to my kids.

Hendrix, beating me to the punch, turned the chest upright, and cleaning up, he sang under his breath.

"I told you 8 pm," I said. "They had to be in bed by 8 pm, Hendrix."

"Which was the plan until time got away from me."

"Clearly." I cupped a small basketball with both hands. "It looks like you didn't even try."

"That's what it looks like."

"Now is where you explain."

"I could. You probably won't change your mind."

"8 pm, Hendrix."

"Okay, fine. I didn't want to throw my guy under the bus." He sighed. "Daniel knocked out Martin's tooth."

"He did what? How?"

"For some reason, he thought it was a good idea to throw a remote control car at his brother."

"Why did he throw his car at Martin?"

"I figured you could provide insight on why your son felt so inclined to chuck a remote control car across the room, unprovoked, by the way, in the exact location of your eldest. Seriously, he just chucked it. Martin was minding his business getting worked in Smash."

"That boy won't be satisfied until I lay hands on him." Hendrix grabbed my hand, stopping me from barging into the boys' room.

"It's okay. I took care of it."

I sighed. "So Daniel knocked out Martin's tooth."

"Martin was crying, so I let him stay up with me for a little. It's amazing how the Tooth Fairy can calm a kid down. Then Daniel came out crying because he heard us talking, so I had to calm him down. Next thing I know, I had two kids crying for their mother."

"So, you wipe their tears away through song and dance?"

"Kiss me."

"I'm serious. You didn't listen, Hendrix."

"I'm listening."

"The house is a mess."

I'm cleaning."

"This is going to throw off their sleep schedule."

"I wanted to let them stay up as a treat...you know what, that's no excuse. Sorry."

"Thank you."

"For what, exactly? Pissing you off?"

"For watching them. For being honest. It's not what I wanted to hear, but it is what it is. You did me a favor, after all. I should be more appreciative."

"I thought you were off this weekend."

"I was, but they needed me to cover a shift."

"I would never go to work on my day off."

"You can't ignore your boss."

"I stay ignoring my boss. They pay me at work, not to sit at home waiting for them to call."

"Going in when they need you shows good character and work ethic. A good reputation will take you far in life."

"My job is not my life. If I die tomorrow, my boss will throw my crap in a box and hire somebody new. At most, I might be the subject of an email. I don't owe my job my health or sanity."

"Well, everyone can't be you. Some people need the money."

"I get it. I get it. I live at home with my dad, so maybe I'm speaking from luxury when I say it's not all about the money to me. What about the principle?"

"What about it?"

"You don't have to bail out your job. McDonald's is a billion-dollar company with what? Thousands of restaurants in the world? They'll be alright if one is short-staffed for a day. God forbid people have to wait a little longer for their sweet tea and nuggets."

"If everyone were like you, the world would come to a halt."

"If everyone were like me, more people would be happier. Or so I like to think." He hugged me from behind as I reached to pick up the plates on the coffee table. "You need to get some sleep."

"I need to clean-"

"Vita."

"Hendrix, everything isn't a game."

"Vita, I made the mess, and I'll clean it up."

"It's okay."

"I got this." He smiled.

There's that smile again, I thought.

. . .

All signs pointed to him being gone. The living room was back to normal, and the lights were off. I nearly had a heart attack as I checked on the boys, seeing Hendrix's figure standing over Martin in the dark. He turned to me, grinning and raising a balled-up paper towel over his head.

He came from the boy's room, tossing up the paper towel, his smile as big as ever. "Tooth acquired," he said. "Is ten dollars doing too much?"

His lips looked juicy.

I moved my fingertips in a circular motion against my thighs; feeling the tingling pulsation, I bit down on my bottom lip.

I caressed his cheek, letting my hand stay there as I lowered my head slightly and stared into his eyes. I breathed heavily. When he put his hand on my waist, I couldn't breathe at all. We kissed. He moved his head back, and our lips barely touched-mine quivering. We lived in unison. Our gaze never broke from one another. He stopped smiling and stared with a passion that made me crumble inside.

I want him, I thought. Why wouldn't I? He's perfect.

I took his hand and led him to the guest room. Just as he closed the door, I wrapped my arms around his neck and attacked him with kisses. I felt all of the passion and desire that left my cheeks warm and my body trembling on his lips. He broke away from our kiss to bite my bottom lip gently.

He smiled-so did I. Lowering my head so that his lips were to my forehead, I rubbed his stomach and moved my hands down into his shorts. He looked ready--felt ready. He grew in my hands, and when he was fully erect, I stroked him from tip to base. He tore off my shirt and buried his face into my chest, kissing, licking, and caressing my breasts while I kept stroking.

He grabbed hold of my wrist and took my hand from his shorts. Then he lay me on the edge of the bed, kneeled on the floor, and slid my shorts and panties off.

There was a warm pulsation of my clit and increasing wetness, waiting to feel his tongue. He kissed, nibbled, and licked my body, letting me know he knew how to work his mouth. His teasing continued down to my inner thighs for a minute of kissing but stopped short of the prize, leaving me quivering in desire and anticipation.

Lick it, baby.

So he did.

I was floating. Floating. Floating. With a high-pitched moan into a pillow, I orgasmed.

I was still floating, still shaking, and still trying to catch my breath when he stood and took off his shorts. He was throbbing hard. Leaning over me, using his hand to hold himself up, he guided himself into me. Deeper. Deeper. At the moment where he was inside me, and that's it, he somehow brought me closer to cumming a second time with a peck on the lips and a smile. The thrusting, neck licking, and heavy moaning in my ears increased the goosebumps across my body and the satisfaction of being stretched.

He must have read my mind because he brought his face to mine. He was so sexy. I made him sit on the edge of the bed and bent over to let him taste me from behind.

"You taste amazing," he said.

I got on top and rode him with our faces so close that we took in each other's breath. The way we gazed into each other's eyes, I could have erupted from the passion alone. The longer we went on, the harder and faster I went.

Although we were close, I wanted him closer. I nuzzled my face into a sloppy kiss, interrupted by moans. He was floating as well. Like he lost all feeling in his body, he went limp and fell back onto the bed.

With the intense throbbing and his face scrunched up, he was about to cum. Hendrix telling me through the groaning and mumbling was just a formality. I took him in my mouth just as he came.

I crawled into bed and lay on my side beside him. So he kissed me.

We tasted great together.

I moved my head to his sweaty chest. Nowhere else felt right in the world. I moved my head back to look at him through the dark.

"I like you," he said. "I like you a lot."

"I like you too."

"Is it too soon to say I want to keep you forever?"

"A little, but I wouldn't mind if you said it."

"I want to keep you forever."

I felt warm. "Say it again."

"I want to keep you forever."

"Again."

"I want to keep you forever."

"One more time."

"Victoria. Vita. My chicken nugget. I would be one happy man if I could be yours forever."

"Sounds like someone is in love."

"I'm not in love. I'm in the act of falling."

"How close are you to the ground?"

"Maybe I'm close. Maybe I can't even see it yet." He shrugged. "Who knows?"

"Are you scared?"

"Scared of falling in love?"

"No. Scared of getting hurt."

"I would be if it was with anyone other than you."

I kissed his chest. "Today has been perfect."

"And we'll make tomorrow perfect. And the day after that."

"And the day after that."

"As long as you want me around, just tell me what you want, and I'll try my best to make you happy."

"I don't want you to leave yet."

"Good because I didn't want to leave either."

"But I guess you have to." I rolled onto my back. It's probably best if you aren't here when Martin and Daniel wake up. They might get the wrong idea."

We got dressed and made our way to the front door. He stood there, waiting for me to take his hand off the doorknob and lead him back to the room.

He can't stay, I thought.

He walked outside and stopped on the welcome mat, gazing at the sunlight that barely peaked over the houses.

"Hershey changed his mind," he said, facing me.

With tears rolling down my face, I smiled. "I get to see my boys."

"You had this the entire time."

"We had this."

Chapter 6
Hendrix

The music playing over the speakers occasionally stopped for a cashier to request a price check over the intercom. Seconds later, commercials tried their best to persuade us to take advantage of the Inland Empire's best deals.

A decent number of customers roamed the aisles. Employees, in their white uniforms, looked like milkmen.

I put a cantaloupe into the cart's seat and strolled through the produce section, and examined each fruit or vegetable in large bins, starting at those under the misters. The bright colors of all the fruits and vegetables, the smell of fresh fruits, and the mist against my face always made me take a second stroll through the section before leaving.

Whenever my dad bought his cigarettes, the son in me couldn't bear to accompany him to the register, where his coughing and gasping turned every head.

I was at the back corner of the store, killing time by the prepackaged salads when I heard him coughing at the registers. So I could breathe again, I needed him to stop coughing. Looking into the aisles as I passed, I connected eyes with a man in a gray suit who turned onto the cereal section from the opposite end.

Do I know this guy?

If we were strangers, we would've been on our way after acknowledging each other's existence with a head nod. From the hesitation to look away, there was a history.

Then, it all came to me.

Hershey.

I saw the exact moment when he recognized me; the intense look of deep thought turned to eyebrow furrowing anger.

Fuck a Hershey, I thought.

The rustling carts and their wheels squeaking and rolling against the ceramic tile echoed over the music playing over the speakers.

I walked down the coffee aisle with no intention of buying any. I loved the smell far more than the taste.

Hershey passed the aisle like he was on a mission. Clearly, the mission was to confront me because he doubled back into the aisle, sat his basket uncomfortably close to me, and stared at the shelf. Then, he turned around.

"Hey, my man, do I know you?" He asked.

He knew who I was. He didn't forget the man who kissed his girlfriend—the man who his girlfriend chose over him.

Victoria and I are together now, I thought. You fumbled your chance to be with her, so go on, man. Enjoy your day.

"Yeah, I know you." He mockingly laughed. "You're the kid from that night. What a night that was. You remember me, right? Hershey."

"Sorry, man. I have no idea who you are." On my way out of the situation, he stepped in front of the cart.

"You don't remember me? I'm Victoria's husband."

I gave him nothing.

"You know, my Victoria. Precious little thing. Arm looks like a coloring book. You kissed her. That Victoria."

"Sorry, I think I would remember someone named after a mediocre chocolate bar."

"What can I say? It's a family name. If my father had his way, I would be a Maurice, after Maurice White of Earth, Wind, and Fire. My mother-- God bless her soul-- thought it would be a tad cretinous to name me after a musician. Don't get me wrong, "September" is a cookout classic, but I'm happy to say my parents put in a little effort and love into naming me."

"Oh, that's what's up. How did they land on Hershey? Let me guess; she ate a ton of chocolate when she was pregnant and said, 'eh, why not?"

"Hershey is my uncle's name."

"Adorable." As I went to stride off in victory, Hershey yanked the cart to a stop a second time.

"Hey, buddy, about what happened with Victoria-"

"You mean when you cheated on her or was there something I missed?"

"Look, kid, the unequivocal response would have been to knock your teeth out. That should tell you something. There's no ill will from my end. Victoria is a beautiful woman. I would've done the same thing."

"Cool. I would have to be an idiot to let that opportunity pass me by."

"That's why I put a ring on it." He smirked. "I took her out to The Dramatic Scenery of Big Sur. You may not know what that is, seeing how, you know, FAFSA disbursements are generous, but let's be real here. You can't afford it." He chuckled. "It's this beautiful remote location up north. I took her to this secluded beach tucked away between coastal bluffs. That's where I dropped down to one knee. You should have seen her face. I've known her for years, and I don't know if I've ever seen her that happy."

"Cute."

"Look at you. Looking like your metabolism never lets you down. You can't tell me you aren't doing well with the ladies. Of all the options, what do you want with a twenty-five-year-old mother of two? Go out and live before you waste the apex of your life playing house."

I thought, as I smiled and moved the cantaloupe to my left hand, about swinging on him. I wanted him to say another word- to give me a reason to knock him into the bags of coffee and then sweep up the spilled grains with his milk-dud-looking head. The chance never came because he ambled along, his focus on his cell phone in hand.

I kept myself composed in front of him, all the time fuming inside. I paid for the cantaloupe and walked outside. Dad, smoking on the curb outside the store, glanced back at me from over his shoulder to notice me shaking in anger.

"Take a deep breath there, buddy," he said and then coughed.

"Don't call me buddy."

"Didn't mean to offend you, son. Do you want to tell me what has you about to bust all the grapes in a fruit fight?"

"For once in your life, be serious."

"I'm not used to seeing you all charged up, just trying to get a laugh out of you."

IHOP was across the parking lot. I put the cantaloupe in the backseat of the car on my way there. A fast walk kept a distance between my dad and me. Cancer and age expanded the reach between us, making his wheezing impossible to hear in real life, although I heard it in my head.

. . .

We had become such regulars at IHOP that the staff knew us on a first-name basis and committed our orders to memory. Before they even handed us the menu, they asked, "the regular for you two today?" They even sat us at the same two-person booth, where our knees touched.

By the time I slid inside the booth, I was calm. Thanks to Victoria. It was hard to be angry after the night we had. I imagined her curly hair hanging over her face, and I heard her sweet voice that made me giddy inside. It took everything in me not to call. I did send a heart emoji, though. She replied with heart eyes.

We're acting like teenagers, I thought. I like it. No. I love it. I'm falling for her, and I'm close to the ground. Can I tell her that, though? What would she think? She can't think of anything that I haven't thought of myself. I'm falling for a woman this soon. Is it too soon, or is the time just right?

I sighed, sitting my phone face down on the table in enough force that if I cracked the screen, I wouldn't have been surprised.

"I think I'm falling in love," I said. "Don't be mad, but it's Victoria. We've been seeing each other for about a month now."

"Hmm."

"Everything slows down when I think about her, and finally, for some of the few seconds in my life, I can think. And because I can think, I realize that everything will be okay, even with you. I feel like I can do anything as long as I have her by my side, and it's so stupid."

"It's not stupid."

"It is, though. I never thought of myself as loveable until she made me realize I'm worth the time. And it's all in her eyes. The way she looks at me, it's like I'm her now and forever more."

"That's a long time."

"Right? Why do I feel like I'm wasting my time if I'm not with her? Breathing seems so pointless if we're not together." I sighed. "I shouldn't be this dependent on someone. And it's not like I want to be because it's killing me. This could end tomorrow, and here I am, so damn invested. I want to punch myself in the face, but at the same time, I want to hold her all day and all night. I don't even want to be here right now. I should be with her. Who cares she's working, you know? I'll sit in the corner until she gets off." I slammed my face into my hands, grunting.

"You know what you need? Alcohol. Let's go to a bar after this."

"It's not even ten."

"Come on, Hendrix, it's your day off. Why stay cooped up in the house? We have an entire day ahead of us. Let's go out and have some fun. Me and you. Father and son."

"What's wrong with eating pancakes and going home?"

"We've been eating pancakes and going home for months now. It's the same old thing over and over. I'm losing my mind. If I eat another short stack, God, take me out the moment a pancake touches my lips." He folded his hands in prayer and bowed his head.

I slapped his hands. "Are you serious?"

"Half serious. I might keel over right now if we don't do something."

"Like what, Dad?"

"Let's go to a strip club."

"You're too old to be talking about the strip club. You need to stop worrying about butt cheeks and start focusing on your health."

"Okay, I see what's going on. You get a woman, and you're too good for some random butt cheeks."

"You know what? Yes, yes, I am too good for random butt cheeks. For the first time in my life, I have a great woman, and it's not like it's any of your business...She has a great ass. I don't need to see random ass."

"Alright. Alright. Nobody asked you to have sex with a stripper. You don't want them, and they sure as Hell do not want you. That's Strip Club 101. I'm sure God took his time on your lady's ass. That doesn't mean you can't look at random ass. Lots of random asses. Tell me how that doesn't sound like Heaven."

"I'm not going to a strip club."

He sighed. "Fine. I'll make you a deal. If you take me to a club, I'll tell you where your mother is."

"Fuck you, Dad."

...

I stopped to admire a garden outside a home that looked straight from the early 1900s.

We stood on the opposite side of the white picket fence, separating us from the freshly cut grass with the lines from the lawnmower, garden growing fruits and vegetables, marked with a sign that read, "Martha Black's Farm," and a house that neither of us could afford. That didn't stop me from dreaming.

"This, right here," I said, "is the aesthetic I need in a house."

"It's nice."

"It's more than just 'nice.'" I finally took my eyes off the house and moved them to her. "You don't like it?"

"It's a little too *Love it or List it* for me. Don't get me wrong. It's cool. It just feels more like a dream than real life."

"What does that mean?"

Two boys, neither older than ten years old, burst through the front door of the house, shooting imaginary blasts from their palms and making blast sound effects with their mouths. On the lawn, they argued about who hit who first. Their parents sauntered to the bottom of the steps, hand in hand. They drank mimosas with their free hands with no care in the world. They waved at us like we weren't some random couple standing outside their home.

"That," she said.

Their sons resembled both of them, yet only one of them, depending on the angle.

Under her breath, Vita sighed, trying to play it off. A smile and kiss with pursed lips couldn't make me erase what I saw: She saw herself, Hershey, Martin, and Daniel in the family.

. . .

Leaning back with her hands propping her up, I lay in between
Victoria's legs, my head in her lap and back flat against the short,
spike-like grass.

The kids on the playground shouted and shrieked like only
kids know how to do when having fun as they bounced from
one piece of equipment to another.

We sat in our own little world, separated by a field, where it
was just us two.

"So, your mother isn't dead?" She asked.

"If she did, it wasn't when we thought."

"That's a swerve."

"The crazy thing about all of this is my dad made us believe
her ashes were in an urn on the fireplace."

"Who's ashes are in the urn?"

"Our dogs."

I showed her a picture of my mother on my phone. My mom
looked to be my age in the picture. She was tall with a honey
complexion, and she wore a black shirt tucked into high waist
jeans.

Victoria, smiling, held my phone beside my face and looked
back and forth between me and the photo.

"I've never been to the strip club," she said.

"I don't know why he can't go by himself. Jokes on him. I'm
not sure I want to meet my mom."

"That's a lie."

"I'm serious, Vita. For my entire life, it's always been my dad
and me. Sure, my sisters were around too, but he was like my
best friend, mentor, and more. He taught me how to drive, talk
to girls, change a tire; he even taught me how to cook. He wasn't
the best at everything, but he did what he had to do. I'm good."
I plucked a blade of grass from the ground and let it blow away
in the wind. "I've gone this far without my mom. Why do I need
to see her now?"

"Because no matter what happened, she's your mom. You
can play it cool all you want, but a mother leaving her kids isn't

something you just shrug your shoulders at. It has to be one of those things that wake you up in the middle of the night."

"Yeah, back when I was a kid. The thing is, I'm not a kid anymore, Vita. I'm done crying over a woman who could care less how I feel." I took a moment to reflect. "I'm over it. She chose that, not me. I'm not running back to her like she wasn't the one who left. Let's say she wants to come back into our lives, fine. I'm not going to force my mother back into mine." I took a long pause. "It's better for everyone if she stays gone. If she did try to come back into our lives….Jesus. I rather she stays gone."

She leaned forward, and with her hair brushing against my face, I took in its scent of lavender and vanilla. I moved her hair from over her face, and while I stared, lost in the world where only we existed, she blew a dandelion into my face. I rolled from her lap. Laughing, she leaned back, using her elbows to keep her back from the ground. I crawled to her.

"We got this," she said.

"I guess."

"You can't do that. You can't always be the ray of light in my darkness, and then turn around and not let me be the same in yours." She sat up. "Whether you decide to see your mother or not, you should take your father out. He needs this."

"He needs to rest."

"That's what you think he needs. If you knew you were dying, would you just wait around until it happens, or would you live your life as much as possible before the bell tolls?"

"If I were sick, I would be fighting for my life."

"If you were sick, your father would be right there for you no matter what. Do the same for him."

I grunted. "I guess I'm going to see some random ass tonight."

"That's the spirit."

"You should come with us."

"This is much-needed father and son time. Don't be 'that guy."

"Oh, I'm definitely being that guy. If you were dying, would you want to hang out with your son at the strip club?"

"Who said I would be with you the entire time? Maybe I want some ass in my face."

"You're joking, right?"

"Am I?" She got up. "A woman can enjoy a nice ass in her face too."

Her ass took me back to the first time we had sex. "Agreed."

"Let's go."

"Where do you want to go?"

"I have many places in mind. This one, in particular, is a surprise."

. . .

After about an hour on the freeway, I couldn't tell you where we were going.

"Where are we going?" I asked.

She removed one hand from the steering wheel and shook her index finger to tell me "no." There was no way to tell how serious she was since she wore sunglasses.

She bobbed her head from side to side as she danced to the songs on the CD my dad gave me, her hair draped over her face.

She exited the freeway and drove through a city that I always passed on my way to somewhere more populated and alive. Away from the busiest parts of town, Victoria turned into a residential area that had houses with wide porches and low-pitched roofs. The grass in the neighborhood was like a meadow, long and green. All the potholes sounded like they did a number on my alignment. That didn't slow Vita down; she leisurely drove past the parked cars way too close for my comfort.

"Seriously," I said, looking out the window. "Where are we going? Big Sur?"

"Big Sur?" She laughed. It sounded almost like Hershey's laugh. "You know that's up north, right?"

"I'm not stupid."

"I didn't say you were. Stop being so impatient. We're almost there."

She pulled to the curb in front of a small blue house. A behemoth of a tree in the front yard towered over everything for as far as I could see. Its thick branches curved over the walkway leading to the porch.

Vita stared at the house, her thoughts visibly racing.

"What am I thinking?" she asked, mumbling.

"Whose house is this?"

"Mine."

"Yours?"

"My parents."

"We're going to see your parents? I thought you and your parents weren't on the best terms."

"Yeah, they don't talk to me. Good thing I didn't come to see my parents."

"Uh, okay. We drove all the way to your parent's house, not to see your parents?"

"I want to show you something." She kicked the car door open. "You'll love it."

I got out of the car.

She lifted her sunglasses from her eyes, squinted as she looked around the neighborhood, probably reliving years of memories. Her eyes glistened from the light. Her feet resisted the entire time she walked to the house. The piles of leaves covering the concrete crunched under our feet.

"There used to be a swing on the tree," she said. "When I was a kid, I would sit there and wait for my dad to come home. He would always give me one good push before going inside, so I could jump off. He swore I would break something."

"My dad would love this porch. There's a lot of room to smoke."

"We didn't use it much. I think we only sat out here during the Fourth of July. My mom and I would sit on the porch and watch my dad barbecue."

She looked around the street again for neighbors, and then she hurried through an iron gate on the side of the house. I slid into the backyard as the gate was closing.

The side of the house was so narrow that I almost scraped my arm on the fence as I scratched my nose.

The backyard had rows of raised beds filled with fruits and vegetables from the back fence to the house. In the corner where we stood, two chairs were underneath a pergola covered in vines. Along the right wall, they had a garden of flowers. The backyard had no grass, just wood chips.

Everything is so green, I thought.

"Seeing how you love your gardens so much, I figured I'll show you mine," Victoria said. "Well, the fruits of my labor. This is nothing how I remember it. They always said they wanted a bigger garden."

"This is beautiful."

"The garden used to be in the back. It was just the first four beds. I helped my dad put the wood chips down and put some of the beds together. Me and my mom did all the gardening. I promise you she made me read hundreds of gardening magazines. If it wasn't for school or gardening, I didn't read it." She gandered across the backyard, taking in the view. "We planted broccoli over there, carrots there, cucumbers there, tomatoes and spinach there."

"I need one of these when I grow up."

"Do it. It's refreshing."

"I might need some help from the professional."

"I was twelve. I can barely keep a cactus alive now."

She strolled through the backyard, leaning over and admiring the vegetables in the raised beds.

She seems okay, I thought. Is she?

If she wasn't well emotionally, she did a great job hiding it. Then again, she had on sunglasses. Turning around to look at me, she waved and motioned for me to join her. There wasn't enough room to walk side by side, so she took the lead.

"The good old days," she murmured.

"The best thing about the good ol' days is they're never too far away." I gripped her by the hand, squeezing, hoping she would turn around. "They're right here, Vita. You don't have to leave this time."

She turned around. "Remember all that stuff you said about not wanting to see your mother? Me too."

"I bet they would love to see you."

"I'm happy to take your money."

"Then put your money where your mouth is. We can kick back and wait right here."

"They don't want to see me."

I sat on the edge of a raised bed. "They're parents."

"And?"

"We're their kids. We're predisposed to piss them off so much they'll say something they'll regret."

"They called me a disgrace, Hendrix." She watched me grimace. "Exactly. Do you want to hear more because they didn't stop there? Stupid. Irresponsible. A temptress."

"Oh."

"Uncomfortable yet?"

"Okay, okay, I get it."

"If I remember correctly, my dad told me I would ruin Martin and Daniel's lives and that they would spit on my grave."

"Jesus."

"Oh yeah, him too. They cursed me in His name."

I held her from behind and nuzzled my face into the back of her shoulder. "Those kids can't get enough of you."

"I stopped worrying about what he said years ago. I know who and what I am now."

"Okay, but you brought me here for a reason, not just because your parents have an incredibly serene and picturesque garden."

"It was a mistake."

"While I'm inclined to believe that because nobody wants to come to Beaumont on purpose." I kissed her cheek. "This time, I think you're somebody."

"You should've heard what they said to me."

"Years ago. They said those things years ago. Trust me. I get it. I really do. But they deserve the chance to prove they changed."

"Three years is not a long time ago."

"I don't think you know how time works. Three years is a long time for regret to creep up that ass."

She laughed. "Okay." She couldn't stop laughing.

"Three years is a long time for them to regret what they said, Vita. They didn't mean all that."

"Maybe they didn't. I still don't want to find out."

"If that's what you want."

"It is."

"Cool. Just know I support you. Whether that's breaking into your parent's backyard when they aren't home or, you know, meeting them."

"This bridge burned a long time ago. I'm focusing on the future." She started turning her body, and I let her go. She turned around and looked at me. "My future with Martin and Daniel. You and I."

"Me and you. Are you going to let me have you forever?"

She put her hand on my cheek. "I'm thinking about it."

As I leaned forward for another kiss, she twirled. Her hair whipped across my face. She strolled over to a bed filled with tomatoes, peppers, and spinach. At this point, her back was to me, but I knew what she was doing. She picked me a snack. She yanked the vegetables from the plants, which made a loud, tearing noise. Occasionally, she looked over her shoulder, smirking.

She carried a small assortment of vegetables in her shirt and cleaned them off at the water hose. While rinsing one, the others sat on the ground. When done with one, she sat it on one of the chairs under the pergola.

I joined her under the pergola.

"Give me your shirt," she said.

"Why?"

"Because I need it."

"We all need a lot of things. Doesn't mean we deserve it."

"I can't tell you why I need it. It'll make sense when you give me your shirt."

I sighed and unbuttoned my shirt.

She used my shirt as a blanket. The same shirt I bought with my dad when we were at "treatment." The same shirt my dad loved because he said it reminded him of something he had in his "golden years." The same shirt I hated wearing for that exact reason. The same shirt I only wore because I wore it the day

Victoria introduced herself to me. If it weren't for that day, I would have thrown it away.

She sat the dripping wet vegetables on my shirt and sat down.

"We're going to have a picnic," she said.

"You're adorable." I squatted with my arms on my knees.

"You can't get enough of it."

I took a bite of the tomato. My jaw tingled. "You know, I'm not a big fan of tomatoes, but this is pretty good."

Vita took a bite and smiled. Juice dripped down her chin. "That was for me. You're going to get heartburn."

I looked at the house, imagining baby Vita running around the backyard. In the story in my head, she wore her hair in a ponytail and didn't have front teeth, so when she smiled, all you saw were her gums. I wondered which parent she favored. Did she look like her mother, dad, or a combination of both?

Did she get her smile from her mom or dad? Her eyes? Certain personality traits? Which parent did she favor-- personality-wise?

I look like my dad with my mom's smile, I thought. And I think I act just like her because I can't see anything that my dad and I have in common. Just because you can't see something doesn't mean it doesn't exist. We could have a lot in common, and because we're so busy looking for something else, we may not notice it at all.

"Do you want to know what I think?" I asked.

"What?"

"I think you should consider talking to your parents."

"I could say the same to you."

"I'm considering it. Can you say the same?"

"What side of the fence are you leaning towards?"

"I don't know. She left me, and I feel like she should be the one begging for my love."

"Exactly."

Halfway through biting down on a pepper, she smiled. Strands of hair flowed over her face, and as she went to move them away, I leaned forward and grabbed her wrist. We were face to face, the pepper still to her lips. She extended it to feed me.

"Your mother's loss. She missed out on seeing a wonderful man," she said.

"No, she had one. She couldn't appreciate him."

"Question."

"Maybe I have an answer."

"Are you still falling in love?"

"You make it pretty difficult not to."

"Still not going to tell me how close you are to the ground?"

"Now, why would I do that? Just know I'm getting closer."

"I'm floating."

"I like the sound of that."

"I love what you do to me."

A car pulled into the driveway. The engine stayed on for a moment, and car doors opened and slammed. Three sets of footsteps-one being much lighter and faster-came closer.

A young girl asked her mother and father if someone was at the house. Her mother, calling the girl *baby*, told her no. Her father insisted it was the neighbor's car.

We hopped up, and I yanked my shirt off the ground and balled it under my arm.

"That's my parents," she whispered.

"Who's the girl?"

She shrugged.

When we heard the front door close, we bolted from the backyard to the car. Vita sped off.

I was laughing. She didn't find anything funny.

Chapter 7
Victoria

The dress did my body a ton of favors. It hugged onto my body and showed off all my thighs. I stared at myself in the mirror, trying my very best to remember how beautiful I was through the onslaught of negative thoughts.

I look good, I thought.

I unwrapped a towel that had been around my hair since showering thirty minutes ago and blow-dried my hair. After, I did my makeup.

If we were going to a club, I assumed we would drink and dance until we physically couldn't anymore. A strip club had to be different. A room full of horny men foaming at the mouth for naked or half-naked women in a room reeking of lotion, cologne, alcohol, sweat, and funk.

I had never been to a strip club, and a part of me compared myself to the women I hadn't seen yet. I felt worse thinking about Hendrix's dad.

He seemed sweet when we met. Is he anything like Hendrix? What would he think of me? Would he think I'm cute? What would he think of my dress? Was I doing too much? How would he act? Most importantly, would he like me? If he did, would he want me for his son?

I typed a text message where I faked a sickness. My thumb hovered over the send icon.

Hendrix had already met Martin and Daniel, I thought. They liked him. Martin won't stop talking about him. To Martin, Hendrix was nothing short of amazing. You have to meet his dad.

Apparently, Hendrix was good at Smash Bros. The Sunday after Hendrix watched Martin and Daniel, he came over, and he and Martin mindlessly sat like zombies and played the game for two hours. They yelled in frustration, shouted in joy, and made all types of other ambiguous noises. Daniel liked him because he didn't tease or hit him.

The person who I assumed was Hendrix knocked, and I opened the door. Hendrix's father stood with his back to me. The smoke from his cigarette burned my nose.

He wore an olive long sleeve shirt, jeans, a knitted black scarf, a black bowler hat, and boat shoes. He gasped and heavily breathed whenever he didn't inhale or exhale.

Seeing him smoke felt weird, considering he had lung cancer, but not surprising considering I met him as he bought alcohol. Hendrix never told me that his father still smoked. I figured that would have been something he would have shared.

"Victoria," Hendrix's father said, "I see why my son fell in love with you. You are gorgeous. I'm talking 'stop a man in his tracks' gorgeous. 'Give her the world' gorgeous."

Did Hendrix tell his father that he loves me? I asked myself. Don't worry about that now. Focus.

I smiled.

"Thank you," I said. "You look dapper, Mr. Harper."

He winked. "My mama called me Colin."

"Would you like to come in?"

"No, thank you, dear. We should be heading out soon. Your boyfriend is freshening up in the car." He took a drag of his cigarette and blew out the smoke. "I tell you, that boy is his mother's child."

"How so?"

"They wait until they get to their destination to put on the makeup-in Hendrix's case lotion. That boy will have a layer of ash on him when he walks out of the house. Plus, they make it a point to be the Cinderellas of the ball."

Hendrix turned onto the walkway from the driveway and smiled when he saw me. He looked like a model in his white button-up, black blazer, black pants, and gray boots. He came to me, and I smelt the lemon-scented lotion that made his skin pop under the porch light.

We kissed.

"So," he said. "Are we ready to go?"

"Hell yeah," his father said.

"Ready than ever," I said. "Let me grab my purse."

"You're going to need it."

Hendrix waited outside while his father went back to the car. I came back with my purse, and Hendrix wrapped his arms around me.

"You look beautiful," he said.

"So do you. We look good together. Oh, by the way, your father's compliment was better."

"What did he say?"

I walked in front of him and gazed back to give him a wink.

We got in the car, and Hendrix drove to the club. His father sat in the backseat, behind Hendrix, smoking. His window was open, and the air pushing into the car made a loud, throbbing bass noise that drowned out all the wheezing and coughing.

A twenty-five-minute drive later, where Hendrix's father coughed half the time, we exited the freeway. Trees stood higher than most of the buildings. Blocks of clubs, bars, restaurants, and shops, of varying architectural styles-- all made up 'downtown,' the heart of the city.

The traffic lights that stayed red longer than green kept traffic backed up for blocks.

The clusters of men and women, enjoying the nightlife, turned their bodies or stepped into the street to avoid running into one another.

A pickup truck jerked to a stop to avoid hitting a group of college students who drunkenly lurched into the street.

We parked on the fifth floor of a nearby parking structure, which looked too sketchy to cost $15.

A line formed outside the elevators. Most people took the stairs. Some of the people, like Hendrix's father, enjoyed a cigarette.

Everyone going to the strip club stood out from everyone else. Everyone else dressed casually. Those who were going to the club looked the part; provocative and stylish.

A group of us packed into the elevator, and when the door opened, everyone tried to exit at once. The closer we got to the club, the more the people dressed casually broke from the crowd and went into the stores and restaurants.

At our destination, we stood in a small line in the lobby of a strip club. The cloth walls muffled the music blaring from inside.

The bouncer patted everyone down, then directed us to a cute woman in a black dress behind a register. Way too many people were drunk so early in the night, needing to put their arms around their friends to stay up. Since it was a Monday, entry was free. Hendrix's father realized that he had left his ID in the car. Before he could leave, the bouncer, in all black, called us to the front of the line. The bouncer didn't ask for Hendrix father's ID. He stared long and hard at Hendrix and his ID before he let him inside.

The bass in the song, seemingly shaking the room, went through my chest the moment Hendrix pulled open the door. At once, we all cringed. By the end of the night, I just knew my ears would be bleeding. The stage was in the middle of the room, and on both sides were booths. The bar extended along the right wall. The few people inside drank as they waited for the next dancer to take the stage. If they were lucky enough, a dancer sat with them.

The women had the cutest outfits. I wondered where they bought them.

"I'm going to get a drink," Hendrix's father said.

"I think I'll get one too," I said.

"I'll grab a table," Hendrix said.

Hendrix's father and I gathered at the bar and admired their endless alcohol choices along the shelves. Hendrix's father ordered Hennessy straight. I ordered a rum and coke. When the bartender gave us our drinks, he took his as a shot and ordered another- he did the same with the second. We paid, and I joined Hendrix at the booth.

He scrolled through his phone. I held his hand under the table while dancing in place. We watched as his father did The Slop in the middle of the walkway. In this gorgeous one-piece, a dancer joined him for a quick dance as she made her way to the stage. The DJ called her Leah.

Leah had to compete against Hendrix's father for everyone's attention. For the most part, the few people inside focused on him, the gentleman dancing in the middle of the strip club. Leah smiled at him even when she climbed up and down the pole, removed her clothes, or rubbed her breasts into someone else's face.

Two dancers joined him, and they rolled their bodies and shook their asses on him. He had the most satisfied grin on his face. After a song, he came back to the table with one of the dancers. She was white with blond hair and wore a long-sleeve fishnet top, a G-string, and heels. Hendrix's father was gasping and breathing heavily, smiling.

"Are you okay?" The dancer asked. She had to yell over the music.

"Yeah," he said, gasping for air. "I'm just dying."

"You were dancing pretty hard."

"No, seriously. I'm literally dying. I have cancer."

The girl hugged him, pushing her breast into his face. "My dad died of cancer."

"I'm so sorry for your loss."

"No, no, let's not talk about that. Let's focus on you. How are you feeling?"

"It's been rough, honestly."

"I bet."

"I want to make the most of my time before God decides it's my time."

"Awww." She lowered her fishnet top and forced him to motorboat her breasts. "Titties in your faces because fuck cancer."

"Titties in the face because I have cancer." With his hands on her breasts, he gawked at Hendrix. "Are you seeing this, Hendrix?"

Hendrix would have rather seen anything else, as long as it wasn't his father grabbing a fistful of a stripper's breasts.

"Not to be in your business, so it's totally fine if you don't answer, but what cancer do you have?" The dancer asked.

"Stage 3 Lung Cancer."

"That's what my father had."

"How old were you when he passed?"

"12."

"You poor baby. That must have been awful."

"The worst."

"You poor thing, a girl shouldn't have to grow up without her father."

Hendrix and I moved to the chairs in front of the stage to give his father more privacy. Hendrix made sure he put as much distance between him and the stage as possible.

Leah twirled on the pole in ways I didn't know was possible. She groped me and forced my hands onto her body, covered in glitter. She earned every dollar I threw.

Hendrix tried to play it cool, so it wasn't obvious he watched his father. The dance ended, and Leah crawled across the stage for the balled-up and sweat-drenched dollars on the ground.

Back at the table, Hendrix's father and the blonde girl took shots of tequila. We joined them. My chest was on fire, but it was a good pain. Leah joined us, and we took another round. Hendrix sat there on his phone, trying his best to ruin our good time with his melodramatic sighs and eye rolls.

Hendrix's father talked to Leah and the other dancer about school while Hendrix and I watched another dancer, who overused the move where she slammed her hip onto the floor. We came back, and they were standing by the table.

"We're about to leave," Hendrix's father said.

"Together?" Hendrix asked. "Who do you think you are? Hugh Hefner?"

"I'm no Hugh Hefner. I'm just a man, Hendrix. A man who God is looking down in favor."

"Where are you going?"

"Who cares. Anywhere but here.'

"Really? You did all that begging. You did all this to get me to come with you just to be here for forty minutes? We could have stayed home."

"Then, I wouldn't have met these two lovely ladies, right here."

"I'll go grab the car."

"No need. We'll take an Uber."

"To anywhere but here? That would be an expensive fare."

"You would be a lot cheaper. Where do you lovely ladies want to go for the night?"

"Well, when you figure it out, let me know."

"We can't go back to my house," the blonde girl said. "Every other night, my mom is out, living her best life, now she decides she's old and washed. You hate to see it."

"My roommate stayed home this weekend," the other girl said. "Colin, why don't you show us your house?"

"Unfortunately, since I can't work, I couldn't keep up with the mortgage. The bank foreclosed my house a couple of months ago."

"Aww...Where have you been living?"

"With my brother. Sadly, going there is out of the question. He has kids, so you know how that goes. The crumblesnackers need their sleep."

"How about a hotel? We can grab alcohol on the way."

"I like this plan."

"We can go back to my place," I said. "It would be a lot cheaper than getting a room."

"I like this plan even more."

A kiss on Hendrix's father's cheeks and the women left and returned in a flash with their bags.

We left the club, and outside, I had a ringing in my ears from exposure to the loud music. A combination of alcohol and pride had Hendrix's father walking with a bounce in his step.

For some reason, the dancers had never changed into less distracting clothes. Disgust, approval, confusion, anger, or lust, Hendrix's father greeted everyone with the same boyish smirk and nod.

Hendrix apologized to everyone.

"Are you sure about this?" He asked in a whisper.

"Anything for your father."

"I appreciate you looking out for him, but you don't have to do this. You're volunteering your mother-in-law's house for my dad to get cozy with some strippers. He can take that debauchery to a hotel."

"That's too much of a hassle."

"Not really. The hotel is down the street. We can drop them off, and he can Uber back. That's way better than hearing my dad getting freaky with two dancers." He paused. "My dad likes threesomes. I'm learning too much about my dad tonight."

"You would have more fun if you loosen up and stop hating."

He let out a noise that sounded like a huff and laughed. "Oh, so I'm hating because I'm concerned about my dad taking home two strange women? Okay, cool."

"You weren't having fun before that."

"I was...kinda."

"You looked like someone held a gun to your head."

"It was cool. I wouldn't go back. I have too many student loans to be living recklessly in the strip club."

"Can you just say you weren't having a good time? It's okay. The strip club isn't for everybody."

"I was. It's entertaining watching my dad on the hunt. If he's having a good time, then I'm having a great time."

"See, and you weren't going to take him. He needed this."

"It's still kinda weird seeing him with a woman that's not my mom."

I interlocked our fingers.

The blonde girl knew of a 24-hour liquor store. It was down the street, past the parking structure, and there, we bought tequila and whiskey.

. . .

Most people had gone home by this point, and fewer people walked down the street.

Hendrix's father sat in the backseat sandwiched between the two girls, his arms around their shoulders as they giggled like teenagers.

"So Colin," the blonde hair girl said, "are these your kids?"

"Oh no," he said. "Hendrix, Victoria, and I worked together before the cancer."

"Do you have any kids?"

"Two daughters, Eve and Vanessa. They moved away for college and never looked back."

"They didn't come back when you told them about the cancer?"

"They came to visit once. That's about it.'

"Aww."

"My grass has been stepped on a little more than yours in this thing called life. As you get older, you get used to the sad world we live in, ladies. So many people are living for themselves, even the ones you love. Why would I need them, though, when I have two of the greatest friends ever?" He patted Hendrix and I on the shoulder.

"That's so sad. Well, don't worry about them, Colin. We're the only girls you need to worry about tonight."

They rested their heads on his shoulders. He grinned and winked at me when I looked back.

Hendrix rolled his eyes. He drove with one hand on the wheel and the other on the gearshift.

"What is this?" Leah asked, holding a crumpled stack of papers.

"Exactly what it looks like, my dear," Colin said.

"People go cemetery hunting? That's a thing?"

"Right?" Hendrix said. I caressed his hand from the conviction in his voice.

"As Jesus entered Jerusalem," Hendrix's father said, "the people of the land spread palm branches under his feet. When The Lord decides it's my time, I want to rest underneath palm trees."

The light turned green as Leah yelled, "Chinese Fire Drill."

Everyone, except Hendrix, switched seats. Now, I sat in the backseat, behind Hendrix, with both dancers. The blond-haired woman leaned across Leah.

"Is that bae," she whispered.

"I did pretty good," I said.

"You did, bitch."

Her breath reeked of alcohol, and I was sure mine did as well.

. . .

By the time I could turn on the lights, Hendrix's father took a whiskey bottle to the head. He and the girls passed the bottle around, taking one sip before passing it along. It was cold in the house-much colder than outside-and I turned on the heater.

Hendrix went to the bathroom, and the rest of us went into the kitchen. We made mixed drinks and casually sipped them as we sat around the kitchen table.

"Oh my God," Lead said, scooping up one of Martin's toys from the counter. "Transformers was a whole vibe growing up."

"Not that you can do any wrong in my eyes," Hendrix's father said. "That's what you would call a Gundam. You see, Transformers are sentinel beings. Gundams are mechs."

"Not just any Gundam," I said. "Wing Gundam Zero. It's Martin's favorite. You wouldn't know by the way he leaves it lying around."

"You have an adolescent brother?"

The realization that Hendrix never told his father about Martin and Daniel tightened in my throat. "Son." I swallowed the knot. "I have two sons."

"You and Hendrix aren't playing," Leah said, laughing.

"He isn't the father."

Leah raised my head by the chin. "Queen, Hendrix looks at you like every other girl is trying to be you. Hold that motherfucking head up, bitch!"

"You think?" My eyes, on their own, shifted to Hendrix's father.

"Of course, queen."

"I make it a habit to sweep outside my own door," his father said. "The world will talk, Victoria. You gotta decide when it's worth listening to."

"You have kids," the blond-haired girl said, "And a fine ass boyfriend who doesn't care! You're a queen. Now, can we stop being lame? I'm trying to get fucked up. Let's play a game or something!"

"What game?" I asked.

"I vote Medusa," Leah said.

It was a game where everyone looked down at the table. On the count of three, we looked up and stared at someone. If two people stared at each other, they took a shot.

"Do you have shot glasses?" Leah asked.

"We have red cups," I said.

"It'll do."

I grabbed cups from the pantry.

"What happened to your bae?" The blond-haired woman asked.

"He's not much of a drinker," I said.

"Awww, tell him he can still hang out with us."

"Hendrix is going through it right now," Hendrix's father said. "Not to put his busy out there like that... his mother died."

"That's terrible."

"Come on now, let's not ruin the night with all this sad stuff. Let's play."

The game began around the kitchen table. Our heads were down, and the blond-haired girl counted to three. We all looked up; Hendrix's father and the blond-haired girl looked at one another. I stared at the blond-haired girl, who stared at Hendrix's father. He and the blond-haired girl shouted "Medusa" and took a shot of tequila. Their faces scrunched as they brought the glasses back to the table. In the second round, Hendrix's father and I looked at one another. We shouted, "Medusa." He and I raised our shot glasses, nodded at one another, and took a shot of tequila; it burned going down and in my stomach.

Hendrix strolled into the kitchen and sat beside me. I placed my hand on his thigh. We filled him in on the game, and to no surprise, he declined to play. His father coughed, leaned over the table while covering his mouth, sounding like death itself was near. The girls put their hands on his back in their way to comfort him through the hacking.

Hendrix stared at his father, ready to take his father into his arms or walk away. The coughing spell ended with Hendrix's father struggling to breathe for several awkward and painful seconds, where every eye fixated on him.

"I get it. I sound like shit," he said. "I'm all right. Let's go."

"Are you sure you're okay?" The blond-haired girl asked.

"I had to get it out of my system. I'm all ready to go."

"Are you sure?"

"Come on, baby. I've been doing this for a while. Trust me." He cleared his throat. "I have a crazy idea."

"What is it?"

"We should play a game within a game. Every time I cough, we drink."

"That's fucked up," Leah said. "Fuck no."

"How are you guys going to get all self-righteous about something that has nothing to do with you? I'm the one with cancer. If I'm not worried about it, why are you? We all came out to have fun, right? And that's what we're doing. I know I have cancer. Shit, even on a good day where I manage to go about my life, this cough reminds me as quickly as I forgot. My life has been consumed with this shit. No matter where I go or who I talk to, the conversation always finds a way to go back to my cancer. How are you? Are you okay? I'm so sorry. I'm tired of being the sick guy. I know I'm sick, but that doesn't mean I can't have fun like everybody else. Let me be a person again. I'm okay with this. You should too."

"Fuck it," Hendrix said and downed a shot.

"Let's fucking go," Leah screamed.

His father and the girls cheered. They screamed louder when he took a second. The liquor went straight to his eyes, and in that moment, with his eyes glazed over, he was one step closer to being gone.

"Let's go," Hendrix's father said.

Leah began counting before we could bow our heads. On three, I watched Hendrix gaze at his father. From the cheering and screaming, the girls had to drink.

They took their shots, and then his father coughed. We took shots. We fell into a pattern the next couple of rounds. Each time, I stared at Hendrix, who stared at his father; his father coughed, and we downed shots. In the last round, Hendrix and his father finally connected eyes. His father smiled, but Hendrix didn't, and they drank. They drank again when his father coughed. Everyone laughed in drunkenness, except Hendrix and me.

Back when I walked into class at the beginning of the quarter, I never imagined I would be in a committed and loving relationship with anyone other than Hershey. Back then, I spent most of my day with Martin and Daniel, with very few interactions with adults.

I looked across the room with a silly grin and fought back giggles. Hendrix. He looked gorgeous. I lay my head on his shoulder and nestled my cheek into his shirt.

I tried to stand and almost fell over. Hendrix's father and the girls walked crookedly to the living room, giggling. Hendrix stayed at the table, gazing where his father once sat.

"Talk to me," I said. "Is it about your dad?"

"He's dying, Vita," he said. "My dad is dying, and we turned it into a game."

"He wanted to have a good time."

"I could give two fucks what he wanted, Vita. The man is dying, and instead of going to strip clubs or making drinking games out of his sickness, he should focus on his health."

"You should tell him how you feel."

"So he can tell me what? He wants to feel human? That it's his life? I've tried to reason with that man every day and want to know what he does? He turns it into a joke."

"You're right. It's not a joke."

"Why did I turn that shit into a game?"

"Baby, we were just having some fun."

"After tonight, you guys will never see him again. I have to be with him. I have to watch his health deteriorate! Nobody will be taking shots when he's resting under his beautiful palm trees. Oh no, that shit won't be funny then."

"You'll have me."

He swirled the last few cups of tequila before finishing the bottle in a shot to the head. He slammed the bottle to the table. His eyes, glassy, slowly moved to me. He laid his head on the table and stared at me with a goofy smile. He squeezed my hand.

"I love you, Vita," he said.

I smiled. "You fell?"

"I fell a long time ago."

"Me too."

"We're so bad. Don't tell anybody."

"I'm telling the world."

"You're crazy. We're crazy. We love each other." He chuckled. "We love each other. Man, I love the sound of that."

"You have to lose your mind to fall in love. Putting your complete trust and emotional well-being in the hands of someone is the craziest thing you can ever do."

"I like it."

"I like it too."

"That makes me happy."

"Good." I rubbed his head. "You look amazing tonight if I didn't say it before."

He looked to be holding his breath.

"What are you doing?" I asked.

A childlike smile came across his face as he exhaled. "How can you take my breath away so easily?"

"Still not better than what your dad said."

"What did he say?"

"He kinda ruined the whole surprise of you loving me. Not entirely, though. I loved hearing you say it."

"I love you."

I was floating, and I was sure I was blushing because my cheeks were burning up.

"Say it again," I said.

"I love you, Victoria."

"That's not my name."

"Vita."

I smiled. "Now, say it right."

"I love you, Vita."

He took my hand and stumbled from the kitchen. The girls performed their dance routines as best they could in the living room, without a stage or pole. Hendrix's father tipped them well.

The girls giggled and took a gulp apiece from a bottle of whiskey before passing it. They made out, making way too many sucking noises and using a lot of tongue. They stopped to turn to Hendrix's father and beckoned him over with lust in their eyes.

Hendrix led me into the bathroom and kicked the door shut. In the dark, he bent me over the sink. He gritted his teeth and moaned, loving my wetness covering him. My legs buckling more by the second, I let out the loudest and most high-pitched squeak.

"Shit," I said, moaning.

I wanted to tell him I loved him, how happy he made me, to never stop loving me or thrusting. All I could do was moan and curse. I lay there, taking all of him, tip to balls, moaning, and inching closer to orgasm.

"I'm going to cum," I said.

"Me too."

I didn't want the moment to end, but his moans and the love in his eyes aroused me to a knee-buckling orgasm. He dug his fingers into my waist and thrust harder and faster until his shaft pulsated and throbbed. He wanted to cum inside. I could tell that much because he pulled out at the very last second to finish on my ass. In the moment where we both gasped and sweat like crazy, we gazed at one another in the mirror.

Then he squatted and ate me from behind.

"Oh shit," I said, squirming away and laughing. "Okay. Okay."

We cleaned up, and he got dressed.

Whether it had played the entire time or we barely noticed, now, music blasted from the living room, rattling the walls, medicine cabinet, and mirror. A combination of the dancers and his father moaning and groaning cut in and out of the music.

"I see where you get it from," she said.

"Really? I'm not trying to hear all that." Hendrix sat on the floor, with his legs extended, and I lay on his lap with my head up. We gazed into each other's eyes while he played in my hair.

"Do you know what I like most about you, Vita?" He asked.

"I was hoping that you liked everything about me evenly."

"Eh."

"Oh, what happened to 'You're so perfect, Victoria? You're what God envisioned when he made angels."

"Whoa there. I never said all that. Are you perfect? Yes. But I'm not owning the other thing. That's way too cheesy."

"Like you aren't cheesy."

"Can I finish what I was saying?"

"I haven't decided yet." I smiled.

"Well, too bad. You can listen if you want."

I covered my ears with my hands. "Nah, I don't want to hear it."

"Very funny," he said.

"Fine. I guess I need some entertainment since we're locked in here. What do you like most about me?"

"You make things easier. Sometimes life gets too hectic. It starts moving so fast that I can't think, and everything starts to spin. I fall into this world where nothing makes sense, and the more I try to get out, the further I slip into the madness. When I'm with you, things are just easier. You don't take away all the anger, sadness, confusion, and uncertainty, but you do remind me that everything doesn't have to be bad."

"Whoa. I do all that?"

"And more."

"When I had Daniel, my world started to fall apart." I rolled onto my side. "I had two kids with a man who looked down on me, and he never had to say it. It was how he spoke to me like I was a kid. After my parents disowned me, I lost the little self-esteem I had left. Add in all the lying and cheating...I was a mess." I took a minute to gather my emotions. "I bet you're wondering why I stayed. I loved him. It sounds so ridiculous to say, but I did. I stayed, holding onto the small chance that Hershey woke up and realized he needed me. I didn't care if he wanted me as long as he needed me, even if it was just a nut. I watched the person I loved most, love everyone except me. And it's happening again." I paused and thought about the little girl's voice. "They had another child."

"Adopted. That girl sounded at least six."

"Adopted, pushed out of my mom's vagina. Does it matter? They have the daughter they always wanted. That's why, after all these years, they never tried to reach out. I have Facebook. Why didn't they try to reach out to me on Facebook? They have accounts. I saw them!"

He caressed my cheek. "I know exactly how you feel."

"Babe." I broke down crying. "I miss them so much."

"I can't sit here and give you advice to try to make you feel better because honestly, I don't know what to say or do. I'm right there with you."

"I need you to tell me something. Grab a toy, tell me a joke, something. Don't wait until I need you the most, not to be you."

He stayed quiet so long that I thought he somehow vanished like everyone else I loved in my life. "The truth is, we're going to care no matter how much we tell ourselves we don't. We should stop looking for their love and focus on the people who care about us. I know that's probably not what you wanted to hear." He sniffled. "I got nothing here, Vita."

"It's what I needed to hear."

"But it's not what you wanted."

The music stopped playing, and so did the moaning. Hendrix's father, singing along to Donny Hathaway's "A Song For You," broke the silence. His voice slurred in heartbreak, pain, and drunkenness.

Hendrix and I left the bathroom. His dad lay on his side in a white shirt and boxers, crying and writhing through the song. He hit a high note, and in a vocal run, his voice cracked into wailing. The dancers slept on the couch in their bras and panties. Feeling Hendrix trembling, I turned to him and noticed he cried at the sight of his father. There was nothing I could say or do to soothe his pain. Squeezing his hand felt like the most sensible thing to do.

Say something, I told myself.

What was I going to put him to ease with? I was equally a mess.

Hendrix dropped to the floor, beside his father, who put his head in Hendrix's lap. They both sobbed.

"I'm scared," his father said.

"Me too, dad," Hendrix said. "Me too."

Chapter 8
Hendrix

On the drive home, after a long day of work, my nausea finally ended. All I needed was for my head to stop throbbing.

I walked through the front door, and barely surveying the situation I entered, I was cornered by Eve. Her eyes cut deep, saying everything she wouldn't say-- couldn't say.

"What I do now?" I asked.

"To the strip club, Hendrix," she said. "Really? You took our dad to the strip club?"

"He wanted to go, so I took him."

"Listen to yourself, Hendrix. You took our sick and dying father to the strip club. For what? In what world was that a good idea? If he was that thirsty, you could've directed him to PornHub or OnlyFans. What were you thinking?"

"Look, I'll take a rain check on the dysfunction. I'm too tired for all this." I made it halfway up the stairs and stopped.

Vanessa, glaring, with her hands on her side, stood at the top, and dad leaned against the wall in the hallway, his arms crossed.

"You better get in the mood, Hendrix, because we're having this conversation now," Vanessa said. "You hear me?"

"What do you want to hear, Vanessa?" I asked. "That I'm sorry? That I was irresponsible? That no matter how much you do around here, all I do is slack off? Tell me, please, just tell me so I can say it and save everybody the drama."

"How about you take responsibility for your stupid decisions. You took our dad to the strip club, Hendrix. Do you understand how irresponsible that was?"

"I'm a grown man," dad said. "I can go wherever I want."

"Dad, I'm talking to Hendrix."

"And I'm talking to you, young lady. Sick or not, I'm still your father-I'm all of your father. I'm not a freaking child. I told my son that I wanted to go to the strip club, so if you have a problem, you come to me, and I'll tell you to get over it."

"It's not even that. I don't care what you told him. I don't even care if you went. I care that he took you. He could have told you 'no,' something any other responsible adult would have done. Hendrix never had to grow up because he never had the chance to fail. You always bail him out."

I moved past Vanessa; she grabbed my hand, and I snatched it away. I went to my room and closed the door. Vanessa and Eve barged in and stood over me as I lay down in bed.

Here it comes.

"What?" Vanessa asked. "You had that good of a time?"

"I guess so."

"Vanessa and I decided we're taking dad to his appointments from now on," Eve said.

"If that's what he wants," I said, pulling the blankets over my head.

"It's not about what he wants," Vanessa said. "It's about what's best."

"Alright. Well, he has an appointment today at 2 pm."

"I'm glad you're handling this responsibly. What's the address?"

"Ask dad. He'll tell you."

"We already asked. He won't tell us."

I didn't reply. I pretended to fall asleep, and eventually, I was. Seconds later, Vanessa snatched the blanket from over me. With my eyes closed and groaning, I rolled onto my other side. Vanessa threw the blanket into my face. I sat up, balling up the blanket, and knocked over bottles of lotions and perfumes when I threw the blanket into my dresser.

"What?" I asked.

"Oh my god, grow up," Vanessa said.

"Have you thought for a moment- for one second-why your father doesn't want to tell you something like that? Or why you even have to ask months later? You wouldn't have to ask if you paid a little more attention to your father."

"What are you trying to say, Hendrix?"

I stood and looked her in the eyes. "That you have some nerve coming back home acting all high and mighty like you've been the most caring and loving daughter in the world. Before you knew dad had cancer when was the last time you came to visit or even called, huh? I'll save you some time. It was a while-- long enough that we were more surprised when you did pick up the phone and called. It may be hard to believe, and I want you to hear me out. Dad and I have been functioning pretty damn well without you, Vanessa. You left, and the world kept spinning."

"Shut up, Hendrix."

"Do you want to know something funny?" I laughed, and when she didn't answer, I kept talking. "Dad and I knew he had cancer months before we told you. Go ahead. This is the part where you yell and scream, telling us how irresponsible we were because we didn't tell you. Oh wait, never mind, we did call, and you ignored us as usual. When we did get a hold of you, what did you tell us? What was it again? 'You'll call us back.' Yeah, that was it. Hey Vanessa, just in case you forgot, living that busy life of yours, you never called back. I guess you were too busy for the dad you love more than me!"

I violently shook as my body pumped out adrenaline.

"Hendrix," Eve said, "You need to fix your attitude because all that disrespect is unnecessary. If not out of respect for us, for dad. You know this type of environment isn't good for him."

"Oh my god. Can you stop acting like he's a freaking child?"

"He's sick."

"He isn't sick enough to take you shopping or buy you a new car," Vanessa said, shaking in anger. "You haven't been the perfect child yourself. The only time you call dad is when you blow through your rent money on clothes and makeup."

Vanessa said something. I had no idea what she said, but I knew it was to me. Suddenly, I'm telling them how I felt about them without any regard for their feelings. All of the years of anger and frustration came out of me, and I kept closing my eyes so I couldn't get a good look at their faces. Eventually, I stared directly into their eyes, going back and forth. Tears streamed down their faces, and I didn't know if it was the hangover or if I wanted to see them cry; regardless, I kept going. As they stood there speechless, I found my dad in the master bathroom, sitting on the bathroom counter, with his back against the mirror. When I came in, he gave a half-assed smile.

"About time you stood up for yourself," he said. "You feel better?"

"Not really." I sat on the edge of the tub, resting my arms across my legs and leaning forward.

"Vanessa has been out for blood since she came back. She had to figure you were going to throw a punch eventually. She just didn't figure you would use the old Rope-a-dope. Me neither. Poor Eve just got caught in the crossfire."

"I'm tired, dad. I'm just tired of being her punching bag. She was right about almost everything you said, but I don't need someone to tell me how fucked up I am. I already know."

"Give yourself some grace. You're way too hard on yourself."

"Aren't we all?"

"Some more than others."

I sighed. "Where does this family rank on the scale of dysfunction?"

"We aren't as dysfunctional as we seem. Every family has problems. Ours is finally coming to the forefront. It's the cancer."

My chest stung. "And when you..."

"-Die."

I sighed. A tight knot sat in the middle of my throat. "Yeah."

"Then the fighting ends. I'll be damned if my kids turn their backs on each other." He tapped me with the back of his hand. "Speaking of our dysfunctional family. You held up your side of the deal, so I guess I have to honor mine."

"I'm alright. She left, and I'm over it."

"Are you sure? You're a little emotional right now. Let's revisit this later. See how you feel then."

"I'm not chasing behind my mother. She wanted to leave, so I'm going to respect it."

"Oh man, I'm glad to hear you say that." He laughed nervously. "Because I have no idea where your mother is."

...

My eyes followed her every curve.

"Look at me," I said.

She gazed deep into my eyes. The moment would last forever if it were up to us.

"I want you," I said.

"I know."

"I want you so bad."

"Then why are you talking. Fuck me."

She dropped to her knees, staring at my crotch and smiling. She grabbed and stroked my dick, laughing. It hardened each time she slowly moved her hand back and forth with spit as lube. Now, rock hard, she stroked me with everything in her, and I, moaning loudly, hoped to feel the warmth of her mouth soon. The more unceasingly and loud I moaned, the harder she smiled and the harder she stroked.

The tingling sensation in my groin of a quickly approaching nut spread down my spine. One more stroke and I would have burst over her hand and my stomach. Vita stopped, hopped up, and passionately kissed me. She backed away from me and wiggled to take off her jeans. She wanted me to take her.

I kneeled and pulled down her panties to her thighs. She was ready for me. I smacked her ass, and she moaned.

"Harder," she said.

I smacked her ass harder. I could imagine just how sweet she was, and I buried my face into her, running my tongue in between her lips, licking up her wetness. She tasted fantastic, as usual.

She tried to crawl away, moaning. Oh, no. I pulled her back into my face by the thighs. She glazed my face from my nose down, and I loved it more than anything in this world. She quickly stood, pushed me back onto the bed, and with her hands rubbing my sweaty chest, she rode me as I held onto her hips for dear life.

"I'm-I'm about to cum," I said.

"I know, baby. I know."

She leaned forward, wrapping her right arm around my head, and bounced until my body went numb and my arms fell to my side. I could only moan before I burst inside of her.

She slowly lifted, and cum dribbled out. She lay beside me, spreading her legs, and fingered herself with her middle and index fingers. She deepthroated the same fingers.

"You taste good, baby," she said.

My body still limp, I lay on the damp sheets. She slid down to my partially erect dick, wrapped her lips around it, and sucked the tip with short flicks of the tongue. I squirmed in unbearable pleasure, and if I could speak, I would have had to decide if I wanted her to keep going or stop. My toes curled, and I tossed my head back, pushing it harder and harder into the pillow. I couldn't scream or moan. I just lay there trying not to make a sound. She smiled, watching me squirm.

"Oh my god," I said, breathing hard. "I love you,"

She took me from her mouth. "I love you too."

"Maybe we should get up and do something productive."

"This is productive."

"You know what I mean."

"What's wrong with lying here all day?"

"Just enjoying one another's company."

"Yeah, that would be perfect."

"Do you know what else is perfect?"

"Let me guess: me?"

"Yup."

I buried my head between her legs until she got hers too.

Chapter 9
Hendrix

The smell of the holidays took over the house, a mix of turkey, ham, and cakes. For the past 24-hours, dad and I prepared Thanksgiving dinner-or in our house, Thanksgiving breakfast, lunch, and dinner. Yesterday evening, we baked cakes and pies, washed the greens, and chopped the onions and celery for the dressing. Throughout the night before, resting our eyes for a few moments, we cooked most dishes.

Now, at 9:30 am, what looked like every pot we owned covered every inch of the stove and counters. The macaroni and cheese baked in the oven.

Through the heat, sweat blanketed me.

The songs from the CD he gave me played on his phone. Vanessa ate a slice of sweet potato pie at the kitchen table, mostly covered with cakes in bowls or wrapped in foil.

I wiped down the little counter space there was with a wet rag. Dad checked the macaroni and cheese, then sat on the couch in the living room.

He had on a black T-shirt and jeans. For some reason, he had his gun holstered.

"Oh god, dad," Vanessa said. "Do we have to do this today? On Thanksgiving? I think you're safe."

"It's my God-given right to bear arms, and I'm thankful for it," he said. "If I don't arm myself to stand against tyranny today of all days, can I call myself a Black American?"

"Who are you standing against?"

"The Native Americans got shot in the face so we can eat some turkey with our families. I'm ready to stand my ground in case anyone wakes up with pilgrim ambitions."

"This isn't back then anymore."

"Damn right, it isn't." He patted his gun. "You're damn right."

Vanessa looked at me, holding in a laugh.

"What's so funny?" I asked.

"You and that baby apron. Why do you still wear that thing?"

"I love it. Why wouldn't I still wear it?

"Look at it." She tossed a piece of pie crust into her mouth. "Don't you think you should get a new one? It's a tad bit small, don't you think?"

My dad and I wore matching aprons: white with blue writing across the chest. His read "Chef 1," mine "Chef 2." We had bought them at some store in the mall that no one ever went into-that was back when I was ten. Back then, it dragged to the ground, and now it stopped just below my waist.

"What? I happen to like my apron," I said.

"No. You don't say. That thing is looking like an ascot."

"It's not that small."

"Close enough. You should invest in a new one, seeing how that thing isn't doing much but make you look silly."

"Buy a different one? I'm going to act like I didn't hear that." I shook my head in disgust. "Buy a different one. This is the only one to buy."

"Because God forbid you wear one your size."

"Okay, Vanessa, let's say I buy a different one. How do dad and I differentiate chef one and two?"

"How will we ever know?" She stood and grabbed a glass plate from a cabinet.

"The macaroni and cheese has another ten-fifteen. Other than that, enjoy."

I washed the dishes in the sink, having to scrub hard to wipe off food that seemingly fused to them over time.

Vanessa made a plate of dressing, greens, yams, ham, green beans, and a roll, topping the mountain of food. She ate back at the table like she waited all year to eat.

The first bite terrified me the most. For years, I'd spent the holidays learning to master dad's undocumented recipes, sometimes not to a tee, which damaged my ego, although Eve and Vanessa never hated the outcome.

"How is it?" I asked.

"Great," she said, swallowing. "Hey, about the other night."

"Yeah, it kinda went off the rails. I was way out of line."

"We were all tripping. You're still annoying, but I love you."

"Love you too."

 "Did Eve say when she was coming back or where she was going, for that matter?"

"No idea. She just got up, got dressed, and left."

"How's that square going to ditch us on Thanksgiving?"

"Are you sure you haven't heard from Eve? You have a thing for not checking your messages."

"When she left, she said she would be back this afternoon. My phone is right over there. Check if you want."

A coughing spell pulled dad from his sleep. He hurried to the bathroom, holding his left shoulder. He cleared his throat and spat, with long periods of wheezing and heavy breathing in between. His coughing became rougher and drier. Soon after, gagging and throwing up. When he stopped throwing up, he gasped. After a few seconds of wheezing and heavy breathing, he threw up again. He stopped throwing up, groaned, and said, "Shit." His voice echoed from his head being in the bowl.

He hobbled from the bathroom, wiping his mouth with his arm, and lay back on the couch, groaning. For the first time since mom left, he wore his gold wedding ring.

"Dad," Vanessa said. "Dad."

He didn't answer.

"Dad, are you okay?"

He didn't answer.

She sat on the back of the couch, running her fingers across his hand, and kissed him on the cheek. She came back into the kitchen and sat on the counter beside the sink. After washing a cup, I held it out so she could grab it; water dripped onto her legs.

"Really?" She said, "you're getting me wet."

"That's disgusting, Vanessa. I'm your brother."

She used the cup to sling water into my face. "Stop being gross. You know what I meant."

"And you know dad will have a fit if he sees you on his counter." I sat the cup upside down in a pot on the dish rack.

"These dang Silestone Quartz countertops." She laughed, tapping the counter. "I remember when he got these dang things. He was so excited. They were all he talked about."

"His Silestone Quartz countertops." I chuckled, thinking about how often he mentioned them when we were younger. "I swear I saw him eating off them one night."

Her laughter became more unrestrained. "You're stupid. No, you didn't."

"I promise you. He had a sandwich-no plate or napkin. Tomato just dripping. He tried to play it cool when he saw me."

"Those were simpler times."

"No coughing. No wheezing. No gasping."

"Too bad we can't go back. Back when he wasn't sick."

"Do you ever think we're responsible for all of this?"

"What? For him being sick? Hell no. He has cancer. Don't think some shit like that."

"Cancer that he probably got because he smoked. He smoked because we stressed him out."

"We aren't our mother."

"Why did she have to go?"

"She didn't choose to die, Hendrix."

Guilt weighed on my shoulders; I was a few seconds from telling the truth. "Yeah."

"He smoked because he lost his wife. He would just stand out on the porch, staring down the street. It was like he was waiting for her to pull back into the driveway."

"Do you remember when she died?"

She shook her head. "Only what dad told us about the accident."

"But you were seven. You had to remember something. A wake? A funeral? Something."

"Dad said mom never wanted a funeral. Let him tell it; she always wanted to be cremated. I asked to see her after the accident, but he told me that I was too young."

"It just doesn't make sense."

"It does now. I've accepted it. I don't think I would have been able to handle seeing her on a table, dead."

"Hear me out, though, did anybody see her dead body other than dad? What hospital was she taken to? What happened to the car? Where's the death certificate?"

"Hendrix, don't do this to yourself. It's not healthy."

"I used to hear you praying for God to send her back."

"That was a long time ago."

"He never answered."

"Even He isn't that almighty."

I wanted to tell her. I tried to tell her so badly. I balled my hands, which were still in the warm water, into fists. I looked back and forth between the dishwater and Vanessa, gritting my teeth and trying to find the words to tell her mom was still alive.

Mom isn't dead, I said to myself. It's not that hard, Hendrix. Don't be like dad. She needs to know. She deserves to know mom never died. Just tell her, you pussy.

I pulled my hands from the water and snatched a towel from the drawer below the dish rack. I paced across the kitchen, stopping to bang my head on the refrigerator.

She's not dead, I thought. She's not dead.

Just as Vanessa put her hand on my shoulder, the front door opened, and Eve shouted all our names. A set of footsteps accompanied hers. Unlike the light clicks from her heels against the floor, the second set made a thumping noise.

A clean-cut Hispanic man wearing a white dress shirt tucked into his black slacks stood with her. She had on a woven white dress and black heels. They were holding hands.

Dad sat up on the couch.

"Marc, I want you to meet my family," Eve said. "This is my twin brother, Hendrix, my sister, Vanessa, and that handsome man on the couch is my father. Family, this is Marc."

Marc, in a rush, jogged to dad and shook his hand.

"Nice to finally meet you, sir," Marc said.

"Dad isn't feeling too well today," Eve said.

"On Turkey Day? That has to be one of the worst feelings. I hope you feel good enough to enjoy some turkey, at least."

Marc exchanged introductions with Vanessa and me before Eve insisted on giving him a tour of the house. She took her time presenting the Harper family history or sharing a fond memory of every room and decor piece. They walked upstairs, their footsteps loudly thumping.

Vanessa and I turned to one another at the same time.

"Marc," Vanessa said. "Since when did she have a whole boyfriend?"

"Fantastic question."

"This is an Eve thing to do."

Her bland tone made it difficult to tell if she had an attitude or not.

"I'm bringing my lady."

"That's different. Dad knew about your girlfriend. Nobody knew this guy existed until right now."

Eve and Marc came back into the kitchen to end their grand tour. She went on about the Silestone granite countertops that dad got when she and I were twelve. Vanessa and I sat on the loveseat in the living room. Dad, lying on his side, staring at the wall, rolled onto his other side. I heard smacking as Eve and Marc kissed, and looking at them, I saw their tongues going in and out of each other's mouths. They walked to the back of the couch and stared down at dad. Eve kissed him on the cheek.

The alarm on my phone went off. *Shit, the mac, and cheese.* Dad and I jumped up to check on the macaroni and cheese. I looked over his shoulder, and the heat rising from the oven sizzled my face and arms. The edges of the macaroni and cheese were black, and the top was browned. Dad used a folded-up towel to take the dish from the oven and place it on a trivet. Then he lay back down on the couch.

Vita called. She said she was turning onto the street, and I went outside just to meet her at the curb. She wore an indigo long-sleeved dress, black boots, and a black fedora, with a small brim.

"You're early," I said.

"I hope that's okay."

"I get to see you more. That's definitely not a problem."

"We have dinner at 6' back at the house. I wanted to come early to spend as much time with your family as possible."

"I can't believe you went back."

"Only temporarily. I need to save enough money for my own place and then find a way to break the news to the boys. I think Martin is starting to suspect something is wrong. He walked in on me, sleeping in the guest room the other night."

"We got this."

"We do." She checked out my apron. "So, what's up with the baby apron?"

"My dad bought this when I was younger. He's chef one. Every time we cook together, we wear our matching aprons."

"Look at my baby being all adorable again."

We walked inside, hand in hand.

"How's your dad feeling?" She asked.

"Eh. Thanksgiving is always hard on him."

"Mom-related?"

"It's his and my mom's anniversary."

"Oh."

"Yeah. He tends to mope around, but it hasn't been this bad. He hasn't said a word all morning."

"This must be torture for him."

"Maybe we can take him to another club."

"Oh, gosh. I'm done with alcohol."

Hand in hand, we stepped into the kitchen. Vanessa was the first to greet Vita, and then everyone else said their 'helloes,' hugging and exchanging their names.

I went upstairs to my room to get dressed; Vita came with me. She picked out a burgundy sweater and black pants. Back downstairs, everyone sat in the living room with glasses of wine; Eve and Marc sat on the loveseat, Vanessa in a chair in the corner, dad still on the couch. Vita and I sat on the floor, our legs crossed.

We conversed about what we did for a living, and Vita and I were the only ones who didn't have some long fancy title, so far up the hierarchy that they made their own schedules, including deciding to work remotely. The conversation turned to relationships. Eve and Marc shared they met on a dating site and casually dated for three years; however, it didn't get serious until earlier this year. Marc, born and raised in Fontana, relocated to Texas after college for a job.

Marc had his arm around Eve and his legs crossed. He took a sip of wine.

"How did you two meet?" Marc asked Vita and me.

"I'm dying to know that myself," Eve said.

"We met at school," Vita said.

"Awww, high school sweethearts, aye?" Marc said.

"No, college. We met this quarter."

When dad sat up, groaning, turning everyone's attention to him.

"All this love in the air is beautiful," he said. "It reminds me of a time when I was young and in love. Thirty-two years ago today, I married the woman of my dreams."

"Lucky woman," Marc said. "I bet you were a stud back in your day."

"I like to think she finds me handsome. Found me handsome. She left me."

Eve and I got up at the same time and sandwiched him on the couch. She held his hand.

"Mom died in a car accident when we were younger," Eve said, looking at Marc.

"Dead," dad said. "Left me. It's all the same. She's gone all the same."

"Oh, daddy. You have to stop doing this to yourself. She's dead."

Grunting, he looked at Vita. "Do you still have that ring?"

"What ring?"

"Of course, you don't. What am I thinking? Why would you? You're with Hendrix now."

"I mean, I still have it."

"He didn't take it?" His eyes lit up. "Next time you visit, I would love to see her ring again."

"I thought you had her ring."

"I do." His eyes weren't bright anymore, and he leaned down back onto the couch. "I wanted to compare the two. That's all."

"Am I missing something here?" Eve asked. "What ring are you talking about?" She looked at Vita when dad didn't answer. "What ring are you two talking about?"

"Your mother's ring. I have a ring that's identical to the one your dad gave your mom."

"How do you know that?"

"I saw your dad in the grocery store a few weeks ago. I didn't know he was your dad then. He saw my ring and said it was the same one he gave his wife."

"Dad," Vanessa said, "I thought you didn't have mom's ring. Why haven't you shown us?"

"It's not important," dad said.

"It kinda is, Dad. Why wouldn't I want to see my mother's ring?"

"Let's see it," Eve said.

"Not today, girls. My heart can't take it."

Vanessa and Eve stood.

"Where are you going, babe?" Marc asked.

"To see my mother's ring," Eve said.

They hurried to dad's room. His attempts to get up to stop them ended with him grimacing and dropping back onto the couch. He looked at me helplessly and worriedly, and I ran after them.

Eve and Vanessa rummaged through his nightstands to pull out stacks of papers, envelopes, and pictures. When they didn't find anything, they made their way to his counter, which had all his jewelry. I blocked them.

"Are you seriously going to ransack his entire room for a ring?" I asked.

"It's not just a ring.' It's mom's ring," Vanessa said. "He always does this. He always conveniently forgets something like this. Why wouldn't he tell us he had mom's ring?"

"Why wouldn't he have it?"

"Hendrix, dad will pull out their wedding photos with the quickness. He has her ring. You don't find it odd he never showed us?"

"Photos are one thing. Maybe seeing the ring hits different."

"It hurts so much to see her ring that he's begging to see a ring that looks like it? Okay."

"I don't know. People are weird."

"Dad is weird."

"Exactly."

"Aren't you at least curious?"

"To be honest, no."

"Well, we are."

"Haven't you seen it already? I mean, you were seven when she died. You of all of us should remember."

"That was years ago."

"I can't believe he never mentioned her ring before," Eve said. "I can't believe we didn't either."

"It didn't even cross my mind until now."

"See," I said. "We can't be upset at him for forgetting."

"I can promise you he didn't forget."

"It's dad. You know he's extra. Come on, y'all, it's Thanksgiving. Let's get some turkey in us and enjoy being around loved ones. We can turn dad's room upside down another day, okay?"

"Fine. But the turkey better be good."

"Duh. I cooked it."

About halfway down the stairs, we heard dad going on about mom. We hurried into the living room. Vita and Marc sat on each side of dad, looking down at his phone. We stood behind the couch and watched dad scroll through wedding pictures we had never seen before. When he got to a picture of mom holding out her hand to show her ring while he stuffed his face with cake, he stopped and stared at it. He wasn't lying. Mom and Vita's rings looked identical.

"Jeez," Marc said. "How much was that ring?"

"More than a few paychecks," dad said. "I tell you one thing, though, she was worth the blood, sweat, and tears."

"I bet she was a happy woman."

"She was." He smiled. "She was. That was thirty-two years ago."

"Are you ready to see how the food turned out?" I asked him.

"You all grab a plate," dad said. "I'll get something later."

Everyone, except our dad, made a plate and sat down at the kitchen table. I sat beside Vita; Eve and Marc were on the opposite side, and Vanessa was at the head of the table. Eve, Marc, and Vanessa poured themselves more wine while Vita and I drank cranberry juice. Eve and Marc fed each other, and Vanessa watched in disgust. No one spoke, and the only sounds were the heater and forks clanking against plates. Vita didn't have much on her plate, and when she finished, she went back for more.

Dad lay back down on the couch during a coughing spell. When he stopped, he gasped for air.

And we went on like it didn't happen.

"I have to know," Marc said. "Who cooked this food? This is some of the best cooking I've had in my life."

"Chef 1 and Chef 2," Vita said, pointing in the direction of my dad and me. "I didn't know you had it in you, Hendrix."

"Don't give me too much credit," I said. "I'm lost in the kitchen without my dad. I just follow his lead. That's why I'm chef 2. All the praises should go to him."

"Is it possible for me to speak with the chefs?" Marc asked. "Privately."

"I can save you some time," Eve said. "If you're looking for recipes, look elsewhere. I can't even get Chef 1 and 2 to tell me their secrets."

"I respect the sanctity of a family recipe. I just need a quick word with your brother and father. No need to bore you fine ladies with guy talk." He stood.

"Now?" I asked. "Like right now?"

"It will only take a second."

We stepped outside. Dad and I sat--him, in his wicker chair.

Marc's body tensed, and he stuttered at the sight of dad's Glock 48.

"You can ask away whenever you're ready," dad said. "Unless you're going to force me to stand my ground, you're fine."

"I'll make this quick," Marc said, staring at dad's hip. "I love Eve, and she loves me. And we love each other."

"I get it. There is a lot of love passed around between you and Eve. Trust me--I heard the kissing."

"I've been meaning to ask her something important for some time now. Listening to you speak about your wife only exacerbated my desire to be with your daughter." He nodded at me. "Your sister...for the rest of my life. With your blessings, of course."

"To tell you the truth, I have no idea who you are. Eve never mentioned you, not once."

"Not even in passing," I said.

"And here you are at my house on Thanksgiving, my favorite holiday, on my anniversary, asking me to give my daughter away to a stranger."

"That's pretty bold, Marc."

Dad stood and stepped to Marc. "What did you expect me to say?" He paused and snapped, searching for Marc's name. "Marc, right?"

"Yes, sir," Marc said.

"You didn't answer my question, Marc."

"Sir. I expected you to be a little hesitant because you are right; you don't know me."

"If we're being honest here…Can I be honest with you, Marc?"

"Of course. I'm asking a lot right now. It's best if we are as transparent, given the situation."

"I'm leaning towards a 'no,' Marc."

"With all respect, sir, I can't accept your answer."

"You expected me to be hesitant."

"I also expected you to say 'yes.'"

"Why?"

"Because I love her."

"Well, we hope you love her, Marc," I said. "You want to marry her."

"My entire life, I dreamt of a woman like Eve. When we met, I knew I didn't want anyone else. I want to be her everything and more."

"Do you promise to love her forever?"

"Yes."

"Through thick and thin?"

"Absolutely."

"Even through the good and the bad?"

"Of course."

"I do."

"Huh?"

"I do, too," dad said.

Marc looked at dad. "Wh-what?"

"I now pronounce us Father-in-law and son-in-law. Congratulations, Marc. Welcome to the family." He patted Marc on the shoulder, grinning, and walked inside.

"Was that a 'yes?'"

"Mmhmm," I said, putting my hand on his trembling shoulder. "My sister means the world to me, Marc. If you want to marry her, then I'm going to go out on a limb and say, she means the world to you. I don't know anything about you except your name, but if Eve loves you, I love you."

"Thanks, man." He pulled me into a hug.

We came into the house. Marvin Gaye's "I Want You" played on dad's phone in the living room.

Eve waited in the archway of the kitchen. Marc pulled her into his arms. The best way to describe their kisses was sickening.

Dad went upstairs, and I went back into the family room. Vanessa was gone. Vita ate a slice of pound cake, dancing, admiring the water-colored paintings on the walls. One was a portrait of a girl smiling. That thing always gave me the creeps.

I held her from behind, and together, we swayed from side to side to the music. She fed me a piece of cake. In a perfect world, we would relive that moment in a white dress and a tux.

"What was all that about?" She asked.

"I'll tell you later. Have I ever told you how much I love the smell of your hair?"

"Maybe. You tell me so many flattering things that it's hard to remember them all."

"Have I told you I love you today?"

"Now that I don't remember."

"Well, I love you."

"I love you too."

She turned around and rested her head on my chest as I held her tightly.

Eve and Marc walked into the family room.

"Aww, you two are adorable," Eve said.

"Thanks, sis," I said.

"You're welcome, Hen-Hen."

"Can we not do this right now?"

Eve laughed. "But that's your name. Don't be embarrassed, Hen-Hen. Your girlfriend needs to know your real name sooner or later."

"Hen-Hen?" Vita asked.

"Please don't call me that," I said.

"Why not? It's cute."

"No, it's not. It's stupid, and I hate it, but for some reason, they insist on calling me it."

"Calm down, Hen-Hen." She pinched my cheeks.

She looked so cute, I thought. Don't smile, Hendrix, I said to myself. Don't smile. If you do, she'll never stop calling you that dumb name.

Vita walked to the kitchen, giggling. My dad and Vanessa came back downstairs, and he started to fix himself a plate. Vita offered to do so. He agreed and sat down at the table. She brought him his plate and joined me.

Marc looked around. He had his hand in his pocket and had a look in his eye that told he planned to propose right there.

"Don't be this tacky, Marc," I whispered to myself.

"Can I have everyone's attention for a second?" He asked.

He gave this drawn-out speech about how he never knew what love was before meeting Eve and that he was glad to have met her. Halfway through, Eve put the pieces together and grabbed his hand, ugly crying, making him do the same. He could barely talk from all the sobbing and stuttering.

It felt like a stage play. Dramatic.

Eventually, Marc dropped to one knee and finally pushed out the words, "Will you marry me?"

Eve covered her mouth as she squeaked and screamed, "I do. I do."

She erupted into his arms, and they kissed.

The ring wasn't from *Tiffany's* or big as Mom's, and that's saying a lot because it hurt my bank account just looking at the thing. Eve ran around, shoving her hand into our faces like we couldn't see it from across the room. She was crying and screaming, and the entire time she sounded like she was hyperventilating. She ran to Marc, and he picked her up and spun her around. When he sat her down, they discussed wedding ideas. Using Pinterest, they decided on tangerine, orange, and yellow as their colors. Marc wanted to have their first dance to John Legend, "All of me." Then they stopped talking and stared into one another's eyes. Eve let out a loud squeak and jumped back into Marc's arms.

Dad ate the entire time. He never looked up from his plate. When he finished eating, he poured himself a cup of Orange juice and drank it back at the table.

Eve stood beside him.

"Daddy," she said.

"Yes, sweetheart," he said.

"I'm getting married. Can you believe it?"

"I can't say that I do."

"Daddy, I know a lot is going on, and this may sound tacky...please hear me out. Traditionally, the bride's family pays for the wedding-"

"Seriously, Eve," Vanessa said.

"As I was saying, daddy. Traditionally, you would have to pay for the wedding. Marc and I aren't traditionalists."

"Clearly."

Eve rolled her eyes. "We might need some help, though."

"You are seriously asking your sick father to pay for your wedding?"

"I don't want him to pay for my wedding. I just need his help." She turned to dad. "Let's just ignore her, daddy. Now, back to the wedding. Marc and I already have a lot of ideas, and I know you'll love them."

"Eve, can I talk to you upstairs?"

"As far as colors go, we're thinking about tangerine, orange and yellow. Well, you probably heard that-"

"Eve, now."

Eve rolled her eyes and kept talking about her wedding. She mentioned getting mom's ring, and Vanessa called her a "self-proclaimed princess."

"Well, at least I'm not a bitch."

"You know what, Eve?" Vanessa got into Eve's face.

"What?"

"You think you're so goddamn special. I'm sick of this princess shit."

"Be sick. No one cares what you think, Vanessa. All you do is huff and puff and try to blow down everyone's house. Are you so unhappy with your life that you have to try to ruin everyone else's? That's why you're the only one here without someone to go home to at night, other than dad, but at least he has a reason! What's your reason, Vanessa? That you're so ornery that no one wants to be around you? Jesus Christ, buy a vibrator, suck a dick, or shut the hell up because I'm tired of hearing you bitch!"

"Can we not do this today?" Dad asked.

They refused to shut up or calm down. Words transitioned into pushing. Eve knocked into dad when Vanessa pushed her. Marc got in between them, and they shoved him out the way with ease.

Dad didn't look like he was breathing. His eyes glazed over as he sat there, almost in a trance from the foolishness.

Eve and Vanessa kept yelling. Dad, with his hands shaking, tossed a cigarette from his pocket into his mouth. He rolled down the spark wheel of a lighter he pulled from his pocket, but he moved too slowly to gain enough force to ignite a flame. He kept trying. Nothing.

I kneeled beside him, waving my hand in his face.

"Dad, are you there?" I asked. "Dad, can you hear me?" I glared at Vanessa and Eve. "Attention, Eve and Vanessa, you're upsetting, dad!"

They wouldn't stop yelling, and the more they screamed, the heavier he breathed. For a second, I thought he had a heart attack.

"Dad," I said, hectically tapping his leg. "Dad? Dad, say something." I turned to Eve and Vanessa. "Guys, shut up!" I turned to dad. "I didn't mean to yell."

The air in my lungs thinned. I paced, trying to think. I couldn't gather my thoughts with all the screaming.

Is it finally happening, I thought. Is he dying? Should I call 911? This is what he wanted. This is what I wanted.

"Can we not do this right now," he said. "Please, not today. I don't want to do this. Not today. Not today."

Vita went to grab my dad's hand to move him away from the fighting, and he snatched his arm away. He stood, unholstered his Glock, and lay the muzzle against the side of his head.

Other than me, everything stopped: the time, Marc, Vita, Vanessa, Eve. My legs wobbled as I paced. In the deadly silence, I heard my heart pound.

"I haven't been going to my treatments," dad said.

"What?" Vanessa said.

"Since we're showing our asses and all."

Victoria

The door opened enough for Hershey to stick out his head.

I leaned forward, rubbing my arms. My teeth chattered to the cold wind that pierced my skin.

"I know," I said, "I'm late."

"Knowing something doesn't mean much without the appropriate actions."

"Something came up. I tried to leave, but I couldn't."

"Something more important than your family?"

"There isn't anything in this world more important than my family."

"Then why weren't you here?"

"I already told you. There was an emergency. I couldn't leave him alone."

"So that's where you were? You picked a man over your family." He closed his eyes and nodded. "I see. Goodnight, Victoria." He closed the door.

The door locked. I unlocked the door, pulled down on the lever, and pushed; it didn't budge.

"Hershey," I whispered. "Hershey, open the door. I'm freezing my ass off out here."

"Enjoy the cold. You're going to miss it when you burn in hell."

I ran back to the car, holding my fedora on my head. In the car, I rocked back and forth, running my hands together. I started the car and turned on the heater. It took a few minutes before the car was no longer blowing cold air. The air vents pointed towards me, and the heat, on the highest level, toasted my skin. A great feeling that quickly burned. I turned the heater off and sat in my car, feeling the rumble from the engine. The wind whistled and pushed against the car.

It was in the 9 o'clock hour. I didn't know the exact time-I hadn't looked since I left Hendrix's house at 8:27 pm. It wasn't late, and I told myself that I could go back to Hendrix's home. At Least I felt wanted there.

When I had left earlier, Martin and Daniel stood by the door, and the sadness on their faces was the last thing I saw. That was then. Now, I looked up, hearing the door close. Hershey came around the walkway. He held the car handle until I unlocked the door, and he got inside. He leaned forward, blowing into his hands.

"I need you to be honest with me," he said. "No bullshit. No sugarcoating. Is this the end for us?"

"It looks like it."

"Come on, kiddo."

"Don't call me that."

"Jesus." He sighed. "Two months ago, life made sense. What happened to us?"

"You had sex with another woman."

He sat, nodding his head repeatedly. "Life comes at you fast. I didn't believe it until now. My kiddo isn't my baby anymore.."

"I'm the mother of your children, not one of them."

"Victoria, can you relax for a second? It's a nickname. No different than honey or babe." He thought to himself. "You're right. You aren't a child."

"Thank you."

He sniffed and wiped his eyes with his hands. His demeanor made me uneasy. I heard him sobbing as I stared at our home, as I thought back to the years I cried in bed while he went out with other women.

Years of lying and cheating came to this. He called out for me in a soft and high-pitched voice. He felt my pain-or at least I hoped. I wished that when he caught a reflection of himself in the window, he questioned if he was good or beautiful enough to be loved other than when it was convenient or when he wiped the tears from his eyes, he hoped the person who caused them would never hurt him again. I expected the last few weeks of sleeping alone felt like torture and made him realize how much value I added to his life.

He broke down into whimpers.

I turned my body to him and watched him try to hide his face with his coat.

"I can't feel sorry for you," I said. "You had me. All you had to do was love me, and I was yours forever."

"I'm not looking for sympathy. I'm looking for my wife."

"You don't have a wife, Hershey. You had a little girl too stupid to realize you never appreciated her. She waited and waited for the lies and cheating to end so that she could be your wife. You never stopped. Unfortunately for you, that girl grew up."

He moved his coat from his face and stared into my eyes. The lights from a passing car revealed his face. Now, I saw his eyes swollen with tears. I had to look away.

"I want to try again," he said.

"There isn't anything to try. You and I are over."

"I want to try this family thing again."

"Thing, huh?" I chuckled.

"I want to be a family, Victoria. You, me, Daniel, and Martin."

"We'll always be a family, Hershey." I put my hand on his shoulder, and he looked up, smiling. "But not in the way you want. You made that dream impossible."

"And Hendrix made it real?"

I stayed quiet.

"Kiddo, please."

"For Christ's sake, stop calling me Kiddo! I'm not your kiddo!"

"Please don't do this to our family."

"Do what? Be happy? Find someone who appreciates me?"

"This! I fucked up. Every day, I wake up sick to my stomach at the idea of losing you? I know what I did, Victoria, and I'm sorry! You hear me? I'm sorry for cheating!" He recomposed himself, breathing heavily. "I'm sorry, baby. I strained this family, but you don't have to break it. The kids need us together. I need you, Victoria."

"But you don't want me."

He grabbed my hand, rubbing it against his face wet with tears, kissing my palm. "I want you."

"I've waited years to hear you say those words."

"I want you. I want you. I swear to God, I want you and no one else."

I pulled my hand away. "It's too late, Hershey."

Neither of us spoke. I listened to the wind and rustling of the trees. My head was down, and I glanced at Hershey. He gazed outside the window, still sniffling.

I remembered the first time I met Hershey. I was so young and dumb, hoping for the best from a world I didn't understand. Young enough to fall in love with the first cute guy who showed interest. Stupid enough to convince myself I was still in love with the cute guy who wanted everyone else. I thought back to the first time we had sex. He wanted it more than me. He had his hands in between my thighs, which I had clenched together.

I love you.

My destiny.

Forever.

He repeated the same tired words every time he knew he was losing me throughout the years. The first time he used "forever" was when he popped back up after leaving after learning I was pregnant with Daniel. Three summers before that day, he came over every day when my mom and dad were at work. We spent the entire day together, falling in love. Back then, he came up with my pet name: kiddo.

He sighed.

"I love you," he said. "You're my destiny. You may not believe it, but you're my first, last, and forever."

I chuckled.

"What's funny?"

"Nothing. I'm sorry."

His words sounded sincere. After he repeated himself several times, I realized he meant it. He loved me. He thought we were destined to be together forever. Most importantly, he wanted to be with me forever. A somber feeling wiped the smirk off my face.

"Do you mean that?" I asked.

"I never meant something more in my life." He looked at me and held my hand.

I looked down at our hands together, realizing they interlocked, and we gripped tightly. The little girl inside me kept them together.

Don't be stupid, Vita, I told myself. This is what he does. He tells you everything you want to hear to get you, and when you come running back like an idiot, he hurts you again. He doesn't love you, you aren't his destiny, and he damn sure doesn't want you forever. Look at him, though.

I've never seen him like this before- crying, heartbroken. This wasn't the Hershey I knew. I never saw him this passionate.

Victoria, I thought, maybe he does love you. Maybe you are his destiny. Maybe he does want you in his life forever.

I went back and forth with myself until my head throbbed.

"Have I told you I loved you?" He asked. "I'm ashamed to admit that I never valued you. I had everything I could want or need at home, and it wasn't enough for me. I can't take it all back no matter how much I want to, but I would in a heartbeat. I hurt you. More importantly, I betrayed your trust, love, and this family. I know it won't be easy to regain your love and trust, Victoria. I'm willing to try again and I hope you're feeling the same."

"Hershey, I can't."

"Don't second guess love. You mean the world to me. Give me one more chance to prove I'm the husband you believed me to be. That's all I need. I swear we can be a family forever--you, Martin, Daniel, and I. No one else."

My hand trembled, and he leaned in for a kiss. I snatched my hand away and moved my head back. I turned towards him, my feet in the seat, my chin on my arms, which lay over my knees.

"I'm sorry," I said.

"You don't love me anymore."

"I love Hendrix."

He fell back into the seat, sighing. "What do we tell them?

"The truth. We tell them we aren't happy."

"I'm unhappy because you want to leave. If you stay, I'll be the happiest man in the world."

"Then, I'll be unhappy."

He sighed again and rubbed his head. "When do we tell them?"

"The sooner, the better. They already know something is going on. We might as well tell them now. No need to delay the conversation."

"What about tomorrow?"

"I get off at four. I can head straight over."

He opened the car door and went to get out until he heard me pull my seatbelt. He turned back to me. The coldness of the air, pushing into the car, sent a shiver down my spine.

"You're leaving?" He asked.

"I think it would be best if I didn't stay. The boys might get the wrong idea."

"We would hate to make them happy."

"Hershey." I placed my hand on his knee, and it wasn't romantic, yet, he took it as such because he tried to hold my hand; I pulled it away. "I didn't choose a man over, my sons. A friend tried to commit suicide. I figured it was best if he wasn't alone. He needed me."

"So did your children." He got out and slammed the car door.

I sat in the driveway for ten minutes, nursing the stinging feeling in my chest. To the pain, I lay my head on the steering wheel. When the pain eased a bit, I left. For two hours, I drove through the city. The lights, coming and going, as I drove past, felt hotter and seemed brighter. After, I ended up at Hendrix's house. Endless thoughts swirled through my head. I called, and he let me inside, where I curled into a ball in his bed. I tossed and turned most of the night, and eventually, I stopped trying. As Hendrix slept, I read articles on the effects of divorce on children.

I lay next to the man I loved as I thought about another man. Hendrix always made me happy, except at that moment.

Tomorrow, I'm going to break my boy's hearts, I thought. They're going to hate me. That's at best. At worst, they fall into a depression or lash out in violence, according to the articles. I don't want to break their hearts, but it's either theirs or mine right now.

...

Hershey waited at the end of the driveway, his hands on his hips. He did a poor job of hiding his stress. He walked to the car and opened my door. He smiled without showing teeth, trying his best not to say anything offensive.

"There's no coming back from this, Victoria," he said.

I nodded.

He sighed, closing his eyes, and massaged his eyes. "There isn't anything that will make you reconsider?"

"Afraid not."

I got out of the car, and together, we walked into the house that I wanted as a home. I expected to hear the patter of feet against the floor upstairs, Daniel screaming and yelling at the top of his lungs for no reason, and the noises from Martin's video games blasting from the television. No one or nothing made a sound inside.

"They, uh, had a busy day with grandma," he said. "They went Black Friday shopping, so I let them take a nap. And don't worry, it's only been thirty minutes. I won't let them sleep over an hour. I know you don't like that."

I stood by the door, looking around, and Hershey motioned with his hand for me to join him in the living room. He sat on the arm of the couch.

Once designated for special occasions, the living room looked lived in with smudges and handprints on the glass coffee table, footprints on the red oriental rug, tiny stains on the white couch, and the silk drapes still pulled back to let the sun in were wrinkled. The dysfunction caused by the whirlwind that was my children was too much to take in at first glance. I hesitantly sat in the living room, my body sunk into the couch cushions. Crumbs dug into my hands.

"How was work?" He asked.

I wore my uniform, and I smelled like fries and burgers.

"It was work," I said. "Is it okay if I take a shower?"

"Victoria, this is your home, no matter what happens to us. You don't have to ask to do anything."

I went upstairs and peeked into Martin's room. Martin and Daniel lay asleep in bed. Daniel sprawled out, snored, and Martin slept in the fetal position. I slowly walked towards the bed, and the floor creaked as I leaned over and kissed them on the cheeks. I went into Hershey's room to shower-it used to be our room.

As the water warmed, I strolled around the room that always felt more like mine than his. The room was dirty from the lost opportunity of us being a family. If he tried harder, I wouldn't have been visiting my own home; I wouldn't have been so uncomfortable; I wouldn't have locked the door. If we tried harder, we could have been a family, him cooking and me cleaning as the kids slept.

The water steaming and fogging the mirrors snapped me out of my daze. I hopped into the shower, letting the hot water run over me as I watched the door in the mirror in the small chance Hershey tried to enter. The emotions were too much not to cry. When I stopped crying, I ventured downstairs in a shirt and jeans from the closet. He never cleared out my closet--our closet.

Hershey still sat on the arm of the couch, looking down. I sat down on the couch.

"I should wake them up," he said, standing.

I grabbed his hand, and he interlocked our fingers. "I'll go with you."

He sighed. "Here we go. The end of our family."

"Do you remember what we're going to tell them?"

"That we're unhappy."

"Let's try to make this as easy as possible for them. We need to make sure that we're honest with them, though we don't want to go into full detail about everything. We need to make sure that they know that you and I will still be here for them no matter what. We need to tell them about any changes that are going to happen. We also need to make sure we are civil. That's most important. We don't need them to think we hate each other."

"I need for this not to happen."

I stayed quiet.

He sighed. "I don't think I need a reminder to be civil, Victoria."

"You weren't civil last time. I was just making sure."

I led him upstairs. Halfway down the hall, Hershey stopped. I tried to keep walking, but he wouldn't let go of my hand, and his feet planted on the ground.

"Hershey, you're hurting my hand," I said.

"Victoria, you need to stop this right now." He spoke with bass. "We're a damn family!"

"It's over."

"Because you want it to be over. It doesn't have to be over, Victoria. Jesus! We can work through all of this shit."

"Not anymore."

"We can, baby. All you have to do is give me a second chance. Give us a second chance. Don't walk away from us."

"I'm not leaving them. I'm leaving you. I'm tired of having this conversation, Hershey. There's nothing you can do or say that can change my mind. I've made my decision."

He let go of my hand, and his arms fell to his side. Just as we walked into Martin's room, they sat up in bed, yawning. They smiled when they saw me, and with a burst of energy, bum-rushed me.

"Mommy," Martin said, wrapping his arms around me. "You didn't come back yesterday. What happened?"

"Mommy had an emergency," I said.

"What's that?" Daniel asked.

"Something really scary happened."

"Scary? Was it a monster?"

"No, mommy didn't see any monsters."

"Then what was so scary? A ghost? Did you see a ghost?"

"No ghosts either, baby."

"Daddy sees a ghost." He laughed. "Booooo." He ran over to Hershey.

Hershey picked up Daniel and sat down on the edge of the bed. Daniel wasn't wrong. Hershey did look like he saw a ghost.

"Mommy, are you going to be home today?" Daniel asked.

I sat beside Hershey and extended my hand to Martin. Martin took my hand and climbed on my lap.

"You know that Mommy hasn't been home a lot lately," I said. "Well, Mommy and Daddy have decided that it would be best if I have my own house. You'll still get to see me. Every week you can come over and hang out with Mommy."

"Will you still cook me and Martin dinner?" Daniel asked.

"Mommy and Daddy will both make dinner, honey. How does that sound? Two meals. Doesn't that sound like fun?"

"Who's going to wash my clothes?"

"Mommy and Daddy will wash your clothes."

"Are you leaving because I hit Martin yesterday?"

"No, of course not." I held back tears. "It's not because you hit Martin. But don't think that's an open invitation to hit your brother."

Martin hopped from my lap and looked back and forth between Hershey and me.

"You're getting a divorce?" He asked.

Neither Hershey nor I could respond.

"Is it because of us?"

"No, sweetheart." I hugged Martin. "Mommy isn't leaving because of you or Daniel. I love you both so much."

"Then why are you getting a divorce? Can't you stay together?"

"Sometimes, things happen. Mommy and Daddy are not happy anymore. You or Daniel didn't do anything."

They bombarded me with questions, and I couldn't think of the right words to speak. As long as I didn't blink, the tears would stay lodged in my eyes. They had the same heartbroken expression on their face as Hershey. He wouldn't talk. I needed him to say something, so I had the chance to think. I looked at him several times, hoping that he would help explain to Martin and Daniel that they weren't to blame. He didn't. I extended my hand to Martin, refusing to take it, too busy looking at Hershey. Then he looked at me. He never took my hand.

Hendrix

One of our regular hostesses forked over the menus. She was young, probably younger than me, with red hair and blonde eyebrows.

Dad and I sat next to each other. What was the point of looking at our menus? We knew what we wanted.

Eve and Vanessa stared intently at theirs, flipping to the end and starting over at the beginning. The waitress we get most days walked to the table, with her notepad in hand, and when she saw Dad and me, she smiled.

"I brought the entire family today," dad said.

"Is that right?" She said, putting her hands on her hips and looking over the family. "What brought the entire family to this old place on Black Friday? I remembered the days where we ate leftovers for at least a week. Sometimes we were halfway to Christmas before we cleaned out those containers."

"Oh, trust me, we have lots of leftovers. Hendrix and I cooked up a storm. Dressing, yams, greens, mac and cheese, you name it."

"I know where I'll be later tonight."

"Still, sometimes you just want some good ole' fashioned pancakes."

"I heard that. I take it you boys are getting the 'the regular?'"

"Absolutely. Sometimes I wonder why Hendrix and I even get menus."

"Formalities, honey. How about you beautiful ladies? What can I get you?" She took Vanessa and Eve's orders and went back into the kitchen.

Eve took in her surroundings. Not too many people visited. In a corner booth, three men drank coffee quietly. The waiters and waitresses stood around at the front counter, laughing and joking about their day. The chefs in the kitchen sounded like they had a good time as well. Music played faintly from over the speakers. The table beside us had stacks of dirty dishes. A kitchen helper came, put the dishes in a gray plastic container, and headed back to the kitchen. The dishes rattled together as he walked.

A somberness clouded over us. It cast over our thoughts and everything we wanted to say. We sat in silence, where we didn't even want to look at one another.

Eve built enough courage to look at dad, who moved his eyebrows up and down.

"The regular, huh?" She asked. "You two must come here a lot."

"I wasn't exaggerating," dad said. "We come here every time."

"Every time? You never went to a single appointment?"

"There were never any appointments."

"Have you ever been to the doctor?"

"Nope. When I heard the news, I just-"

"Gave up?"

"If that's what you want to call it. I see it differently myself, but that's just me."

"Hendrix," Vanessa said and stammered. "This is your father-our father. I don't get how you could go along with something like this."

I looked up from the table and stared over her shoulder, out the window. "It's what he wanted."

"That's what he wanted." She repeatedly bobbled her head. "I guess I understand his decision, but what I'm trying to wipe my head around is why would you go along with it. Do you want dad to die?"

"You know, I never saw it as my decision. Of course, I don't want dad to die. If I could, I would rip the cancer out of him, but I can't, just like I couldn't force him to go to his treatments. I wanted him to. I begged him to go. I fought him on it. And every time, he fought back because that's what dad does.

I can't win in a stalemate, so instead of fighting, I respected his decision. He was happy; that's all I could ask for."

She sighed while shaking her head. "I hear you. I just don't get it. I really don't."

"Remember when you and I wanted to become professional wrestlers? There was this time where you hit me with a pillow. You hit me so hard I fell off the bed and hit my mouth on the floor."

"Yeah, I remember that. It knocked your tooth out."

"Do you remember what dad did?"

"After the beating? He put a mattress on the floor."

"He put a mattress on the floor so we could keep wrestling." I smiled. "He did that even though he hated wrestling. He thought it was stupid. I don't know if he put that mattress down because he wanted to support us or because it was safe. But he put it down nonetheless."

"We did perfect our turnbuckle drops."

"He knew we would grow up and become the greatest wrestlers of all time if that's what we wanted. I like to think that's why he put that mattress down. He supported us even in our foolishness because that's what you do when you love someone. It's not easy. Trust me on that. I would know. Dad has been through the fire and back for us and never complained. And if this was my chance to reciprocate, I didn't have to like it. He would've done the same for me."

"Putting a mattress down so your kids can wrestle is a lot different than not going to your cancer treatments."

The waitress returned with our drinks, holding them above her head on a black serving tray. She distributed our water and then our other beverages. Eve and I had cranberry juice, Vanessa had apple juice, and Dad had coffee.

"Your food is coming right up," she said, sitting a stack of napkins on the table. "Maybe another five to ten minutes."

"Thank you," Dad said.

She walked off.

Dad poured himself a cup of coffee and added one creamer. Holding the cup to his mouth, he cooled it with his breath and took a sip. In a sigh, he uttered the same noise of satisfaction he made when he smoked before sitting the cup down.

"You should have told us, Hendrix," Eve said.

"You would've snapped," I asked. "You didn't want us to tell you."

"I guilted your brother into silence," dad said. "Trust me, your brother fussed at me the entire time, and come on, you know me, I never listen. If you want to be mad at anyone, be mad at me. I don't want my children hating one another."

"Dad, we fight because that's what siblings do, but we could never hate each other."

"You could have fooled me. Since you and Vanessa came to visit, you kids have been at each other's throats with insult after insult. Believe me; I wanted to tell you and Vanessa. I really did."

"Dad, we love each other, despite all the screaming and yelling. That will never change."

I wonder if she would say that if she knew dad lied about mom dying, I thought. There's no coming back from that. I have to tell them eventually unless there's another dramatic incident where dad feels so inclined to put a gun to his head and confess that she's alive.

"What's wrong, son?" He asked.

"You tried to kill yourself," I said.

"That's what you three keep telling me. I tried to kill myself. I don't remember doing it. The last thing I remember is Vanessa and Eve arguing, and I started feeling light-headed. Next thing I know, a paramedic was shining a light in my eyes."

"I still don't understand how we didn't know you were so depressed," Eve said. "Wanting to take your own life is serious. We didn't just miss that; we weren't paying attention."

"There was nothing to see because I don't want to die. I didn't want to kill myself. Everything happened so fast that I couldn't keep up. I can't hop back into a time machine to ask myself what I was thinking, so I have to assume it was my way of getting you girls to settle down."

"I'm guessing you and mom's anniversary didn't help either."

"Another statement only past me can verify."

I still looked at dad. He rubbed my shoulder while smiling. I guess it was his way of reassuring me that everything was going to be alright. The two waitresses brought our meals, and we ate with little conversation. Dad left a ten-dollar tip, and I paid. On the way out, some of the waitresses told dad and I goodbye by name. Eve and Vanessa grimaced.

As Vanessa drove home, I pretended to be asleep in the backseat.

...

Inside, Vanessa's bags lay against the wall of the entryway. Dad, Eve, and Vanessa carried one bag apiece. I carried two-one on both shoulders.

Vanessa stuffed her entire life into those bags from the look and weight. I waddled to the car and threw them into the trunk.

My car was on the street, parallel with the house, and I leaned against the hood and watched Vanessa, Eve, and Dad come outside to say their 'goodbyes.' Vanessa embraced dad with all her might. Then she hugged him again when they let go.

This might be the last time we're together, I thought. Dad is only getting worse. Our last memory might be us sitting in an IHOP discussing how our dad wanted to kill himself.

Vanessa walked across the lawn to me. She tapped me across the arm and flashed a smile.

"Time flew by," she said.

"Looks like you finally have to get back to the real world, I see," I said.

"Yeah, it has been nice. I've been pushing it with all the vacation time. I need to get back to the real world. I'm not built for this whole "not working" thing. I'm starting to go crazy."

"Those damn dishes."

"Those damn dishes. Next time, I'm bringing all the paper plates and plastic ware."

"It's that bad?"

"I'm not built for the house, Hendrix. Being cooped up for weeks at a time was torture. I was bored. Retirement is going to kill me."

"I mean, I get it, considering you did everything around here. If you were bored, you weren't working that hard." I had that little brother grin.

She grimaced so hard I figured a random pain shot through her body. "I'm sorry."

"Why are you sorry?"

"For being so hard on you. Dad's right. We have been at each other's throats a lot. I was 'we.' He was nice enough not to throw all the shade."

"Oh, don't worry about it. You've been screaming at me my whole life." I gently nudged her. "I have thick skin."

"Only because you have to. Just because you're used to it doesn't make what I'm doing right. I have a magical way of being a bitch sometimes."

"I have a mythical way of turning you into...that word. You want the best for me even when I don't want it for myself. I appreciate that. I appreciate you."

"There are better ways of communicating that than screaming and talking down to you."

I shrugged. "Seriously, don't worry about it. No big deal."

"Can you just take my apology?"

"Apology accepted, Vanessa."

"Thank you." She smiled. "I appreciate it, little brother."

"You're very welcome, big sister."

"Now, give me a hug."

We embraced with both hands. We never did that. We always committed to the one arm, side hug you did in church when the pastor instructed everyone to hug a neighbor. I wrecked my brain to remember the last time Vanessa, and I even did that.

We tightened our embrace.

"Take care of dad," she said, with her head on my shoulders. "Don't let me hear about him putting a gun to his head on your watch."

"He can't. You have all his guns in the trunk of your car."

"Don't let me hear about him doing something as equally stupid. If I do, I'll piledrive you off the bed."

"Don't threaten me with a good time. You were right, by the way."

"I'm almost always right."

"I was irresponsible. Dad was dying, and I sat back and let him get worse. I shouldn't have taken *no* as an answer."

Vanessa lifted her head from my shoulder and broke from the hug. "Is it what I would have done? No. But that doesn't make what you did wrong. Whether I like it or not, Dad was happy, and that's all I care about."

"It's still rough knowing we're going to lose him one day."

"We won't lose him. Think about mom. Have we lost her?"

"Technically."

"Don't start. We haven't lost mom, and we won't lose dad." For a second, she almost shed a tear. "At least you get to be with him. The next time I see him, he might be in a casket."

"I would trade places with you in a heartbeat."

"I guess we're both in a lose-lose situation."

"Maybe."

She slapped my shoulder, smiling. "On a positive note, Victoria is beautiful. I'm glad you finally found someone who makes you happy."

"That's my baby."

"Look at you becoming an adult. Don't mess it up."

"To be fair, I didn't mess up the other ones."

She hugged me again. This time longer than the one before.

Should I tell her about mom? I asked myself. Next time I see her dad might be gone, and that won't be a good time. How did dad keep this a secret for so long?

We broke from our hug.

"Hey, Vanessa," I said.

"Yes, Hen-Hen."

"I hate that name."

"I know."

"About mom."

"What about her?"

"I wish she was still with us."

"Try not to think about that, Hen-Hen. Mom's gone. Let's focus on the family we have left. God called her home. We may not understand why or like it, but he did what he had to do for a reason."

She winked. She walked to the driver's door of her car. Dad and Eve waited for her there, and they hugged and kissed one last time before she left. She waved as she drove off. Dad and Eve went back inside, and I waited on the curb until I couldn't see Vanessa's car anymore. I walked inside, and Dad was in the kitchen, whistling.

Upstairs, Eve stuffed her bags with the clothes that had slowly taken over my room. I sat on the bed and watched.

"I bet you're happy to get your bed back," she said.

"Sleeping on the inflatable mattress wasn't so bad."

"You liar. I saw you in the morning slumped over, looking like your back was on fire."

"It was either your or my back. Someone had to bite the bullet."

"You're quite the gentleman, Hen Hen."

"It reminded me of the good ol' days where we would build forts or go camping downstairs."

She moved a pile of clothes--accidentally knocking some to the floor--to plop down beside me. "I miss you."

"I've been here the whole time."

"It's possible to see them every day and not see them at all. I had no idea you had a girlfriend."

"Like I knew you had a boyfriend. Let alone, someone you wanted to marry."

"My point exactly."

"You want to see me? Let's talk."

"If only we had the time."

I checked the time on my phone. "What? You're telling me we don't want to try to catch up on seven years in two hours?

"I missed out on so much."

"You're wasting time, Eve."

"Alright. How are you feeling?"

"Starting off easy, huh?

"It's been a while. I have to warm you up."

"I'm your brother, Eve. Gross."

She nudged me. "Stop being childish and answer the question."

"About dad?"

"About everything."

"You have to be more specific, girl."

"Okay, let's start with dad. How are you feeling?"

"Confused. Wondering why it has to be our dad. Of all the people, dad is the one who's dying. It's not fair."

"Marc told me that I should pray."

"Did you?"

"A little. It helped for like a day. I don't know if it was the prayer itself or all the crying."

"If it helps, then don't stop praying."

"That's what Marc keeps telling me. Have you prayed at all?"

"I haven't prayed in years."

"Maybe if we all did it, God will hear our prayers before everyone else's."

A crow cawed outside the window.

I laughed just enough not to offend her. "I don't think that's how it works, Eve. But I'll give it a shot."

"I'm so happy to be leaving. I can't be in this house anymore. There's so much death in the walls."

"Dad and Vita make it less creepy. For the most part, I just try to enjoy life as much as I can."

"Sounds like this girl is special."

"I love her, Eve."

She tickled my side. "Aww, have you told her yet, Hen-Hen?"

"She knows."

"So when is the wedding?"

"It's too soon to be talking about marriage."

"Some would argue that it's too soon to be dropping the L-Bomb, but when have you ever been conventional?"

"Falling in love with someone is way different than marrying them."

She pointed to my face. "I can see it all over your face. The way your eyes light up when you talk about her. You better marry her, you hear me?"

That moment I realized I hadn't heard from Vita all day, and I didn't think anything of it since she was with Martin and Daniel.

The crow wouldn't stop cawing, and I closed the window, which didn't do much.

"How did we grow so far apart?" She asked.

"We just did. You moved away and started living your life while I found one of my own. It happens, sadly. It's life. People grow up, apart."

"Not for twins. No matter how much life pulls us, it should never break our bond."

"It didn't. We don't talk daily, so what? That doesn't mean we aren't close." I pinched her side, and I jumped as if I felt it. "See, I felt that. Remember you got in that car accident? I woke up in the middle of the night in a cold sweat, and what did I do? I called you. Our bond is as strong as ever."

She smiled and rested her head back on my shoulder. "Well, I still want to talk more."

"We will."

Dad, still downstairs, guffawed.

"It's nice hearing him laugh," Eve said. "Especially after everything that happened."

I helped her finish packing. She didn't have enough bags because of all the recent shopping sprees, and we packed some of her belongings in a black plastic bag. It took three trips to bring everything to the entryway. We joined dad in the living room, sitting on the couch beside him. He watched a movie and put his arms around us when we sat down.

It was 12:47 when the movie ended.

"I guess I should hit the road too," she said, standing from the couch. "Saying goodbye is the part I hate the most."

Dad made her a plate of leftovers. We took her bags to the car, putting them in the back seat of her brand new BMW 3 Series. We said our goodbyes as Eve cried, and then she left.

Dad and I sat on the porch. He took a carton of cigarettes from his pants pocket and smoked. As usual, he wheezed and coughed. He went right back to smoking when the coughing stopped. It was so casually like he didn't have cancer.

I couldn't wrap my head around the idea of doing something that was slowly killing him, no matter how calming it seemed.

"The other night," I said. "You said you were afraid to die. Was that you talking or the alcohol?"

"That was all me with the strength of Jim Beam. I'm terrified."

"Then why do you insist on smoking? Why don't you want to get treatment?"

"When the doctor told me I had stage 3 lung cancer, the first thing I did was research the survival rate. Statistically, with or without treatment, I was a dead man. After that, I immediately looked up pictures of chemo patients. They didn't look like themselves. I told myself that if I were going to die, I'd rather go out on my terms, doing what I wanted to do. It makes looking death in the eyes easier." He took another drag. "I guess."

Chapter 10
Hendrix

The following day, I strolled down Main Street to meet Vita for coffee. It was another dreary, overcast day. I passed the strip club we went to before, which looked abandoned during the day.

A parking attendant, sporting an orange vest over a button-up, and black pants, checked meters for each car parked at the curb. He waved at me as he tucked a ticket underneath a Ford F150's windshield wipers. People went in and out of shops that still had Black Friday sales posters hanging in the window. A well-dressed man danced outside a clothing store that blasted pop music, joined by a group of sorority sisters judging by their matching red T-Shirts with their letters on the right chest. Their bird-like shrills sounded almost as bad as their attempts of twerking.

I turned to the side to avoid bumping the shoulders of the people walking in the opposite direction. A homeless man with no front teeth held the door open for coffee shop patrons. Most people thanked him. No one tipped, and he had some choice words for anyone who didn't.

I waited outside the shop for Vita.

"Hey, man," the homeless man said. "Can I trouble you for a dollar?"

I patted myself down. "Sorry, no change, man."

"I accept credit cards."

"Sorry."

"Eat my dirty ass."

The coffee shop manager burst from inside, demanding the man to leave, and surprisingly, he listened. He had a bounce in his step from an apparent physical condition, telling jokes aloud for anyone who would listen. The passing crowd parted as they drew near him.

My jacket did little to keep me warm. I walked inside and sat at one of the many tables along the tinted windows.

Two women entered with bags hanging from their forearms, wearing sweaters zipped to the neck and scarves wrapped around their necks, discussing all the "great deals." A group of men my dad's age came in and stood behind them. One man, who had moles, under his left eye, in the shape of a diamond, cracked jokes about a cashier from a nearby shop. He guffawed from his slightly protruding gut, barely able to speak, let alone enunciate himself.

I waited twenty minutes before going back outside. I drew my hood over my head and shoved my hands into my pockets in the cold. Hunched forward and my teeth chattering, I looked down the street for Vita. There were a lot of people—none of them her.

Then, I spotted her. She drove by and turned left at an intersection. Ten minutes later, she made her way down the street with her hands in her pockets. She had on a grey coat, black pants, and black boots. Her hair bounced as she walked. She stopped in front of me, her hair hiding her face, and she left it there.

I moved her hair from over her face and tucked it behind her ear. I kissed her, expecting her to kiss back. She was much more interested in the world happening around us than I was.

Why won't she look at me?

"We got this," I said.

"Some things aren't as easy as you make it."

"Vita, we got this, even if it beats us down. We got this."

"After the last twenty-four hours…I'll have to take your word for it."

"Tell me about it. Vanessa, Eve and I took shifts watching dad last night. Lucky me got the last shift. I've been up since four in the morning."

"I couldn't sleep either. I haven't been sleeping much lately."

"What's on your mind?"

"Martin and Daniel."

"Are they okay? Did something happen?"

"They're fine."

"Are you fine?"

"Never better." Her eyes remained fixated on everyone except me.

"You want me to believe that?"

"One thing I've learned about you, Hendrix, you're going to believe what you want."

"Alright, everything isn't okay. I'm not going to push the issue. Just know I'm here when you need to talk."

"Because you love me."

I wrapped my arms around her waist and kissed her; her lips never puckered. I moved back, with my arms still around her, and stared into her glazed-over eyes. I moved my arms up to her back and held her tightly, my face buried in her hair. She didn't lay her head on my shoulder, like how she didn't hug me; her hands stayed in her pockets.

"I love you, Vita," I said.

She didn't say anything.

"I love you so much." I squeezed tighter. "Whatever is wrong, we got this, baby."

"Do you mind if I grab a coffee?"

"Why would I? That's why we're here."

We went inside. The smell of coffee met us at the door. Three people stood in line in front of us. I stared at the menu written in chalk on a board behind the counter, holding Vita from behind. The cashier talked for the sake of talking, and the customers nodded and smiled. At the counter, Vita ordered a Chai latte with a shot of espresso. I stared at the menu, contemplating if I wanted a drink, but decided not to get one. I paid for Vita's latte before she could take her purse from her shoulders. She thanked me. We stood off to the side, against a window, waiting to hear her name called.

Victoria stood in front of me. After the most awkward few minutes of our relationship, she looked towards me but not at me.

"Do you believe in destiny?" She asked.

"I don't know. I don't think so."

"I do."

"Why do you ask?"

"I'm thinking."

"About?"

"Destiny."

"But what specifically?"

She went to reply right when the barista called her name. As soon as she grabbed her drink, she left the shop without acknowledging my existence. I followed as she walked down the street, examining the items in the windows of each shop.

She never acted like this before. Something was wrong.

I trailed a few steps behind and ran to keep pace.

"Do you believe meeting me was destiny?" I asked.

"Of course. I was supposed to meet you because we met." She stopped at a crosswalk and looked left and right as we waited for the signal to walk. "I think."

"You think? What is that supposed to mean?"

When the sign signaled we could walk, we crossed the street with a medium-sized crowd coming from both directions.

"So, you aren't sure?" I asked.

"I think."

"You think?"

"I think someone can come into your life for any reason. Time will only tell if that person will stay and meaningfully impact your life."

"Okay. I guess I'm following. Keep going just in case."

"The way I see it is everything isn't your destiny. I like to think of destiny as significant events that contribute to my forever. I don't subscribe to the idea that everything in my life happened because it was supposed to happen, like it or not. I was destined to be born, the same way I was destined to have Martin and Daniel, to fall in love, to die. Everything else is random occurrences that will probably have no bearing on my life in, let's say, three months. It came, it happened, it was nice, and now it's over."

"So, you're looking at destiny from a macro level? When it's all said and done, and you look back on your life, who made the greatest impact? Who defined your life? Who do you even remember? You're not worried about the random people, like the mailman, the grocery store cashier, or even like-"

"You."

"Me?"

"If you and I end today and we never see each other again for the rest of our lives, could I say you're a part of my destiny?"

"By your definition, I guess not."

"And that's the scary thing about destiny. I don't know what mine is."

"Victoria, what are you getting at?"

We stopped in the middle of the sidewalk. I stared at her as she sipped her latte and looked past me with glazed-over eyes. Some of the passing individuals moved around us, and others walked between us. I went to caress her cheek, but she continued down the street, turning at a stop sign. Fewer people were on the road than before—a steady flow of cars passed by now and then. There were a few shops with cars parked outside. She began to walk faster and turned onto the next street. She never looked up to read street names and kept going until we stood in a parking lot of what looked like it used to be a grocery store.

A retail store was across the parking lot, full of cars and people walking inside and out-some pushing carts and others carrying bags. Somewhere amongst it all, a child cried at the top of their lungs.

Vita clenched onto me. I couldn't and wouldn't fight if I tried. And why would I? She held onto me like I was her destiny.

She stepped back. Her hand on my neck sent chills down my spine. She kissed me on the cheek, then gave me a peck on the lips. Every time her soft lips lay against mine, and our tongues caressed, butterflies fluttered in my stomach, and my heart raced. The moment always left me speechless, grasping for words to describe just how happy she made me. Our kisses, no longer gentle, were fierce yet passionate, and our tongues explored one another. I ran my fingers through her hair and gently bit down on her bottom lip. She bit my upper lip, staring into my eyes. I smiled. Then we kissed again. Her lips touched the depths of my soul, and an unyielding and steady desire made me never want to let her go. She was my flowers, moon, stars, and sun. All I desired was to lay around with her head on my chest as I played in her hair. She took me from reality to a place where only she and I existed.

She made me feel a happiness I thought was impossible. I questioned if our love was real. It was. As I saw in her eyes, I only felt "forever" on her lips.

Inches away from one another, breathing intently, we stared into one another's souls. She cried without making a sound. Tears fell, and they kept falling faster than I could wipe them away. She smiled, gazing at me like I was the only man in the world that she ever wanted. The smile faded into nothing. Still, on my neck, her hand trembled, and taking her into my arm, I felt her quivering. She embraced me as if we would never see each other again. I tightened my embrace as she pushed her face deeper into my shoulder.

"I love you, Vita," I whispered in her ear.

She cried harder. From the way she gasped for air, I thought she was dying, and I knew for a fact that she was not okay. I moved away, and when I took her hand, interlocking our fingers, my body tingled from numbness, my heart raced and stalled at the same time, and a knot clogged my throat. My fingers brushed her wedding ring.

I opened my mouth to speak, my lips quivering. Nothing came out. I could've cursed her out, walked away like we never met, or burst into tears while begging her to stay. I could have done so much to save face. Yet, I stood there in silence.

I thought we were something, I thought. She made me believe she loved me. I thought we were supposed to be together forever. You thought wrong, Hendrix. You thought wrong.

Looking into her eyes, I told myself not to cry, but before I knew it, tears rolled down my face. I caressed the ring with my fingers.

"Destiny," I said.

"Destiny."

I couldn't fathom how we ended up at that point because I couldn't get past how much love I felt on her lips. I wanted to leave, but all of the confusion, restrained love, and unrestrained anger kept me standing there, breaking down more by the second. I closed my eyes, wishing I didn't have to see her because as long I did, I wouldn't have to resist the urge of begging for her love and affection.

I opened my eyes; she wasn't there anymore. I wasn't in the parking lot either. I was lying across my father's lap, crying just as hard. He patted me on the back, telling me everything would be okay.

Vita, what happened to us?

. . .

Seeing her in class stuck needles into my heart and tossed salt in the wound. Every day, I walked into the classroom, forcing myself not to look at her. Being creatures of habit, I sat in front of her and left as soon as the instructor spoke.

Once, she had rushed out of class with her phone in her hand. Her scent trailing behind tore my heart apart and reminded me of times we would never have again. I couldn't stop myself from reliving every moment we had together in that second. The way she had looked at me, touched and kissed me made life itself worthless if it wasn't with her. She had held me in her hands, delicately. I thought back to the first time I realized I loved her. She kept me sane, and she still did. I loved her with all my heart. That's why I couldn't stop smiling until she came back into the classroom.

My heart fell into pieces. The pieces, still beating, spread out across the room. There was love, hatred, solitude, and loneliness staring back at me as if I was a fool.

Once class was over, I saw her sitting on the stone bench, waiting for Hershey or her mother-in-law.

I walked past her to the car- on my way to a home that we would never share.

. . .

A provocatively dressed crowd danced to the blasting music that vibrated and shook the room.

Many of them bumped my table in the process. The several whiskey shots I drank had me feeling like I could walk on water or fight anyone who looked at me the wrong way.

The blonde dancer from before spotted me from across the room and danced her way through the crowd while holding two shot glasses above her head. Alcohol spilled with each step. Her red dress left nothing to the imagination, and my eyes locked on her skin, glistening in the strobe lights. Somehow, she effortlessly strolled in her stripper heels.

We stared at one another as she approached and slid into the booth.

"You're Colin's best friend, right?" She asked, yelling over the music. "How is he?"

"Alive."

She glanced across the club at the sea of bodies. "No girlfriend tonight?"

"No girlfriend tonight, tomorrow, or the day after. We broke up. She went back to her ex."

With a grin, she slid a shot to me. "It's whiskey."

"Maybe if I didn't still have to drive home. Sorry."

"You don't look like you should be alone tonight or tomorrow or the day after." She rested her hand on the back of mine.

"What the hell. Let's do it."

We clicked our shot glasses together and drank.

The DJ transitioned the song to an early 2000s hip hop song made for twerking. She turned every head in the club with her dancing. If I didn't take her home, someone else would have. The bros and horny college kids waited for their chance.

"Dance with me, Hendrix," she said.

"Whoa. I'm way too drunk for all that."

She straddled me in the booth, slow winding with her face buried into my neck. Her breath against my skin slowed my breathing. As the DJ signaled an upcoming song transition by blending two records, she lifted her head from my neck. Her eyes studied me.

"Your girlfriend leaves you, and what is the first thing you think to do?" She asked. "You call me. I'm flattered."

"Would it ruin the moment if I said it wasn't the first thing I did?"

She put her index finger, wet with alcohol, against my lips. "Don't ruin my fantasy."

"I'm your fantasy, huh?"

"Maybe you're one of them. I can't say for sure. Don't want to give you a big head now." She looked long and hard into my eyes. "What can I say? I can't resist a cutie."

"What are some of your other fantasies?"

"Oh, if everything goes according to plan, you'll find out soon enough."

"Is that right?"

"Let's go."

"Where are we going?"

"To the moon and back. Does it matter? You don't have to worry. I won't hurt you."

She led me from the club. The ringing in my ears drowned out the conversation from the line of people waiting outside. The heat outside left me gasping for air. Beads of sweat glued my clothes to my body. Wet jeans were the closest thing to torture, besides not having Victoria.

We walked several blocks to an apartment complex across the street from her university.

A walkway led through the complex. Along the path, light posts and trees arched over the walkway. She took me inside her second-floor apartment, and I sat on the black leather couch as she went into the bedroom. She came out with a brownie in a plastic bag and broke me off a piece.

"I'm going to make you feel good tonight," she said.

Like every day since Victoria and I broke up, she poisoned my mind. What was she doing? What was she wearing or thinking? Did she ever replay the past and smile at the memories we made in our short amount of time together? She didn't because I wasn't her destiny.

I could only assume I lost my mind when she broke my heart.

Live your life because that's what she's doing, I thought. She's kissing that man. She's letting him touch her. But why do you care? She didn't want you. She never wanted you. You were a detour on her road to her destiny. She always wanted Hershey, but he didn't want her, and in that moment of heartbreak, your love became convenient.

The blonde girl kneeled in front of me.

"Did I lose you to her already?" She asked.

"To who? Victoria? Nobody is thinking about that woman."

"Stay with me." She extended the brownie. "You're with me now, baby. I'll take care of you."

"I'm only thinking about you, baby."

"You don't have to lie to me, Hendrix. I don't care if you're thinking about her." She traced my lips with her finger. "I'm not the jealous type."

"I'm telling no lies here."

She stood, turned her back to me, and bounced up and down to clap her butt. She twirled around, giggling.

"I've been there before. Heartbroken, lonely, afraid...shit, adamant that you'll never find love again, all the while wanting someone so much it hurts to breathe. Those lips can lie to me. Those pretty eyes of yours can't."

I snatched the piece of brownie from her hand and popped it into my mouth. "Now, what?"

"We wait."

She went back to the bedroom and came out with a purple bong. She took bong rips, the air in the bong water bubbled.

"Are you still thinking about her?" She asked. "No lying. You won't hurt my feelings."

"It's hard not to."

She took a bong rip, held in the smoke, and blew the cloud into my mouth.

"How about now? Is she still on your mind?"

"Yeah."

She took a bong rip and blew the smoke into my face. She asked me again, and when I answered yes, the process continued. As long as I nodded, 'yes,' she kept blowing smoke into my mouth, and eventually, the contact high kicked in. I dropped back onto the couch, and the air blowing from the vents took me away. I bounced through a different world in a foreign body. My heart thumped to the rhythms of a song I imagined played as you fly into the sunset. A song that only existed in my head. I danced in a state of serenity. Nothing mattered, not my dad's health, not my mother, not Victoria.

She turned on a song that matched the tone of the music playing in my head. It was the acoustic version of space. I danced from star to star, and there was no blackness, just a swirling yellow. I couldn't feel my body. Who needed it? I danced until my heart was content. She stood and rolled her body like waves as she seductively danced in front of the television. A white light trailed her every movement. Hours into the song, she danced her way to me.

"Are you still thinking about her?" she said. Her voice echoed.

I shook my head.

"Good. It's only you and I at this moment, Hendrix. I want you to think about how much you want me. Dream while awake. Dream about my lips all over your body, baby. I'm going to suck away every ounce of pain."

She danced, trancing every inch of her body with her fingertips and biting on her bottom lip. She moved her fingers to her thighs, and listening to the words I never spoke; she played with herself. She tilted her head back and let the moment take her away like I wasn't there, watching and lusting. Her body trembled as she inched closer to cumming. She opened her eyes and settled them onto me, searching deep into my being, expressing everything she wanted to do to me. I was afraid and aroused at the same time.

She slid her fingers from her pussy.

My mouth opened on its own to taste her glistening fingers. She slid her fingers into my mouth, and damn, she tasted like freshly spun cotton candy. I sucked on her fingers while she played with herself with her other hand. We both gyrated our bodies in dance to the song that had no end.

She moved away, twirled away in dance, past a line of palm trees swaying side to side, and turned off the lights. In the dark, having no idea where she was, I trembled, fiending for her touch. Her presence lingered over me. I felt the warmth of her body coming down on me. The moment built.

My eyes were closed. Even if they were open, I was still in space, so I wouldn't have been able to see her.

She wasn't modest, not from the way she wildly tossed her head back and forth to swallow me from tip to base, drool bubbling from her mouth and covering me. The music drowned in her moaning, choking, and slurping. Taking me from her mouth and fighting to speak through gasping, she asked a question to feed her ego: "You like it, baby?"

I sat there with my eyes closed without saying a word. It was the only thing I could do—that or push her head back down.

She teased me by licking up the spit. When she got to my head, she wrapped her lips around it, never sucking, only going back to licking. I thought of the wait as torture until she went back to sucking. My toes curled, and I needed to do something with my hands. Curl my fingers around her head? Leave them at my side? No, I held onto the couch with dear life so she couldn't suck my soul from my dick.

I thrust my hips lightly, meeting her each time she pushed her head forward to take more of me in her mouth. She stopped, keeping her lips wrapped around me. I took it as her way of begging for me to take control. I grabbed her hair and made love to her face. She gagged but never fought.

I let her head go. She moved her head back, gasping and giggling. She took me into her hands and sucked on the tip. I put my hands on my head and tensed my body, trying not to cum. My legs shook, and I fought to squirm away; she had other plans. She kept sucking until my body jerked forward, and I let out a loud groan as I burst into her mouth.

Now adjusted to the dark, my eyes focused on her as she got up and performed her on-stage routine, minus the pole, of course, gasping for air. Spit dripped down her chin, and she smeared it across his breast.

The same song played.

"This song is so good," I yelled.

"You're good."

I revved up a growl, which turned into a crazed scream. "Fuck, I'm so high!"

"Hell yeah, baby. That's what I like to hear."

She jumped on my lap, grabbed me by the cheeks, and shoved her tongue into my mouth. Our tongues went at it in a passionate war, seeing who could get the other more excited. I grew harder against her wetness in no time.

"I'm so glad you're single," she said.

"Fuck Victoria."

"Fuck that bitch." She growled, so I joined her. "You're going to fuck me."

She hopped to her feet, nearly tipping over. Kiss after kiss, her lips moved down to my stomach, where she looked up with a grin before taking me back into her mouth again. The slow and deep rhythm and coat of saliva massaged my soul and pulled out an animalistic groan.

Through the moaning, I managed to say, "Shit. Baby. Baby?" I twisted my body to pull away from her.

She looked up at me from her knees, wiping saliva from her chin with the palm of her hand and licking it up like a cat. "What's wrong, baby? You don't like how I suck your cock?"

"Heavens no. It's definitely not that. You, ma'am, are an angel. You're just going to kill me. Let me treat you."

"Gotta love a man with champagne taste."

She lay down, and I kissed her inner thighs on my way to her pussy. I was fully invested in her pleasure as she choked me with her legs. Doing so only made me want to lick her more as she covered my face in her juices.

By this time, we both wanted each other. She let me get up. Looking at my beautiful baby lying there, ready for me, I slid on a condom, which magically happened to be on the coffee table, and slowly pushed inside her.

"Fuck me with that cock, baby," she said. I could tell by her eyes that she was ready.

I pushed completely inside of her in slow and deep strokes. As she got wetter, I went faster and harder. The entire time we were looking at each other with flames in our eyes. She pulled me down for a kiss mid-stroke.

She pushed me back and dropped to all fours. She spread her cheeks for me to slide inside. Like the last position, I started slow, making sure she felt me deep inside with every thrust. We could have stayed in this rhythm, although that would have gone against what she told me with her eyes. We no longer held back. Her neighbors probably heard everything from the animalistic and merciless groaning to the hard slaps to her ass. I gave one final thrust before she called out.

"Let me get on top," she said. "Let me ride it."

I let her. The entire time she slowly rode me, she had a smile. We both finished at the same time. She dropped and buried her face into my neck. When she caught her breath, we kissed for what felt like hours until I throbbed against her, and she rode me to orgasm a second time.

The same song still played. We ended up on the floor, her lying on my chest. I drifted off, asleep. I woke up, and she was squatting in front of me, taking bong rips. Her back was to me, and her pussy looked amazing. I still floated within a sunset.

"What time is it?" I asked.

She turned around without saying a word. She smirked and seductively moved closer and closer. My heart pounded rapidly against my sternum. She leaned forward, her ass in the air, and we kissed. We tasted *us* on one another's lips as we kissed with fire guiding our tongues. Not long after, she straddled my lap, and our hands explored one another's bodies. She lay her hand on my cheek.

"You're such a beautiful man," she said. "Wait right here." She left and came back with her hands behind her back. "Come here."

I followed her into the dark bedroom.

"Lay down," she said.

I lay down in bed, and she handcuffed me to the headboard. She straddled me and leaned forward, putting us face to face. Her lips trailed down my body with kisses. She took me into her mouth. In the dark, I listened to her gagging. She could have made me burst into her mouth whenever she wanted. She wanted us both to enjoy the moment as long as we could. When she decided I was going to cum, she kept sucking. I wanted to love it, but she kept going long after I came.

Pleasure turned to pain before she stopped and lay beside me. I still couldn't see her, but I felt her breathing against my face.

The same song continued to play on loop.

"This song is amazing," I said.

"You're amazing."

"I love this song so much. I need this to play forever. At my wedding, when my kids are born, when I die. This song would hit so hard when I'm resting under the palm trees."

"Palm trees are so fucking lit."

Together, we danced while lying in bed until the strangest thing happened: I had a fleeting thought of my mom.

"What's wrong?" She asked.

"My mom never died. My dad said she did, but she's alive."

"Your life is like an M. Night Shyamalan movie."

"Crazy thing is my sisters don't know."

"You have to tell them. If you do, I'll blow you every day until you find a girlfriend."

"When you're a kid, they say not to talk back to your parents, like it's the ultimate sign of disrespect. But what are you supposed to do when your parents are flagrant? Sit back and shut up?"

"Say it."

"Kids have the innate ability to spot bullshit, and you know what parents do when they get called out? Play the "Parent Card," because God forbid if the person they brought into this world puts them in their place." The music took over my body. "I'm done living in the chaos of my father. I'm dancing free from the chains of generational curses. I'm walking away in stride from the flames that are my father's guilt and rejoicing that his sins are not my burden anymore."

"In Jesus' name, awoman!"

. . .

The sun blaring through the open blinds woke me up in the morning.

The blonde girl sat on the edge of the bed-one foot under her thigh and her other leg hanging off the side. She only had on a yellow bra and a white thong, and her hair was a mess. Leaning forward, she ate cereal out of a red plastic cup. I went to get up. The handcuffs, bounding me to the bed frame, pulled my arm back. I lay there naked. The room, bed, and I reeked of regret--sex, weed, and sweat.

What are you doing, Hendrix? I said to myself. Look at yourself, man. You're handcuffed to a random stripper's bed. The drinking, drugs, the spontaneous sex. This isn't you. Casual sex isn't going to make getting over Victoria any easier. I know you want her, but listen to me when I say, 'she doesn't want you.' She doesn't. You have to get that out of your head. She made it very clear, whatever you had wasn't anything but a distraction on her way to her destiny. Whatever that fucking meant. Whether she truly loved you or said it to make herself feel better, she loves Hershey more. You were the side piece, a rebound at best. You made yourself too convenient.

I felt empty.

The blonde girl looked terrific from behind—the front too, from what I could remember.

She crunched on her cereal and loudly rinsed it down with the remaining milk in the cup. She left and came back, and that's when she saw me.

She had a palm tree tattoo down her sternum. The foliage arched over the breast.

"Good morning, sexy man," she said.

"Good morning."

She crawled atop me and kissed from my stomach to my lips. Fruity pebbles, milk, and weed lingered on her breath. "You were so high last night."

"I felt so weird."

"That's a good thing."

"It was like I was dancing on stars. Everything was yellow, and you were like water. What did you give me?"

"If the weed made you feel good, I hope I made you feel great."

"From what I remember, you were the best I ever had."

"So, you shouldn't be thinking about whatever her name is then."

"Why would I when I'm here with you?"

She smiled. "You charmer you. It's sweet, and I am flattered, but you're lying, sexy boy."

"I have no reason to lie."

"Hendrix, I know who I am, and I'm not Victoria. You might not mind being here with me, and I love that, but we both know you would leave me in a heartbeat if she called. Good thing I'm not the jealous type. I might have felt a way about you screaming her name last night."

"That didn't happen."

"Yes, yes, it did." She walked over to the dresser and enjoyed a joint from a visibly used ashtray. She held the smoke in as she walked over and blew the cloud of death into my face. "I don't care if you love her or not. I'm not trying to make you fall in love. I just want to make you cum." She kissed me. "Over." She kissed me again. "Over." And again. "And over. Then maybe you will forget about her."

"After a couple more nights like the one we just had, I won't know her name by next week."

"When that day comes so will you...in my mouth, on my face, inside of me." She stood straight and left the room. "Hungry?"

"Starving."

"I have cereal." She returned with a box of frosted flakes and fruit pebbles. "Frosted Flakes and Fruity Pebbles. Take your pick."

"Frosted Flakes."

"Your wish is my command." She went into the kitchen, and I listened to cereal pouring into plastic.

"You know, I could pour my own bowl if you take off these handcuffs."

She came back with a red solo cup. "You're already a prisoner of the mind. You might as well be one physically. I think you look all sexy vulnerable. Don't worry; I'm not a serial killer."

She sat on my lap and fed me.

When I finished eating, she placed the cup on the nightstand and removed the handcuffs. My wrists, red and sore, throbbed.

"You should slap me," she said.

"Why would I do that?"

"Because I've been bad. I kept you handcuffed all night. You didn't like that, huh?"

"Not really."

"Then slap me so I won't do it again."

"I'm good."

"Do it."

I slapped her across the face.

"Harder," she said.

I slapped her harder; she held her face, smiling.

"Are you still thinking about her?" She asked.

"No."

"Ooh, are you thinking about anything in particular?"

"Yeah, someone."

"Who?"

"Someone I'm about to fuck."

"Sounds like one lucky girl."

She got up and pranced away with me following. At the door, I grabbed her hand, and she turned to me.

"Where are you going?" I asked.

"To give you two some private time." She winked. "The condoms are in the top drawer."

I threw on the condom as she waited, bent over with her hands on the wall.

To her, I was Papi, and she was my little slut. I pulled her face to mine by her hair. She loved begging for me to spank her hard enough to leave bruises.

"I want to ride," she said.

I lay down on the bed, and she was about to get on top until she noticed how covered I was in her wetness. She removed the condom and sucked me instead.

"Look into my eyes," I said.

In her eyes, I saw a life with the woman I love fade.

. . .

Two weeks is a long time not to know someone's name, especially if you're dating, I thought.

April. But everyone called her Amy. I wasn't sure how the nickname made sense, but I went with it. I usually called her bae, and I had occasionally wondered what her name was, but she was always so excited when I called her by the pet name that I forgot all about her real one. She would pounce me. Seriously, she would pounce me to the ground or against a nearby wall and rip off my clothes as fast as she could.

Right now, she sat beside me, putting her hair in a ponytail. The couch soaking wet from the two rounds of sex. We both lay naked, reeking of the musk of sex and the slight hint of her fruity-scented lotion that she had put on right after she got out of the shower that morning.

"We're bad at this," I said.

"Bad at what? You aren't talking about sex because that's amazing. You lay down; I give you the greatest ride you ever had. I bend over; you make me scream out to Our Father." She giggled. "Damn, I want you again. Let me know when you're ready for another round."

"Whatever is happening between us."

"What is happening?"

"Your guess is as good as mine."

"What do you think is happening?"

"I don't know. At times it feels like we're dating. But there's this fleeting thought that we're in this small gray area between a relationship and being acquaintances, and instead of trying to figure it out, we fuck instead."

"That sounds pretty accurate."

"I take it you're talking about the latter. I barely know you, and I'm not exaggerating. You've been The Blonde Girl smiley face, smiley face in my phone until a few days ago."

"You don't know my name?"

"I just learned it."

She tossed her head back in laughter. "Really? That's hilarious. Look, I'm not the committal type. I like to think of myself as self-aware, and to be honest, I would be a terrible girlfriend. I like you. I mean, I like you a lot, but if we dated, I would fuck someone else."

"Damn."

"Not for any reason other than I don't think one man can satisfy me. Don't get me wrong, you, sir, are orgasmic. But when I cum, I'm trying to cum again. I don't think I've ever not horny. God didn't build you men like that. You have to let the horse rest before you hop into another race, and I don't have the time for that. I'll cheat on you, and I don't want to hurt you or anyone else, so I belong to the world." She nudged me. "Not to mention, I'm a terrible cook, I don't iron, and my idea of support is a blowjob after a long day."

"That doesn't sound so bad."

"Yeah, it sounds great now. Trust me. You don't want this. You'll want a conversation at some point, and that's where things will go downhill."

I burst into laughter. "You don't know how happy I am that we aren't a thing."

"You don't know how happy I am that you don't want us to be one. That conversation would've been awkward. I like you. I don't want to end up regretting you."

My phone rang from Amy's room. Before I could get up, she brought my phone. A local number that I didn't recognize. I answered, and my heart dropped when the woman said she was calling from the local community college regarding a job position I applied for a few weeks ago. My heart sank further, and it kept plummeting when she told me her name: Victoria.

Everything she said at that point fell on deaf ears. We ended the call, and I finally realized that I didn't get the interview day, time, and location. As soon as I was about to call back, an email came through with all the information. Seeing her name in her email address cut me deep.

Amy rested her head on my shoulder and then grabbed my crotch.

"Was that Victoria?" She asked.

"It was about a job. I have an interview."

"Then why are you over here looking like your dad just died? Do you know how many of my friends can't find a job? The system is fucked, Hendrix. We are playing a game we can't win. How does one get experience if every job requires experience? I say it's a form of systemic oppression. Keep the everyday man down by restricting education and opportunity."

I stared at the email address. Victoria. I tasted vomit settling in my throat. I loved and hated her for the same reason. She wasted my life. I should have been with her, not some random woman who I barely remembered her name.

Amy, I told myself.

Her name was Amy. I didn't know how you got Amy from April. I didn't know how I ended up with her. I didn't want Amy. I didn't want anyone else except Vita. No Victoria. But Vita… Victoria wanted to be with Hershey.

"Something is on your mind," Amy said. When I looked up at her, trying my best to get out of my thoughts and feelings, she had this promiscuous look in her eyes. "I guess it's true what they say: you can suck a man dry, but just because he cums doesn't mean he loves you."

I laughed. "I'm pretty sure no one has said that, ever. And what's all this talk about love? I thought you said you aren't the relationship type?"

"It's just a saying, sexy boy."

"I don't think you know what a saying is. Someone other than you have to say it for it to be a thing."

"Another reason I'm not dating material. My jokes don't hit." I zoned out.

"Would some sloppy head help?" She asked.

My heart raced. Life moved way too fast with no indication of slowing down. My loan interest accumulated, memories of college felt like distant memories; my father got sicker. Eventually, he was gone.

My older self, much more haggard, sat in the front row at his funeral beside Vanessa and Eve, who paid for the service because I was jobless, barely getting by.

A heaviness pressed down on my chest.

Amy turned her body to be parallel with mine and put her legs across my lap. Our life played out in her eyes. We had an extravagant wedding at a chapel, filled with pews of our loved ones; kids that looked more like her than me, but they had the energy I had as a child, and they bounced around everywhere, never getting tired; a white papillon with tan spots because the kids wanted one. In every vignette running through my head, I looked miserable.

I grabbed my things and left. I didn't say anything, and neither did Amy.

. . .

After weeks of what I had hoped would be quality family time-- my sisters and I flipping through photo books, late-night conversations, and even longer discussions of the future state of our family-things finally went back to normal. It was just my dad and me again. It was nice not being harassed through text from the moment we left the house.

From one of the few benches, we took in the ambiance of a carnival that made its way into town. The cold of steel seeped through my jeans.

On the opposite side of the endless wave of attendees, in the middle of the once-abandoned dirt field, spun a carousel filled with families with small children. Screams from the spinning teacups accompanied the quintessential circus music playing from the carousel and pulled me back to my times on the ride, clinching onto the horse for dear life.

The music must have looped a thousand times while I sat there, watching groups disembark and new ones claim their seats, anxious to see a kid who looked as terrified as I did back in the day. The cold numbed both my left cheek and fingers, and my dad returned with two cups--I had no idea he even left-- when I spotted the boy within the mass of people. His mother tried her hardest to pry the boy from around his father's leg.

"It's just a carousel, kid," I muttered.

"My eldest's exact words to this boy I used to know," dad said, "followed by 'they're fun.' The boy replied, 'that's what they want you to believe until it's too late."

"Dad, in case you've never heard this before, you are one weird dude--extremely difficult to follow at times."

"The first time I took you to a carnival, you and Vanessa had that exact conversation. You should have seen the look on her face. For a second, you knew something Vanessa didn't, and in that moment, you two looked at me like how Dylan looked at that Goku guy."

"You mean Krillin...you know what? Go on."

"My point is you and Vanessa needed me, but this Super Saigon couldn't save you both-"

"-Saiyan."

"That makes more sense. Well, against my better judgment, I chose you." He handed me a cup. "I validated the irrational fears of a boy's imagination over the sensible and caring sentiments of his oldest sister. She wanted her brother to be okay. While Vanessa reluctantly rode the carousel, you, Eve, and I got hot chocolate."

"I don't remember that."

He rose his cup as if he was giving a toast and took a sip. "That's probably for the best. The way your sister looked at me. She still gives me the same look...like I love you more. Her persistent nagging says everything she won't."

"Dad, that's what Vanessa does. She nags-"

"How else would she have a moment like this with her father?"

I glanced over the carnival (the carousel, teacups, funhouse, Ferris wheel, food trucks, and booths of games of chance and skills) while repeatedly telling myself, *dad doesn't have a favorite.*

"You and I have a toxic relationship, son." He sighed with the cup gingerly to his lips. "You came into this world afraid of your own shadow...Timid... and I called myself protecting you from it." In a downward swipe of the hand, he knocked my hot chocolate to the ground.

"Seriously?"

"My baby boy ain't my baby boy anymore."

"Hear me out, I might be biased, but I like to think you did great."

"Let's hope your sisters agree."

"They do."

"I'm Goku, remember? I think I can handle hard-hitting truth. If your sisters feel a way, let me have it."

I took the hot chocolate from his hands and enjoyed several long sips. "You're right. Our relationship has been unhealthy— lately. You threw your world on my shoulders, dad, and sat back and watched. You need to tell Eve and Vanessa. It's your lie to tell, not mine."

"I receive that."

I left him on the bench as I stood in line to ride the carousel. High-pitched voices coursed through the assortment of conversations and the same looped carnival music, expressing their eagerness to reach the front of the line. When the carousel slowed to a stop, and the ride attendant opened the gate, children skittered to their desired animals, and in fate, one seat awaited me: a horse.

My dad stepped from the crowd to the steel gate surrounding the carousel, a cheap grin on his face, as the machine jerked to a start. *Was he proud of me for facing my lifelong fear, or was he mocking that it took so long?* Either way, he knew I was dying to get off from boredom. That and the sharp tingle of numbness crawling up my leg.

Chapter 11
Victoria

On the third trip outside during my weekly grocery unload, the Toon Link plush stared at me from the crinkled plastic bag wedged in the corner of the trunk.

"If it ended amicably," Hershey's Mother said from over my shoulder, "it would still make a lovely gift."

"He won't even look at me."

She patted me on the back before taking the rest of the bags inside.

Christmas lights and decorations had gone up so quickly after Thanksgiving that it seemed plausible they were always there. They snatched my attention, pulling my gaze from one house to another and then back to where Hershey and I cohabitated. Our home…His home stood out as the painfully bland house in the otherwise vibrant neighborhood.

I considered texting Hershey and asking him to bring home decorations. But I chose to wrap Christmas gifts, including Toon Link, instead. It was the better option.

…

He placed his hand on the side of my face, letting it stay there, as he gazed at me like I was his forever. I closed them for a second to meet his puckered lips for a kiss.

His heart raced. I felt it. He had longed to feel the warmth of my body against his, and he nuzzled his face into my breasts, wrapping his arms around me and pulling me closer.

I didn't feel anything.

I held my arms around his neck, and I grinded on him, feeling the tingling sensation of numbness throughout my body. He bit my neck. He told me that he wanted me to grind harder, so I listened. His face held against my neck with his mouth open, muffled the groaning. He moved his hands from my waist to around my back, pulling himself more firmly against me.

I didn't feel anything.

When he said he was cumming, I closed my eyes, gritted my teeth, and tensed my body. Nothing. I felt nothing. No throbbing. Not the warmness of cum gushing inside me.

In the shower, I tried my best to scrub away his cologne that clogged my pores. I did a double-take in the mirror as I stepped from the shower, my face half-visible through the fog. Wiping my hand across the mirror, I looked at myself. I looked like a husk of who I once was. I changed into my work clothes, keeping my eyes on myself in the mirror. A slew of emotions crashed down on me as I combed my hair. Last night, he buried his face in between my thighs, while the night before, he stared into them when he came inside me. The night before that, we stayed awake, kissing. The night before that, every few hours, one of us woke up to kiss the other, who would wake up and kiss back. He had made it a point to confess his love every waking moment, and I believed him.

Still, I didn't feel anything.

He lay on his side in bed, watching me like a predator with his eyes closed just enough for me to think he was sleeping. Years of motherhood taught me how to spot a fake sleeper: the excessive groaning, the switching sides to face you at all times, the not-quite closed eyes that only shut when I turn to him.

With my makeup done, I gave myself one last look over in the mirror before grabbing my keys and kissing Hershey on the forehead on my way out.

Nothing.

. . .

He surprised me at work that day. For the last ten minutes of my lunch break, we made out in the backseat of his car.

Nothing. Still more nothingness somehow heavy enough to leave pressure in my chest.

Hours later, I came home to dinner cooking. The smell of grease clogged in my nose made it impossible to smell anything else. Hershey met me at the door in his apron.

It was too quiet for the boys to be home.

"Where are the boys?" I asked.

"It's you and me tonight." He kissed my forehead.

"What's so special about tonight?"

"Come on, baby. Can't a man just want some uninterrupted time with his fiancée? I figured we could have dinner, drink as much wine as we want." He lifted his apron to expose his abs. "Be as loud as we want. The night is ours, kiddo."

"You know how I feel about that name." I walked into the kitchen and dropped into the same chair where I hung my purse.

He checked the food in the oven, then he sat down beside me, holding my hand. "Interesting. I assumed you only hated the name because we weren't together."

"It always bothered me."

"I see, so is there anything else that you have neglected to tell me over the years?"

"I can't think of anything right now. If you somehow trigger a suppressed memory, I'll let you know."

"Well, say it now or forever hold your peace because, by this time next month, you are stuck with me through thick and thin."

"I better start thinking."

He cooked meatloaf, mashed potatoes, and cheese broccoli for dinner.

I never liked meatloaf. This would have been the hundredth time I told him if I cared enough.

Then he had the nerve to feed me like I was Daniel or Martin. After dinner, I showered and met him back downstairs to help clean. He snapped a rolled-up towel against my thigh before I could pick up a dish.

"Not tonight. My baby isn't lifting a finger," he said. "Take your sexy self upstairs and put on something I like. I'll be up in a few minutes."

In the room, I lay across the bed, taking up as much space as possible. My nose burned from the smell of his cologne trapped in the sheets.

Still nothing.

The lights were off, and moonlight shined in from the windows and cast shadows over the walls. I rolled over onto my side, and when Hershey came into the room, I pretended to be asleep. He cuddled me from behind and tried his best to wake me, kissing me all over, grinding his crotch against me.

I felt nothing.

Feeling the bed move as he got up, I opened my eyes and watched him walk to the shower. The water came on. Minutes later, he sang.

That could have been Hendrix singing in his full glory. No matter how much I cringed while listening to him hit notes, he had no business attempting. I enjoyed it. In the back of my mind, I heard him sing. It was a distant memory of everything I chose to lose.

I chose Hershey. No, I chose my family. I had to choose my family.

Emptiness came over me. I wanted to curse, scream, and yell. Instead, I closed my eyes. It took me hours to fall asleep.

...

I awoke in Hershey's arms, my head on his chest as the illusion of it being Hendrix was just fine.

For the last three months, every day ran into one another, and at the same time, seemed longer. I didn't remember much, except for my days at work or with Martin and Daniel. Whenever around them, I felt something other than the crippling disappointment that overcame me when Hershey walked through the front door or the pain when he touched me. I had found every excuse to get out of sex. Sometimes they worked, and other times he begged and proclaimed his love until I gave in. It got so bad that whenever we had sex, I kept my eyes closed and thought about Hendrix. All the imagination in the world couldn't bring the same satisfaction. Most nights, I didn't sleep, and I spent the day sluggish and unable to think. Sometimes I sat in the parking lot at work in the brand new Genesis G80 Hershey bought me, staring at Stomps and Starlight. Twice, my heart got the best of me, and I drove to Hendrix's house. That was early after Hershey and I got back together. I hadn't gone back to the house since.

The house was quiet. The sun hadn't made its slow ascent over the horizon. I carefully got out of bed and went into the hall, where a faint noise caught my attention.

Was someone breaking in?

No, it was snickering.

Daniel was asleep in his room.

Martin wasn't in his. Instead of sleeping, he played video games in the family room downstairs. When he saw me, he froze.

"You can keep playing, sweetheart," I said. "Which one are you?"

"Captain Falcon."

"Which one is that?"

"The guy."

I sat beside him and watched him win match after match in Smash Bros.

"You're pretty good at this," I said.

"I got good."

"You mean, you got better."

"No, I had to get good. It's a saying…. You wouldn't get it, mom."

"Okay. Can you teach me how to get good?"

He laughed.

"You know, I don't appreciate you laughing at your mother like that. I could get good if I wanted to get good. No cap."

"Oh my god, Mom, you can play if you don't say that ever again."

"What? I'm too old to say cap?"

"Mom."

"Fine. Fine. I get it. Your mom isn't cool."

He plugged in and handed me another controller. I picked Baby Link, whose real name was Toon Link, and Martin killed me before I knew what happened.

"I hope you don't think you got good," I said. "I don't even know how to play."

We picked our characters again. I stuck with Toon Link; he switched to a little pink thing.

"What stage do you want?" He asked.

"Whichever one you like most."

"I have a lot of favorites."

The number of stages in the game took me by surprise. "There's a lot of options."

"Yeah."

"You choose. Just pick an easy one for me."

"There's no easy stage."

"Well then, don't pick a hard one."

"There's no hard ones either. They're all just different. Try them out until you find one you like. You're not stuck."

Halfway through the third match, he taught me how to play. It didn't matter. I was still terrible, but I got better after every loss, and eventually, I got good. In a stroke of luck, I won. Martin smiled as he turned to me and gave me a hi-five. If I knew he didn't let me win, I would have been proud of myself. To keep the appearance of the ignorant parent, I faked my excitement.

Before playing another match, he went to the kitchen and returned with green apple slices in a zip lock bag.

"May I have one?" I asked.

He handed me an apple slice, and I almost choked on it when he said, "I miss Hendrix."

I miss Hendrix, too, I thought.

"You met him like twice," I said.

"Three times. The store once and twice at grandma's."

"Okay, you met him three times. My point stands. You barely know him."

"He was really cool. Where is he?"

"He was a friend from class, honey. We aren't taking that class anymore."

"That sucks. His Toon Link hit different. That's good, by the way."

"Well, I like to think I hit a little different. I just beat you after all."

"You're good. He's really good. He could really show you how to play. I can't even beat level 7 computers."

"I have no idea what that means, but stop doubting your skills." I picked up the controller. "Press play." I felt and sounded vaguely confident. That ended when he killed me almost as soon as he hit the start button. I paused the game and sat the remote down. "Okay, so I'm not good."

He laughed. "See. I bet if Hendrix trained you, you wouldn't've died so easy."

"Well, it looks like I need to call Hendrix."

His eyes lit up in excitement. "Can you?"

I wasn't sad or depressed, just numb. I had been numb since I left Hendrix standing in the middle of the parking lot.

I thought about how I chased after Hershey for years, basing my entire life off gaining his love and approval. I was everything that he could have wanted and more, and at the same time, I was never good enough. Now, I was good enough. Now, he wanted to kiss me. For nine years, I dreamt of waking up beside Hershey. All he had to do was hold onto my dream, and we could have been perfect together. He broke my spirit, and somehow, it grew anew from the heartbreak.

I looked up at Martin; he stared at me. I smiled, and he frowned.

"Are you still unhappy?" He asked.

"Of course not, sweetheart. I'm delighted."

"You don't look happy."

"Looks can be deceiving." I smiled. "See, baby. Don't worry about mommy."

"You look like a sad person pretending to be happy."

"I'm happy, I promise."

"Are you sure?"

"I'm positive."

"If you're sad, you should say something. I don't want you to be unhappy."

I held both his hands and looked into his eyes. "As long as I have you and Daniel, there's nothing else or no one else I could need in this world. You boys are all I need."

"What about daddy?"

As I went to lie, Hershey came downstairs and nagged Martin about playing video games so early in the morning. He turned off the video game and demanded Martin to go to his room. With Martin gone, I motioned with my head for Hershey to come over, and he sat beside me. He leaned back on the couch and sighed, letting out a burst of morning breath.

I didn't love him anymore, and there was nothing that he could do or say that could make me fall in love again. Our relationship had ended a long time ago; it probably never existed. If it weren't for the guilt of seeing Martin and Daniel cry, I wouldn't have given it another shot. I wished I hadn't. Doing so meant leaving someone I loved. Someone who would have given me the world even if he knew I didn't deserve it.

The sun was rising, and the house was still quiet. Hershey sat half-asleep on the couch. He mumbled tiredly about how I looked like a model he saw in some advertisement on T.V. Then, before long, I'm breaking his heart like he did mine. He readjusted himself on the couch, now fully awake. I let it all out, and when I said everything I needed to say, a weight lifted from my shoulders. I got up from the couch, feeling like I was floating.

"I just need one thing," I said.

"I, uh. Victoria, I thought we were okay now."

"I want to keep the ring."

. . .

Sunlight peeked through the clouds and reflected off the ground, still wet from the night before.

Colin pulled weeds from the front lawn with an unlit cigarette in his mouth. A pile of weeds blocked me from parking in the driveway, and I pulled to the curb. He glanced up at me, and to my surprise, he pulled off his gardening gloves and strolled to the car. I rolled down the passenger window, and he leaned inside.

"My, oh my, look who the storm washed ashore," he said.

"I feel like what the cat dragged in."

"And somehow, you still make it look good."

"Thanks."

He shifted his attention to a wrapped gift topped with a red and gold bow in the passenger seat. "Still making Christmas rounds in April?"

"It was a gift for Hendrix-- something to say 'Thank you for being a good friend.' Then, I forgot to give it to him. I figured it would make a great Christmas present." Hendrix's father and I connected eyes with the same bewildered expression. "Oh my God. What am I doing?"

"Now you look like what the cat dragged in, and ate, and shat out."

"Yeah. I guess I didn't expect you to be so cordial."

"The day is still young."

"Why are you being so nice after everything that happened? After everything I did?"

"To be fair, I was just as upset with Hendrix as I was with you. You kids jumped into a relationship head first without addressing the elephant in the room: where did he fit in with that family of yours? You chose not to have the conversation, and he chose to ignore your cognitive dissonance. But he's my son. I have to be nice to him. You, on the other hand, well, let's just say you aren't my son. I told him to stay far away from the beginning, but you two were so adamant on violating the sanctity of a relationship."

"To be fair, I loved your son, Colin."

"That's what you say." He waved at a neighbor driving by and back at me. "Please don't misinterpret my curiosity as rudeness, but why are you here, Victoria? Hendrix is at work, and if he wasn't, I doubt this, whatever it is, is a good idea."

"I burnt that bridge, I get that, and I can't walk out of someone's life and expect them to come crawling back. I came to see you believe it or not."

"Victoria, from the short time we spent together, you demonstrated yourself to be a sweet young lady, and there's no doubt in my mind that if I had the chance to know you, I would have grown to love you. Don't make me think differently of you."

"I wanted to give you something." I pulled out the ring from my pullover sweater and extended my hand for him to take. "I think this belongs to you."

He stared at the ring, reaching into the car halfway and pulling his hand back. He got inside, filling the air with the smell of wet grass.

"I, uh, think you're mistaken," he said almost robotically. "My wife's ring is upstairs in my room. I've had it since she passed."

"Take the ring." We connected eyes. "It's yours."

He fixated on the ring, his hand itching to take what belonged to him. "That's your ring."

"Hershey and I are done...for good this time."

"I...I already have mine. It's-"

"Upstairs in your room, I know. I want you to have it, just in case you lost yours years ago."

"Yeah."

"Hendrix told me everything."

"That boy can't hold water."

"Then it all made sense. The way you talked about the ring. The way you looked at it. This is the ring you got her, not a look-alike, not some ring that happens to look similar. It's your ring."

"Her ring. If she didn't want it, why should I?"

"Some people don't deserve nice things." I nudged the ring closer to him. "Something tells me you aren't some people."

He hesitantly took the ring and held it to his chest with both hands. "When she walked away from everything we built, I swore I would never see this ring again. Thank you for letting me have a piece of her again."

He stepped from the car and closed the door while looking down at the ring.

"Do you want to come inside for some coffee?" He asked, now paying attention to me.

"Maybe that isn't a good idea. If Hendrix comes back, he'll-"

"Hendrix is at work. And if he does come back for whatever reason, this is my house. If he doesn't like my guest, he knows where the door is."

"I don't know, Colin. This seems like a bad idea."

"You aren't the girls at the strip club, Victoria. You're coming in to talk. Talking ain't never hurt anybody."

"I really shouldn't."

"I'm not mad at you yet. If you keep acting silly, I just might be. Come on inside. Hendrix won't be home for a few hours. Even if he does, you know you'll like it."

He was right. I felt warm inside from the possibility of seeing Hendrix, yet, strangely, I also was cold. But we enjoyed one another's company in the kitchen over coffee. I watched him fall in and out of love with Hendrix's mother at a glance.

"The part I don't get is, why leave?" He asked. "Like that? Did I make her that unhappy? There isn't a day that goes by without me wondering if there's something wrong with my love."

"Sometimes, it's easier."

"How is it so easy when you know you're leaving a trail of fire behind you?"

"I said it's easier, not easy."

He still stared down at the ring. "You owed those kids more, my love." He looked at me. "You owed your marriage more."

"We were never married. I waited for that man to propose to me for years. When I was twenty-one, I thought it was the most romantic thing a man could do for a woman. Now, I realize it was his way of keeping a young and insecure girl around. He promised everything I ever dreamt of and made sure they stayed just that: a dream. Stupidly, the anticipation kept me yearning."

"I'm glad you finally realized you're worth more than sitting around and waiting for someone to love you. Especially someone who has done nothing but hurt you."

I curled his fingers around the ring. "Sometimes, we need to let go."

"Then you shouldn't have given me this damn ring. This is one hell of a birthday present."

"It's your birthday?"

He nodded.

"Oh my God, Happy birthday!"

"Well, it's not my birthday yet. Tomorrow is the big day."

"Hopefully, I'm not overstepping my boundaries here, but what year are we celebrating?

"You broke my son's heart. I mean, you broke him into pieces, stumped those pieces into microscopic pieces, and had the nerve to show up at my house unannounced. What boundaries?"

"That hurt."

He winked. "I'll be fifty-five years old."

"You don't look a day over thirty-five."

"I made it to fifty-five." He knocked on the table with the same hand clenching the ring. "Can't say I thought I was going to make it this far. I can't believe I have this old thing again." He tossed the ring up and down. After catching it a third time, he slid it into his pocket.

"Any plans for your special day?"

"Besides being right here? Can't say I do. Vanessa and Eve went back home, so it's just me, myself, and I tomorrow."

"And Hendrix."

"Him too. We'll probably get our arteries nice and clogged with some burgers. I figured it would be less awkward if I didn't bring him up, you know, considering everything that happened between you two. Didn't want to trigger unwanted emotions."

"Nothing happened except for me being an idiot."

"That's love for you."

"For what it's worth, I never stopped loving him."

I looked down at my phone and saw that it was 12:43 pm. Any minute, Hendrix would walk through the front door. Although I missed him, he had no desire to see me. Why would he? I didn't deserve him or his time.

I stood.

"I should get going, you know," I said, "before he comes back."

"Sit down, Victoria," he said. "I poured you a cup of coffee, and you barely touched it. That's rude."

I sat and took a sip of coffee, burning my tongue in the process.

"And don't worry about Hendrix," he said. "That new job of his keeps him out for a while."

"He has a full-time job? Oh my God, that's awesome. I told him he was worrying for nothing."

"Freaking out would be a better way to put it."

"Where does he work?"

"He's an advisor at one of those Cal States. I can't remember. He's happy. That's the only thing that matters."

"That's good."

Without him, most days were hard.

A month ago, I had left Hershey and coincidently moved into a two-bedroom apartment near Hendrix's house. Everywhere else was either too expensive or ghetto. I didn't have much to my name, just a kitchen table, beds for myself and one for if the boys visited, and a plastic container I used as a dresser.

The boys would come to visit every week. Hershey had been surprisingly civil. They were my destiny, but I still felt something was missing with Hendrix gone.

That morning, before something possessed me to stop by, I lay in bed, hugging my pillow. With my eyes closed and my emotions running wild, Hendrix held me in his arms. I kissed him, and as I got into it, I thrust my hips and tried my hardest to remember what it felt like floating.

"Are you happy?" Colin asked, breaking me from my thoughts.

"Huh?"

"Are you happy?"

"I guess."

"I shouldn't do this because you're my son's ex and all. Plus, he wants nothing to do with you, but how about I let you take me out today-- for my birthday."

My chest stung. "Where are we going?"

I finished my coffee as he got ready upstairs. I heard him walking and water running. I went to the entryway and admired the collage of Hendrix, my favorite picture being him as a baby. He was a chubby little thing with big bright eyes. I turned my gaze to a picture of him smiling and holding up his degree. It felt like years since we sat in class together.

Colin trotted downstairs in this colorful button-up shirt with all types of shapes and designs, and I didn't know what to make of it, so I kept staring, hoping I would figure out what he was wearing. He coughed as we walked from the house to the car. Without a destination, we ended up on the freeway, cruising fifteen miles over the speed limit.

He connected his phone to the car through Bluetooth and turned on a funk song. He cranked the volume up from a barely audible low to a car vibrating high. All the images in my rearview blurred through the heavy bass. He danced. No, he was grooving. Every so often, I glanced at him, and anytime he saw me, he sang to me. If I knew the words, I would have joined. I was content in dancing as he sang along without missing a beat. People stared as they passed. Driving alongside a minivan, Colin stared at the woman driving; he never stopped dancing. She was not impressed.

The song ended, and he turned down the music. He was out after three songs. He made a gurgling noise as he breathed. For a brief moment, it sounded like he stopped breathing.

I tapped him on the shoulder. He didn't budge.

I shook him. He didn't move.

My heart skipping a beat, I checked for a pulse. He woke up sometime later, rolling over and smiling at me.

"You are one lucky lady," he said.

"Why is that?"

He winked.

. . .

We ended up walking along the shore at the beach with sand in between our toes. The water was so cold it felt like daggers. As it waded back and forth, I thought we drifted away.

The clouds were darker, and it was colder now. A fresh scent of salt floated through the air. Some people-but not many- lay on towels, and even fewer ran around in the sand. Fewer stood in the water or swam. Most beachgoers had changed into their street clothes and now crowded the pier or boardwalk, enjoying the rides, restaurants, shops, and street performers.

The screaming from the Ferris Wheel and the roller coaster traveled as far as the lights decorating both.

We walked up a set of wooden steps to the side of the pier to a row of porta-potties that no one had cleaned in days. We covered our noses and hurriedly walked past the line of people waiting to use those boxes of dysentery.

The shops, restaurants, an arcade, and carnival booths overflowed with crowds. The carnival workers, dressed in either green or yellow shirts, waved everyone over to their booths and enticed them to play with large stuffed animals. As we walked by a restaurant, the smell of funnel cake sparked our interest. I bought one for Colin, and as he ate, I sang "Happy birthday." Several people joined along and shouted "happy birthday" once we finished singing. He only had one bite of the funnel cake before giving it to me.

"You know what would be a fantastic birthday present?" He asked.

"You eat that $7 funnel cake?"

He pointed to the Ferris Wheel that looked much bigger up close.

"Are you scared?"

"Of what? A Ferris wheel? It's not that big."

"What's with you kids and your irrational fears of things that spin around? Between you know who and carousels, and you and Ferris wheels, I have no idea what to tell either of you."

"Tell us we can make our destiny. Tell us it's all worth it in the end—that no matter how hopeless and directionless life feels at times, we don't have to end up in the same place."

"Hopefully, this doesn't freak you out too much, but you do know earth orbits the sun?"

Instead of engaging him, I stood in line, watching the previous riders disembark and new ones enter the cars. In what felt like destiny, we didn't have to wait to step onto the death trap. The last car waited for us. As the rim jerked into a start, everyone like Colin, who wasn't having an essential crisis, cheered as we inched higher and higher. The entire time I fought to keep the vomit down. Not fast enough, the ride came to an end, and we walked to the end of the pier, where we had more room to breathe and didn't have to worry about bumping into anyone. Along the wood railing, people cast their fishing lines into the water.

We sat on a wooden bench, looking out into the waves. The sound of them crashing put me at peace, so much so, I closed my eyes.

Colin let out one cough to clear his throat. I opened my eyes to see him staring at the ring.

"This ring has brought me nothing but misfortune," I said. "There's so many bad memories attached to this thing. The further it's from me, the better."

"And so you bring it to me?"

"All I know is the cheating got worse after he gave me that thing, so did the lying. A part of me doesn't blame him."

"No?"

"I believed anything. Hershey could've told me he was working late on the moon, and I would've asked him to bring back a rock."

"That's cute, in a sad way."

"Our entire relationship was built and maintained on lies: I was an adult at the time; I couldn't find better than him; I had the perfect family. Convincing myself that I loved him made things easier. I was so pathetic."

"Anymore pathetic than sitting around waiting for a woman to come back after twenty-plus years? If you were stupid, I was a grade-A fool."

"Of all the men in this world, I fell for the one who wasn't built for my love."

"Sounds like you were dating my Lilian."

"Great. More people like Hershey. That's exactly what the world needs."

"Hershey?" He laughed. "You thought dating a man named after a chocolate bar was a good idea? His parents didn't have good taste or common sense-that much is evident. You thought Hershey would? Hershey?"

"Don't do Mrs. Cecily like that."

"I'm just saying. The man's name is Hershey."

"She tried her best. Hershey is just a living testament that sometimes an apple can fall far from a tree. Truth is, he was sweet when he wanted to be."

Colin rolled his eyes. I laughed.

"No pun intended," I said.

"Diabetes will tell you everything sweet isn't good for you."

"And that's why you're looking at a single woman. I found out what I want and need."

"Which is what?"

"Happiness. Love. Respect. Hendrix."

"I hope you didn't think you could come and woo me into helping you win back my son, Victoria. I'm not that easy." He winked. "It will take a lot more than a funnel cake and good company."

"That wasn't my intention at all. Like I said, I burned that bridge. I'm perfectly aware that I might not see Hendrix, let alone be with him, ever again. I'm okay with that."

"Don't you lie to me, young lady. You care."

"I do. It hurts knowing that I may never see him again. I get so angry with myself because I had him. I had the man of my dreams and ruined it for what?" I paused and thought about Hershey. "I felt nothing when I was with Hershey. With Hendrix, I felt everything: happiness, love, and respect. And I threw it all away."

"For a man named Hershey."

"For Hershey."

He sighed, and I could tell that he was annoyed. "Then I have to ask you the question that my son asked me almost every night for a month: If you loved him so much, why did you leave?"

"I was scared."

"Of love?"

"Of hurting my children. Before anything else, I'm a mother. Every day I wake up and breathe for my sons. They wanted Hershey and me together. I thought I could tell them how unhappy I was, but they thought they were the reason I was leaving. I'm their mother, the one person who should always protect them. If not me, who else would? At that moment, I wasn't protecting them. I was the one hurting them. For the first time in my life, I broke my children's hearts, and I didn't know what to do. I wanted to make them smile again. I wanted to be their protector, and in desperation, I did the only thing I thought would make them happy: I stayed. I grinded my teeth and stayed with their father."

"Nothing comes before your children."

"Nothing."

"Parent to parent, I hope you understand why I don't want you near my son."

There was an unbearable stabbing in my chest, and I wanted to cry more than ever.

"I understand," I said.

"If you gave any other reason, I would call it dumb, but it's pretty damn understandable, and that's what scares me. You want to make your children happy, and if their happiness is dependent on you and their father being together, then who's to say you won't run back to Hershey the first time they bat an eye?"

"I won't."

"Why should I believe that, Victoria?"

"Because I don't want Hershey anymore. I love your son!"

"If you loving him meant anything, you would have stayed the first time. It's not just about love, Victoria! Love won't get you through the day-to-day when the honeymoon phase is over, and life happens. It has to be more than love!"

"Hendrix is my life!"

"Cut the dramatics, Victoria. Let's have a conversation-a real conversation. You say you love him, but why should anyone believe you?"

"Because it's the truth."

"That's nice! A moment ago, you told me how you ran from the truth for years. You told Hendrix you loved him right after walking away from a relationship you ran right back to. That's the truth. Your promises are just words, Victoria. They don't mean anything because when it was time to back up those words, you proved you were full of shit."

"I'm not going back this time."

"And why is that? What makes this time different than before?"

"I was dying inside, and not even my boys could save me. I can't suffer with Hershey anymore. I'm tired of feeling empty. I'm willing to give my boys the world as long as it doesn't involve Hershey and me being together. I tried time and time again, and I can't do it anymore. That doesn't make me a bad mother."

"It doesn't. The fact that you tried makes you a great mother. A bad mother walks out on her children. Shit, why did I say that?"

I had so much more to say but figured the time passed. We watched and listened to the waves now. The moment ended when I asked, "how are you feeling?"

"About what?"

"Don't play dumb with me. You know exactly what I'm talking about. Have you put any more guns to your head?"

"Oh, that."

"Yeah, that."

He chuckled. "I haven't seen you since then, huh? That day seems so long ago. They say when you get older, the mind goes first."

"I thought it was the knees."

"I can still get down. I resent the implication." He bumped me with his shoulders. "I wasn't going to kill myself." He noticed a man smoking against the rails. "Well, I guess I kinda am killing myself. So I should say I wasn't going to kill myself then."

"Are you sure you're okay?"

"I'm fine now. Vanessa and Eve took all my guns, so I have to get more creative next time. I just might hurl myself off the pier."

He had the same devious smile on his face as Hendrix. My smile quickly turned into a frown. I got up, walked to the railing and stared at the waves. Colin followed. Leaning forward, he looked down at the water with his arms on the railing.

"Just in case you didn't know, putting a gun to my head during Thanksgiving wasn't how I imagined my night going," he said.

"Duly noted."

"That should be the first line in my book."

"I didn't know you wrote."

"Girl, I can barely write down my thoughts, let alone write a comprehensive story. I can't spell for shit either."

"Can I ask you something?"

"Go right ahead. I'm all ears."

"After everything I put Hendrix through, why are you being so nice to me?"

He shrugged. "I don't know. Boredom. Or I could just have a fetish for heartbreakers. I guess that question is like a tootsie pop."

I smiled, but tears streamed down my cheek. I listened to the flock of seagulls flying above and the waves splashing against the legs of the pier. I closed my eyes and took in all the sounds.

Colin sighed and said, "I'm going to regret this."

"Regret what?"

He stood straight, and we looked at one another.

"Your bridge isn't burned. That boy still acts like you're sliced bread."

I smiled. "Really?"

"Okay, you got a little too excited, heartbreaker."

"Sorry."

"I have no reason to lie to you. That boy mentions you damn near every day. Most of the time, it's bad, but that's neither here nor there. The point is nobody is talking good or bad about someone all day long if they didn't care."

My smile still took over my face.

"Aye, wipe that smile off your face."

"I'm trying. You just don't know how happy I am right now."

"Don't get too excited. You can't just storm out of someone's life and then waltz back in. It's going to take some finesse."

"Why are you telling me all this? You seemed pretty adamant about not liking me."

"I'm conflicted. You hurt him, and I want to hurt you for that."

"I want to hurt myself."

"Exactly why I decided not to be a jerk. You're beating yourself down more than I can. But I can't lie, you won me over, and I liked how happy you made Hendrix. If he'll have you back into his life, then I guess I'll love you too."

"Don't worry about that. He won't."

"Okay, stop with the pity party. This is the life you chose. Look, if it's meant to be, then it's meant to be. If it's not, go find your destiny elsewhere. But something tells me my son isn't the type to be an old man hanging onto a 'What if.'"

He pulled the ring from his pocket. Without looking at it, he clenched it in his hand and pulled it against his heart.

"Goodbye, Lillian," he said and tossed the ring into the ocean.

. . .

My heart must have beat a million times in a minute. Could he hear it too?

My skin crawled. I paced across the kitchen, my legs wobbling. Any minute they were going to give, and the nerves kept me from sitting down. The walls caved in by the second. They scratched across the floor, moving closer and closer. Something rang, blaring over someone hissing. The lights emitted a suffocating heat.

Colin came downstairs, coughing. The thumping of his feet against the floor moved closer. I turned around right as he walked into the kitchen, and we connected eyes.

"Was it this hard to break up with him?" He asked.

The comment knocked the wind out of me.

"Okay, that was a bad joke." He walked to me. "Victoria, relax. You're making me nervous. You got this."

I stopped pacing. I smiled as the walls moved back to their original place, the ringing and hissing stopped, my skin stopped crawling, my legs no longer wobbled, and air burst into my lungs.

I got this, I told myself. We got this.

Whenever I heard those words, Hendrix was by my side, and nothing could stand against me. But Hendrix won't be by your side today, I told myself.

My confidence failed. The walls eased closer, but this time more quickly. The ringing and hissing kicked into full gear, and they were louder than my heartbeat. As I paced across the kitchen, Colin grabbed hold of me by the shoulders.

"Relax," he said.

"I'm trying."

"Breathe. In and out. In and out."

Together, we took deep breaths. I sat at the table and acted as if my mental well-being wasn't on the line. Colin massaged my shoulders.

"Not to add to your anxiety or anything, but I forgot one thing at the beach," he said.

"He has a girlfriend, doesn't he?"

"Shit. That's a good question. Now that you mention it, though, there were a few nights where he didn't come home. When he did, he looked like somebody turned him out."

"Great."

"Oh, here you go. A relationship didn't stop you two before. By all means, don't let it now. They say we go through stages in life, right? Well, maybe you two were destined for one another."

I smiled. "Destiny."

"Sure." He shrugged. "Don't let his poker face fool you. He's been waiting for you since you left. He won't admit it, and why would he? Just keep up the good fight and don't let the stubbornness get to you."

"I think I love him even more."

"Yeah. Yeah. Yeah. That whole saying about distance makes the hearts grow closer or whatever. That's beautiful, and I hope it's true because if you hurt my son again, I'll probably hurt you. I haven't decided how, but I have nothing to lose. I'll probably be dead before I get to trial. Even that won't stop me. I'll come back as a ghost and haunt your ass."

I laughed awkwardly. "Well, good thing I don't intend on hurting him."

"Good, I'm glad we got that out of the way." He sat in the chair beside me, turned his body to face me, and leaned forward with his arms on his knees. "So, what's the plan again?"

On our way back from the beach, the hour drive was three with traffic, and the entire time I asked myself that same question. "What are you going to say?" The answer was always the same: that is a great question.

I looked down at the table and shrugged.

"You're going into this without a game plan?" He asked. "You have to have something."

"I have nothing. I take it a good ol' *I'm sorry* won't do it."

"You wish it was that easy. *I'm sorry* didn't make him fall in love, and it sure as hell didn't get you into this mess, so that wouldn't be my ace in the hole."

"I wasn't betting on it."

"Which brings me to what I've been dying to know...How did you end it?"

"I kissed him."

"And then what happened?"

"He saw my ring. Then I walked away."

"Jesus." He grabbed a bottle of Hennessey from the cabinet above the stove and took a shot. He wiped his mouth with his arm and came back to the table. "You walked away? You didn't say anything? Not a classic 'it's not you, it's me?' or an 'I think we should go our separate ways?' You just walked away?"

With my elbows on the table, I slammed my hands over my face. "Oh my God, I walked away."

"Ooh, that's bad."

"I can't believe I just said, 'Destiny."

"What does that even mean?"

"That we weren't destined to be together."

"Jesus Christ. How does he not hate you? Us, Harper men, and our unrequited love."

"It wasn't one-sided. I loved Hendrix more than I ever loved anyone who wasn't my sons." I stood but made sure my head stayed down. "Why am I even here? You're right. I should go home and count my losses. Save what's left of my dignity. I messed up bad."

"Alright, stop. Just stop. Okay? I've known my son for quite some time, and I can honestly say he looked the happiest when with you. I don't know if it's true, but that's what it looked like. There's no telling how much time I have on this earth, and while I'm here, my job is to make that boy happy. Toys or going to the park might not do the trick anymore, but you do, and I'm going to do everything in my power to make that happen if that's what he wants. So I have two questions for you. Number one, do you swear that you love Hendrix, the whole Hendrix, and nothing but my son Hendrix?"

"Yes."

"Number two, do you promise you will try to make this relationship work through thick and thin?"

"I promise."

"Then sit down and relax. He'll be home any minute."

We waited in silence. After twenty minutes, the front door opened, and I looked up. Hendrix struggled to untangle his headphones. I sucked in my lips to fight back a smile. When he looked up and saw me, he froze. I couldn't tell what he was thinking by the look on his face, but he didn't look at me in disgust, which I felt was a good sign. I stood to greet him.

His hair was a little longer, and now he had scruffy and patchy facial hair. He looked sharp in his navy suit. He walked into the kitchen, never looking away from me. At the table, he stopped. We stood in front of one another, staring for the first time in four months.

I yearned to feel his lips and the warmth of his body. The mystery of him wanting me gave some type of comfort.

Colin sneaked out of the kitchen. Now, it was just us two and awkwardness.

Hendrix and I kept staring. Neither had an expression on our faces. I was close to smiling, but I held it in.

"It's been a long time," I said.

"Yeah."

"Hard to believe it's already been four months."

"Has it been four months since you got back with Hershey? Whoa. Time is flying."

"Hendrix, let me explain."

"Of all the people, you went back to Hershey. Hershey! And why the hell is his name Hershey?"

"Hendrix, can I explain why I went back to him?"

"From the moment I met you, you made me feel like the most important person in the world. Then you ruined everything. You turned around a month later and made me feel like the most worthless human being on this planet! After everything we went through, you walked away without saying an explanation, and now, after four months, you want to explain? You are unbelievable."

"I shouldn't've walked away."

"You think? You left me standing there like a piece of trash! Do you know how long I waited for you? Somehow in some way, I thought you were joking. I stood out there for over an hour, Victoria, which says a lot more about me than it does about you. But I waited for you. I waited for you to come back and tell me it was some bad joke."

"I never came back. I'm sorry."

"You never came back. Instead, you went back to him."

"If you let me explain, I can make everything make sense."

"I thought you loved me."

"I did love you. Hendrix, I do love you."

"Then how could you do that to me?"

I grabbed hold of his hand and tried to pull him closer to his resistance. I forced my arms around him and my head on his shoulders. Nothing would have felt more right than him holding me. He kept his arms to his side like I was a burden.

"I'm sorry," I whispered into his ear. "I'm so sorry. I didn't want to leave you-"

"Victoria, please, let go of me."

"Hendrix, we can work through this. I thought I was protecting the boys-"

"Victoria."

"That's not my name."

"Victoria, let me go."

"Call me by my name, and I'll let go."

He tried to break from my embrace, and I tightened my embrace. Then I told him why I left and how empty I felt with Hershey. He didn't struggle anymore, and I broke our embrace. He stepped back.

"Okay," he said.

"What does that mean?"

"It means 'okay.' I heard you. Do you have anything else you want to tell me?"

"I love you."

He left, slamming the front door. The pictures in the entryway rattled against the wall. Colin strolled downstairs and into the kitchen, shaking his head.

"I deserved that," I said.

"You did."

"You're making this harder than it has to be."

"You think I'm going to make this easy?"

"I don't know."

"He has a lot of emotions built up right now. You gotta let him settle down."

"Or I could leave him alone."

"If you think that's the best route, then leave him alone."

"I think I should." I hugged Colin.

His face was to my ear, and I heard a gurgling noise each time he breathed. He coughed, and then he pushed me back, leaning forward and covering his mouth. I brought him a bottle of water from the refrigerator. He drank as much as he could through the coughing. It wasn't much. He stumbled into the bathroom and leaned over the toilet, hacking up mucus and blood.

I rushed outside. Hendrix sat in the wicker chair with his head down.

"Hendrix," I said.

"Victoria, why are you here? Leave me alone!"

"Your dad." I forced down a knot in my throat. "He's coughing up blood. He doesn't look good. I don't know what to do. Tell me what to do!"

He nearly knocked me over as he rushed inside to his father.

"Dad," he said. "Dad, what's going on? Are you okay?"

Colin breathed too heavily to speak. For a few seconds, it sounded as if he stopped breathing. Hendrix gasped for air, and when his father breathed again, he sat on the bathroom floor against the wall. Hendrix, squatting, held his father's hand tightly.

I sat with him.

"We need to get you to the hospital," Hendrix said.

"I'm fine. I'm fine, Hendrix."

"Dad, you don't look good. We gotta get you to the hospital."

"Hendrix." He squeezed Hendrix's hand tighter. "Let me go if it's time. We made our memories."

...

Rice. Freshly expired bread. Canned beans, corn, and tomatoes. There wasn't much food to pull together a meal. I didn't do much better on my store run, seeing how I brought back $70 worth of food just to microwave tomato soup.

I brought them both a bowl and a roll of saltine crackers. Colin didn't eat much. For the rest of the night, Hendrix and I sat on the ground, against the couch, listening to Colin sleep.

In the morning, Hendrix turned to me-his eyes puffy and red-and said, "thank you."

"Hendrix, can we talk about us?"

"We're good. You're a mother, and me? I'm a guy who plays video games, lives with his dad, and has no idea what he wants to be when he grows up. We're two different people, at two different stages in their lives. I'm getting there because now I get it: you had too much to lose running in circles with me." He winked. "I'm happy for you. I really am."

Hendrix

Victoria still sat on the floor beside my dad. I thanked her again before leaving for work. In the car, before I left for work, I sat with my thoughts. I knew I should've called off work.

Time moved at an unbearable slow since I didn't know if my father would make it through the day.

Students came in and out of my office continuously. Every minute felt like an hour, and in the few moments I had between students, I messaged Victoria to check up on my dad. He was doing better than last night and was up and about. Even then, she refused to leave him alone, calling off work to be with him until I got off. I thanked her, and she replied with a smiling face. During lunch, I called Victoria from the car. I could tell she didn't expect it from the moment of hesitation before she uttered, "hello." Before I could reply, my dad shouted my name.

"I told you I was fine, baby boy," he said. "Jesus said it wasn't my time yet. I have the strength of The Rock in the Fast and Furious movies."

Victoria and I laughed, which quickly faded into silence.

Breaking the moment where neither knew what to say, she asked about my day, which transitioned into a regular conversation about life. Mistakenly, I called her "Vita." Neither of us said anything until I cut through the painful silence with a lie.

"I should get back to work."

The second half of the day dragged to an end. Students came in to complain for the sake of complaining. I didn't message Victoria, and she didn't message me.

On my way home, I sat in standard California traffic, bumper to bumper, because of an accident on the freeway that spread across three of the four lanes. The closer I got to home, the more butterflies fluttered in every part of my body. During my two-hour car ride, I watched the sun inch closer to the horizon.

At home, I sat in the car to gather my thoughts.

Resist, I said to myself. Hendrix, resist. Don't let her pull you back in with her infectious smile that makes life itself worth it and captivating eyes that you could gaze into forever. Who cares that she gives you an unexplainable rush. That's called lust. Resist her. Remember that she didn't want you. Remember how much pain she put you through. She's with Hershey now.

"I didn't see her ring," I said.

I couldn't stop smiling. I recomposed myself at the door, wiped the smile off my face, and with a stern look, I walked inside.

Dad played Luther Vandross's "A House Is Not A Home" from the living room. The couch was in the middle of the room. My dad and Vita put on a puppet show with Stomps, Starlight, and a plush Toon Link. Vita had Starlight and Stomps.

She still has them, I thought.

"Starlight knew she made a mistake the moment she flew away from Stomps four months ago," Victoria said, making it look like Starlight flew, "and ever since, flying no longer felt the same. Instead, it felt like she was drowning." She dropped Starlight behind the couch.

"Starlight's only wish was to see Stomps happy with or without her," dad said, nodding Toon Link's head.

As Starlight, Vita apologized and confessed her love. She was adamant that they would never be together again, although she wanted to let Stomps know how much he meant to her. Starlight poured out her heart and soul to Stomps, not in desperation. Instead, with sincerity and clarification, he replied with one word: "Okay." Sobbing, Vita made Starlight fly away.

I went over to the couch and gently held Vita by the wrist. She stood. Tears poured down her face.

"What are you doing?" I asked.

She shook her head, shrugging. "Making a fool of myself."

"How does all this end?"

"I get it, Hendrix. I look stupid."

"I'm serious. Do they get back together? This is good T.V."

"To be honest, I have no idea how this ends."

"You went through all this trouble to win me over, and you have no idea how the story ends?"

"Did I win you over?"

"There's still some time left in this game. It's your ball."

"How much time is left?"

"Maybe a little. Maybe a lot. Maybe you should call a timeout and figure out a play. That's your call. I just need to know how you think this story ends."

"I can't answer that question, Hendrix."

"Why not?"

"Because I don't want our story to end."

"You ended it, or at least I thought you did. Now, you're doing this, telling me it's not over yet. How does it end, Victoria?"

"Stomps forgiving Starlight. They get out of this shitty stage in life. They get back together."

I caressed her ringless finger.

"I only love you," she said.

"But you went back."

"For the boys. I thought I didn't have a choice. I know that was a lie now. I want you to want me, Hendrix."

"I always wanted you."

"But?"

"There's no but."

We gazed into each other's eyes as I caressed her face. The moment our lips were so close together, where we took in one another's breath, our forever started.

She put her trembling hand on my cheek.

"Vita," I said.

"Yes?"

"I love you more than you'll ever know."

"I love you too. And I know I don't deserve you, but I love you so much-"

I kissed her.

She moved her head back. "I love you so much." She came back in for a kiss.

Dad's coughing ruined the moment.

"Can I come out now?" He asked.

I laughed and said, "Yeah, dad, you're good."

"Is everyone happy?"

I looked at Vita. "I'm the happiest I've ever been."

"Victoria?"

"What he said," she said.

"Good, because I swear if either one of you mess this up, when I die, I'm going to Poltergeist your asses."

"Got it." I fell deeper into a trance from Vita's eyes. "I love you, dad."

"Love you too, son."

"I love you, Hendrix," Vita said.

"I love you too, Vita."

"I love you both," dad said, throwing the plush Toon Link at the back of my head on his way upstairs.

Chapter 12
Hendrix

I lay on my back, with my cheek resting in the moist grass and my legs spread out. I stared at the bronze marker bulging from the glass. Looking across the field, I examined endless rows of tombstones with flowers beside them, and past them, a hill I climbed to where I lay now.

It was the perfect day. The sun was out and the weather fair, somewhere in the 70s.

My dad, slumped forward and coughing, came up the hill. I heard him before I saw him. He stood over me-his legs on each side of my head. His body blocked the sun.

"I think I found the perfect spot," he said. "It's just down the hill, right next to a John Klemm, husband, father, scientist, and preacher. Isn't that quite the combination?"

"What about this spot?"

"How does it feel?"

"I guess it's fine."

"Let me test it out."

He struggled to lay beside me, groaning and grunting the entire time. On the ground, he closed his eyes. His breathing softened, and, eventually, it sounded like he wasn't at all. He lay motionless.

"I like the other spot better," he said.

"Does it matter?"

"Choosing my burial location is an important decision. It determines where you, your sisters, and your new family will come and remember me. That's why I'm asking you. Once I'm gone, I'm gone. I don't have to worry about the background of my grave or hike up here. You, on the other hand, have to live with it. I want you to have a hand in the decision-making."

I sat up and took in the surroundings. There was a white BMW parked on the pathway, almost parallel to where we lay. Two women-one holding a small child and the other with flowers-held hands as they walked past us and down the hill. My dad turned his head so that it was resting in the grass and watched the women pass. He sat up and put his arm around me. The coughing started.

"Soon, that will be you, Victoria, and the kids," he said, his voice hoarse from coughing.

"Okay. So let's weigh the options here. This spot is close to the pathway, and it's relatively cheap; however, you can only have markers, not upright headstones. On the other hand, the spot down the hill is next to the garden, and we can get upright headstones, but it's a hike to get there, and it's more expensive."

"Did I mention the garden has palm trees?"

"Let's go with the garden, then. You love your palm trees."

"I do love myself a palm tree." We took in the sights together, where only nature made a sound. "Now, let's just hope that I don't need that lot until after the wedding."

"You better."

"I think I have another two weeks in me."

"You better fight, old man. We already sent the final headcount."

"I will stay strong for a dry piece of chicken. Wedding food is always dry. Why is that?"

We laughed, and with his arms still around my shoulders, he pulled me closer. Then he took his arm from around me and lay down.

"How much are you two in the hole?" He asked.

"Not much. About $5,000."

He whistled. "Your mom and I forked over about $25,000, just for her to walk out on me. I wish I had a loving, supportive old man that would let me do the ceremony at his house."

"Thanks, Dad."

"Don't mention it. Where's the Honeymoon again?"

"Cinque Terre."

"Cinque Terre? I'm thinking you're going to say Hawaii or the Bahamas. I've never heard of a Cinque Terre a day in my life. Look at you, Hendrix, coming up in the world."

"Vita said she wanted to go, so I'm taking her. She deserves that much."

"Thata boy. Give your wife everything she could possibly want and need, sometimes without her asking. Keep that mindset, son, and you will be the happiest man in the world."

"Duly noted." I stood and brushed needles of grass off my back.

"Ditching me already?"

"Come on, let's check out those palm trees."

He led me to his plot, where we lay under the palm trees, without the expectation of entertaining one another with conversation. There, I closed my eyes and soaked in the rays shining down on us.

"Our secret won't be ours anymore," he said. "I'm telling your sisters tomorrow."

"I'm proud of you, dad."

"You're proud of me? You're proud of me, huh?" He chuckled. "My son is proud of me." He lightly gripped my arm. "I hope I can continue to make you proud, my son."

"You always did."

"That's a lie. I've done things, so many things, that I'm not proud of—things you could never be proud of… and shouldn't be proud of-"

"You had your reasons, and to be honest, all in all, you did a pretty decent job."

"I like to think I did everything within my means to give you kids the world."

"You did." I tapped his head with my own. "You did."

"That's all I ever wanted to hear. Thanks, my son."

"It's the least I could do. You did bring me into this world." I sat up. "I hate to ditch you, but I should get going. Vita is waiting for me."

"Bye, my son."

"I'm going to my mother-in-law's house, not war."

"Every day is war. A war with ourselves. A war with health. A war for security." He slowly pulled out his phone and snapped a picture to capture our smiles.

. . .

After a thirty-minute ride in silence, we arrived.

As we turned onto her parent's street, she sucked in a deep breath. I parked on the opposite side of the street from the house and rested my hand on her knee. She held my hand, interlocking our fingers. Her hands were cold and sweaty.

There was a gray Prius in the driveway.

"What if they don't want to see me?" She asked.

"They want to see you."

"But what if they don't?"

"I can't answer that because I know that they'll be the happiest people in this world when they see their little girl all grown up."

"I was grown when they kicked me out."

"That was years ago."

"It wasn't that long ago."

"Long enough to regret how they treated their daughter."

"They have their daughter."

"My dad has two daughters. It doesn't mean he loves Eve more than Vanessa."

"Your dad also didn't disown Vanessa."

"Vita-"

"Can we just go home?"

"No."

I stepped out of the car and walked towards the front door of the house. Vita opened her door and demanded that I come back to the car. When I knocked on the front door and looked back at her, she closed the door and slid down into the seat. The house door opened just as I looked forward. A short man with a polo tucked into his jeans opened the door. He looked just like Vita but as a man with a beard, mustache, and gray hair.

Vita's sister and mother talked in another room about going somewhere that night. I couldn't make out where.

"Hi," he said. "Can I help you?"

"Yeah, so I'm going to cut to the chase. My name is Hendrix. You don't know me, but I know your daughter."

"Victoria?"

"Exactly."

His eyes, focused on something behind me, welled with tears.

I turned around, and Vita stood behind me, with her hands behind her back. Her father, without hesitation, burst past me, and Vita collapsed into his arms. All the crying and incoherent talking brought her mother and sister outside. Three years of regret plastered over her mother's face, turning into snot dripping sobbing as she joined the embrace.

"Victoria," her mother said, crying.

Vita's sister and I stood on the porch, taking it all in.

"What's happening?" Vita's sister asked me. "Who are you?"

"I'm Vita's fiancée."

"Who the heck is Vita?"

"The final piece of your family."

"Is that English?"

"That's Victoria."

Her face lit up. "You mean…my sister Victoria?"

Thank you ☺

About the Author

Lamar Neal is a poet and author from the Inland Empire in Southern California. His published works include three poetry collections (*Charm Bracelet*, *We All Need Therapy*, and *Pale*) and one novel, *A Misc. Eden*. As a child, he began his writing journey by creating what he considered television series starring his Gundam and WWE action figures. When he isn't writing, he is most likely at home, playing video games, online shopping for clothes he doesn't need, or trying to decide on his next hairstyle.

Follow the Author:

Facebook:

/LamarKeonNeal

Twitter:

Ghostcharades

Tiktok:

Theghostcharades

Instagram:

Theghostcharades

9 798985 222111